I0748317

THE OMENS OF FATE

Emma Bradley

Copyright © 2025 Emma Bradley

All rights reserved.

ISBN: 978-1-915909-38-1

For Milo, and for all the librarians also out there liberating books because they believe everyone should have access to knowledge.

CHAPTER ONE

"He's a sadist!"

Molly stared in dismay as Sammy threw up her hands and slumped onto her bed. Even though they'd been living in Beryl and Harvey's old home for two weeks already, neither of them had made any effort to make it feel more like their own place. She'd built in a small box-room for herself while staying there before, and there was a separate bathroom, but it would never feel like home, not like the workshop did.

"He's dedicated," Molly countered. "He takes his role very seriously."

Sammy folded her arms over the two bulky sweatshirts she was wearing to counteract the lack of heating and scowled.

"He whipped someone's feet off the table and threatened to hit them with a book," she muttered.

"Well, technically they shouldn't have been on the table. Milo is fussy and overbearing, but he's helping us."

Molly bit her lip, tempted to agree with Sammy, except she had to be the sensible one and Milo was technically trying to help them.

Sammy waved a dismissive hand and slouched down

further. One of her black braids was already unravelling fast but Molly still hadn't managed to get the hang of plaiting it yet and they were running out of rope-bands.

"Well you go and get bossed around by him then," Sammy said. "I don't have to."

Molly bit her tongue as the urge to retort something snappy bubbled up.

I can't blame her for wanting to wallow, but she needs to leave these four walls sometime. It's not healthy.

She inhaled sharply and forced her shoulders to lower. With only a year's age difference between them, she had to be the mature one.

"You don't want to go?" she asked one last time.

"No, I don't."

"Fine."

"Fine."

Molly stalked to the front door and glanced in the tiny cracked mirror hanging on the back of it. A pretty face with an upturned nose and wide blue eyes framed by tumbles of chestnut hair stared back at her, and she still wasn't used to it. The glamour she had to wear wasn't getting any easier to hold, even though a few weeks had passed since-

She shuddered. It was tempting to let the glamour slip while she was indoors, to let the hair curl and go blonde, and her eyes to dip a stormier shade of blue, but she couldn't risk it for her own safety. She couldn't force Sammy to go to the library either, even though it would do her good.

If she doesn't want to go, I can't force her. I'm not her keeper, or her-

She couldn't even bear to finish the thought, nausea rising fast at the mere possibility of facing what had happened to Talie, and what had brought her into sharing a living space with Sammy.

"Don't let anyone in," she insisted. "Don't go out either."

Sammy shrugged. "As if I have anywhere left to go."

"You know what I mean."

"Fine."

"Fine."

Molly pushed the door open and stepped into the lane. She didn't bother with goodbye but she turned and locked the door behind her, as she always did. Sammy had a key so she could unlock it any time she needed to, but assuming she was behaving, she wouldn't need to.

There was some small worry that Ru might appear, pretending to still be her best friend in order to steal her away again, but she was spoiling for a fight and ready for him if he tried.

Where once she would have doubted herself, because he was once her closest friend, now that Talie was gone she couldn't bear the thought of even seeing his face.

If he hadn't kidnapped me and taken me to Celeste, she might still be here.

She wouldn't have to keep worrying about making sure there was enough food for Sammy, or keep asking if the couple of dog-eared books she traded for to keep Sammy occupied were enough. They both knew it wasn't.

She's grieving, and her grief is bound to be far deeper than mine.

She glanced over her shoulder and up past the roofs to the vast pane of glass. The entire citadel, all five towers, being walled in by glass meant the seasons and weather were simulated. Molly hunched deeper into her coat as the vents on the level above pumped chilly air down, determined to get her time in the library over with.

She passed the door to her workshop with quiet steps and slowed with yearning twisting in her chest. The royals had all but banned her from setting foot inside the workshop when they left the citadel after the battle, but she wanted to throw everything aside and let herself in. They all insisted it was too dangerous for anyone to be seen going in there, even with a glamour, but she could be quick enough to not be seen.

Too risky.

She sighed. To everyone outside, she was Daisy and Molly had been missing for weeks. The only thing that kept her from dipping into the never-ending despair and never surfacing again was her daily trips to the library several levels down from her own.

As she turned onto the paved lane that led up and down the various levels of the tower, she noticed not many people were out and about. Usually the lanes were teeming with carts and people, but since the battle at the Menagerie, which she'd technically been at least the partial cause of, people were keeping to themselves.

She shoved her hands into the pockets of her jeans and walked fast down the deserted morning lanes to the towering open doorway of the library.

Once she would have looked up in wonder as she

ventured inside, would have admired the tall vaulted stone ceilings and the enormous rows of wooden stacks among several levels. Passageways disappeared into the gloom near the back of the vast hall, but now it was the blessed silence and the calming scent of aged paper that she welcomed. Even the constant swirl of cosy heating seemed to be timeless despite whatever madness raged on outside the library's doors.

Milo lifted his head above the reception desk, the messiness of his sandy brown hair suggesting he was busy doing something scholarly.

"You're late," he announced.

Molly eyed the big clock on a pedestal behind him, partially blocked by his bulky shoulders.

"I'm a minute early."

"Yes, but you take your coat off, fuss around finding somewhere to sit, get up again to find your books, glower at anyone sitting near you, even if they were sitting there first, and that takes at least ten minutes."

Molly sucked in a breath to snap back, but he was helping her. Technically, he was helping the Holly Queen rather than her, but it all added up to the same end.

"Okay."

He frowned. "That's it? I expected some kind of backchat."

"No backchat. I just want to get on."

"Hmm. Sammy isn't with you?"

"No."

"Why not?"

"She..." Molly hesitated. "Doesn't approve of library

rules. She finds them stifling."

It was almost worth the act of betrayal to hear Milo's indignantly high-pitched squawk. It echoed across the stone and startled one of the Fae reading nearby.

"Stifling?!" he hissed like a feral cat.

Molly nodded. The recklessness felt good, rebellious, a tiny hint of control in the chaos her world had become since Talie died.

"That's ridiculous! Doesn't she know how lucky she is to even have access? Through normal channels, you'd never have been able to get her this luxury!"

Molly stiffened. "She's grieving. If she doesn't want to come, I'm not going to make her.""

"You're grieving, yet you're here."

"I don't want to talk about it."

He stared at her for several seconds, until a flash of awkwardness passed across his face.

"That's okay. I have found some things that might be of more interest anyway. Also, I have someone I want to introduce you to."

He beckoned to the lone Fae still reading nearby, or apparently not reading because he stood the moment he was mentioned despite his gaze being fixed on the page in front of him.

I didn't even see him turn it. I need to be sharper than this.

Molly tensed as the man approached, ready to cast a warding if he came to close.

"This is Ace," Milo said. "Anything you say to me, you can say to him. Now, I have an entire archive to catalogue.

Faerie knows how anything ever functioned in this cavernous pit."

He bustled off with a pile of books under his arm and Molly stared after him, horrified.

Ace wiped a hand over his black beard and gave her an easy smile. He stood taller than Milo and slimmer, but the rolled-up sleeves of his dark red sweatshirt suggested he had more than enough physical power if he needed it.

"Well, it's good to finally meet you," he said. "I'm the social one out of Milo and I."

"I don't need social."

Ace folded his arms across his chest. "Maybe not, but it has to be better than being glowered at by Milo all day."

"I heard that," echoed from one of the stacks.

Molly's lips twitched involuntarily. Immediately after, the swoop of all-encompassing guilt stole her ability to breathe. She turned away. Ace was no doubt one of the royal entourage if Milo trusted him completely, one of the queen's trusted few, but they wouldn't be sharing confidences or anything.

"I get glowered at all the time." Ace lowered his voice to a stage whisper.

"That bad at books are you?"

He smiled. "No, I'm his boyfriend which is apparently worse."

"Oh." Molly frowned. "I suppose there's no sense me asking if you've always lived in the citadel then, or how you really got here?"

As Ace tapped the side of his nose, the sleeve of his sweatshirt slid down to reveal a familiar silver bracelet with rainbow beads. A tiny shred of reservation ebbed away as Molly glanced at the identical one on her own wrist, a sign of recognition between the Holly Queen's inner circle. It meant she could trust that while Ace might not be who he claimed to be, he was definitely someone on the queen's side, and therefore hers too.

Ace dropped his hands to his sides and tilted his head from side to side until his neck cracked.

"It's a long story, and I'm sure we'll get to it in time," he said. "For now, let's start groaning through these books Milo found."

Molly followed him back to his previous desk and a tumbling pile of books.

"Do you know what we're looking for?" she asked.

"Any mention of the citadel's past, this mysterious well of power, divergences in the fabric of Faerie, gift replication, among other things." He took a seat and pulled another over for her. "From what I hear, Celeste is issuing rewards for your return, while Phoenix is now commanding the upper levels."

Molly clenched her fists around the back of the nearest chair. She hadn't thought as much about Phoenix as she had Celeste since the fight at the Menagerie, but as the head of the resistance, he was still someone she had to keep in mind. She couldn't trust him, but Celeste was the one on her hit list.

Her Fae connection rippled awake and the familiar burn of her sunshine gift flared. Ace didn't startle as her skin began to glow, didn't even raise an eyebrow. He waited, stoically silent, until she got herself back under control.

"Okay, I won't mention her name," he said. "Probably for the best. Either way, we both know what we're looking for. It's also about forty-five minutes away from when Milo gets hangry so we can risk a walk to the food van."

Molly frowned. "Has he… has Phoenix taken actual control?"

"Mostly. He's set up a drop-in centre, all things told, for Fae to take their issues to. He says he wants to listen but he'll need time to establish himself. According to him, the upper levels do much of the production and so the better offs and nobles on further down levels will start to struggle or have to start treaties with royalty territory."

Molly slid into the seat.

"Most Fae here would see that as a failure."

Ace hesitated. "Not a bad thing to ask for help when you need it, but I know Fae have their pride. "

It complicated everything in some ways, and she hoped at least Phoenix was mourning Talie even a droplet as much as she was.

He won't feel guilty but he knew her longer than I did.

She pulled the nearest book in front of her and eased it open.

"Only forty-five more minutes?" she asked wearily.

Ace grinned. "Basically forty now. Thirty if we make some solid notes."

Molly sighed as loudly as she could and reached out to grab a pen.

CHAPTER TWO

"It's something to do with the royal family," Ace insisted.

He sat calmly at their usual table in the library, three days after Molly had met him. Sammy had refused each time to come with her, but Molly didn't try too hard. She simply took the *pesanas* Milo gave her each evening, with insistences they were on the queen's orders not his, and brought food from Merry's stall in the park on the way back.

Milo stood with his hands on his heavily-sweatered hips, his brow narrowed.

"It's always something to do with the royal family. They're everywhere." He flicked a glance Molly's way. "No offense."

She shuddered. "I'm not royalty. As soon as this is over, I'm going right back to my workshop. Whatever it is to do with, we haven't found anything much that'll help bring the Menagerie to heel."

Milo sighed and Ace reached for another book, his unruffled persistence never faltering. She had to admit that his presence made a big difference. He was a fast reader, efficient note-taker and always ready to look at anything she found potentially interesting. It made it all the more amusing when Milo insisted Ace was utterly hopeless and threw several strops over the slightest things, all of which Ace handled with his easy smile.

"If we only knew what they were planning, it would be a start," Milo grumbled.

Molly sagged in her chair. "They're definitely in league with each other, the Oak Queen and *her*."

She didn't even want Celeste's name in her mind, let alone have to face the fact Celeste was related to her. Even before Talie died, Celeste had been Molly's enemy.

"Explain that bit to me again, Molly," Ace suggested. "How do you know exactly?"

"They said as much. We were sent to the queen's court and I never knew how she got us in there, but then when they took me into the Menagerie, they as good as admitted that the Oak Queen knew all along."

"It's nothing we haven't considered before," Milo said. "Demi's worried the Oak Queen might be playing a much longer game, and she never took well to Faerie and the nether crowning Demi as her equal."

Ace leaned back in his chair to stretch his arms above his head.

"If she has been in league with Celeste all these years with the plan to take over the citadel then unite the whole of Faerie under the family's rule, it would make sense."

Milo nodded. "She has been intransigent to a lot of Demi's plans and suggestions suddenly. It's almost like she's hoping to delay change until the status quo swings back to her."

Molly folded her arms over the desk and slumped her

chin on top.

"None of that helps us figure out how to stop her though. It's not like we can merrily skip in an army while nobody's watching."

A look passed between Milo and Ace. She sat up.

"What? What's that look for?"

Another hesitant glance, then Ace leaned forward.

"We know someone who can realm-skip at will, much like Kainen and Reyan can shadow," he said. "They're hampered by the renewed wards around the citadel of course, but we think we've found a loophole of sorts."

Milo rolled his eyes. "Ever the man of mystery. I've been looking for a way to skip people in and out, and we've found one."

"Wait, one of you can realm-skip whenever you want?"

"Yes, but it's absolutely a secret," Milo insisted. "Demi might not be able to interfere or step foot inside the citadel anymore, but that doesn't mean those who love her can't misbehave on her behalf."

"Wow. That's cool."

Milo sniffed. "It's a big responsibility and a curse when most Fae would either befriend you for perks or use you outright."

"Fair. How does it work then? How can you get people in?"

Milo turned on his heel and hurried toward the reception desk. Molly waited, because that was his 'I have a book for this' hustle, not a 'I'm done talking to you, idiot' hustle. He returned moments later with a hefty tome in both hands.

"Most Fae research other Fae, historical ones, famous

ones, but they often forget to look beyond themselves and their kind," he explained, setting the book on the desk as if it was a fragile infant and opening to the page he needed. "See, here. There are strains of old stone from ancient days of Faerie that have been used to create the citadel for control, to hem them in inside a Faerie circle."

Molly frowned. "Right, but what does that tell us?"

"It's a Faerie circle, a ring of protection, of power. The stone is the boundary of the well of power."

"You mean like an actual wishing well? I've seen pictures of those before."

Milo's head tipped to the side. "That's a good way of thinking about it. The well of power could be manipulated into powering Fae gifts, although I doubt simple wishing is enough to control it."

"Whatever it is, Celeste will be using it to reinforce her control," Molly said. "Tal- someone once told me that the Menagerie is built around the core of the citadel, probably for that exact purpose."

Ace nodded. "Which is something Phoenix may or may not be aware of. Oh, I almost forgot. He's called a meeting."

"Phoenix?" Molly leaned her hands on the table, braced to stand.

"Yeah. He's called it a 'peace talk' and sent people out through the levels with flyers. He says he's calling out Celeste to discuss the future of the citadel."

Molly bit her lip as yet another wary look passed between the two men.

"You mustn't go," Milo said. "It's too dangerous. Demi

would never forgive me."

Molly frowned. "I'd be going as Daisy."

"Still too dangerous," Ace insisted gently. "I've hidden the flyer, so don't think about trying to find out when it is either. Remember you said you wouldn't talk to people outside unless it was an emergency."

"I know I did." She raced through the technicalities. "I won't go hunting for your stupid flyer, don't worry."

Milo sighed. "Somehow, I don't believe you. We can pack up early today. Same time tomorrow."

He gathered as many of their books to his chest as he could carry in his burly arms and set off for the reception desk. Ace lingered long enough to give her a sympathetic smile and set off after him.

Molly shrugged on her coat with her mind firing. Her Fae connection flickered awake enough for her sunshine gift to warm her skin.

On the rare occasion she'd tried to connect over the past few weeks it had been illusive beyond the need for glamouring and warding to protect as she moved between the house and the library. It gave her a tiny ember of hope that she could still access it, and if retribution was the fuel then she'd take it gladly.

I won't go looking for their flyer. She frowned on her way to the doors. *I can't talk to anyone outside the library unless I have to either.*

The flyers would have been delivered through every door and letterbox though knowing Phoenix. If Ace had somehow managed to get hers from Sammy, which was doubtful, then there was another place she could find one.

"Put those books down that carelessly again and I will remove your fingers so you can't hold any!" Milo's feral hiss echoed across the library hall behind her.

He and Ace were likely risking danger to be here, and while she wasn't naïve enough to assume it was solely to keep an eye on her, they were being kind.

It's risky. It's everything I promised not to do.

The lanes whisked past as she strode toward home, the chilly air blasting from vents above leaving hints of frost on the citadel glass. She didn't slow her pace until she reached the opening to her alley, and even then she kept her steps steady as she passed the workshop door.

Kept her gaze fixed on the door to the house at the end of the alley.

Reached a hand out to swipe the flapping slip of paper wedged between the workshop door and the frame.

She shoved the flyer in her trouser pocket and approached the house, her heart pounding as she slid the key in the door and knocked three times before opening it.

"Only me," she announced.

Sammy lifted her head. "Hi only you. I made food. Oh. Where's the stuff from Merry's?"

Molly hadn't thought that far but she improvised fast.

"I figured I'd get double tomorrow, maybe walk up to *Butch's* and get something else as well. Variety and all that."

"That's probably a good idea. Merry's stuff is great but I'm sure the oil is making my skin break out. The food on the side should still be warm though."

As if that's all we have to worry about.

Molly nodded. "Thanks. Toilet first."

She hauled off her shoes and hung her coat on the peg by the door, then shut herself in the tiny bathroom to pull out the flyer.

Scanning past all the forced positivity in the scant wording about opportunities and truth, she found the information she needed.

Tonight, 7pm, the gym.

Her chest squished tight and she lifted a hand to rub the ache aside. She hadn't been anywhere near the gym since the day Talie died.

She re-pocketed the flyer and took a deep breath.

I can do this. She opened the door and tried to smile. *I have to.*

CHAPTER THREE

By time 7pm rolled around, Molly had to keep her hands under her thighs to hide them glowing. Sammy gave her a knowing look when she mentioned going out but didn't say a word until Molly had her coat on.

"Be careful," she insisted. "If you're going to be out all night, orb me and let me know."

Molly would have smiled in any other circumstance as Sammy stood in front of her, hands on hips in a huge purple dressing gown that used to be Beryl's with a large hair-wrap on. As it was, it took all Molly's effort to keep the bubbling anxiety at bay.

"I will, don't worry."

Sammy sighed theatrically. "It's my lot to worry in life."

Molly didn't dare reply. While she was swilling in grief and revenge, Sammy seemed to be pretending the whole thing hadn't happened, like Talie was just off on some extended mission somewhere.

Not a conversation I want to have right now. Or ever.

Molly stepped into the lane and locked the door behind her, then glanced around to make sure nobody was watching. Daisy was meant to be taller but she had compensated originally by shortening her height to conserve energy. Exhaustion needled through her limbs but she firmed the glamour tighter around her and set off toward the main lane.

The paving underfoot was slick from the artificial rain pumping out from the vents above, but her climbing shoes made no noise as she started up the levels. Soft amber lights beamed out of household windows as she passed them, but she lifted her head and eyed the girders and beams instead. The underside of the level above had been her favourite haunt before, and it would be so easy to vault up there and track to the gym that way amid the rooftops and the chimney stacks.

She shook her head sadly and continued on up the circling lane. Taking the Menagerie routes along the rooftops would be dangerous if anyone found her there, and she couldn't risk using her stealth gift either as Celeste could see through it.

Her palms turned clammy as she approached the doors to the gym. A steady stream of Fae were going inside so she joined the crush and slid into a narrow gap between the door and a pile of training mats with her heart pounding.

Memories swarmed as she stared around the familiar space.

Talie glowering at her far more often than she smiled.

Talie super focused on whoever she was sparring against in the ring.

Talie throwing a sparring pad at her head.

She lifted a hand to her chest and rubbed the ache there, mindful to keep a vacant smile on her face. Pretending was easier when she knew there might be something in return, and even the tiniest hint of news about how to take Celeste down would do. She scanned the crowd for anyone that might take interest in her, Milo and Ace especially, but nobody gave her a second glance.

Clapping echoed over the humming crowd and all eyes turned to the largest training ring in the centre of the gym. A spotlight flicked on as the rest of the space dimmed as Phoenix appeared to take centre stage, and Molly's insides twisted at the sight of him.

If he hadn't sent us in there, maybe she wouldn't...

She shook the thoughts away. What happened to Talie wasn't Phoenix's fault, not directly.

Tall and thin, his general presence dominated the room and had the expectant crowd silent in seconds. He'd tied his long silver hair back from his face and, while he smiled readily enough, Molly thought she could see the pinch of tiredness around his eyes.

"Welcome everyone!" Phoenix began. "Thank you all for coming. As I'm sure many of you know, there have been a lot of worries and twice as many rumours about the recent turmoil between the upper and lower levels."

Molly scanned the crowd again as someone took the space in front of her, with shoulders so broad that she panicked it was Milo for a moment. She inched sideways in time to see a screen being set up behind Phoenix.

"Although I've taken the unofficial duty of making sure everyone is okay, we have someone from the Menagerie who is orbing in for consultation," he continued. "Hopefully we can put all the fears to rest tonight. Ah, here she is."

Molly clenched her fists in her coat pocket as a black and white image appeared on the screen. Celeste looked her unruffled self, and despite the black and white orb-cast Molly could easily remember the caramel colour of her curled hair and the deceptive warmth of her brown eyes.

Breathe. Calm. She's not here. She fought the burning rise of her sunshine gift, the urge to incinerate Celeste to a crisp clawing at her resolve. *You can't eviscerate her through an orb-cast.*

Celeste cleared her throat unnecessarily and smiled as her gaze flicked over the crowd. Molly tensed but Celeste only nodded.

"Good evening. I see many faces assembled. Good. Needless to say the Menagerie will consider leniency and forgiveness to all who drop this disobedience. The Menagerie have supported the smooth running of the citadel for years now, and will continue to do so, but we won't tolerate anarchy."

A dissenting grumble rumbled through the crowd but Phoenix held his hands up for calm.

"The Menagerie have helped some perhaps, but definitely not all," he countered. "We're here to insist that you honour the current split and seek no further control over the upper levels, not at least until trades and treaties can be put in place."

Celeste smiled. "I have no need to seek you out or to fight. The Menagerie can lock down like a fortress, and the core of the citadel will always be a strong foundation for us. Perhaps the Fae of the upper levels need a taste of who exactly is in control here."

Shouts echoed up from the lane outside and Molly dodged past random people to reach the gym doors. She peered out onto the night-time lane lit by the lamps in time to see tiles shaking loose from roofs and smashing down.

As the rumbling ceased, Celeste's laughter echoed over the crowd like falling shards of glass.

"You see? I can do whatever I choose. You are all here by our grace, and we have no need to torment any of you. Simply accept the conditions we've put forth, and you can go back to your lives."

"Complete dependence for us, and utter dominion for you?" Phoenix scoffed.

Celeste nodded. "Those are my terms. Anyone who finds and returns my daughter to me unharmed will also receive special reward."

The orb-cast vanished and the gym exploded into uproar. Phoenix raised his hands for quiet as Nia, his second in command, joined him with panic on her face.

The shaking underfoot continued as Molly's mind whirled away from the chaos inside the gym and down the lane. She couldn't evacuate the entire citadel, not on her own in a glamour, but she could make good on the one thing Talie had once asked of her.

"Enough!" Phoenix hollered. "I won't ask anyone to fight but those that can should make a stand now. She won't expect us to rally this quickly. Go about your business and count a half hour. Anyone willing to join us, we storm their front doors before they're expecting us."

The crowd headed for the door as a roaring hum of

people, but Molly clung to her Daisy glamour and inched closer to Phoenix and Nia.

"-not going to cut it." Nia twisted her fingers through her braids, her brown eyes wide with frustration. "We can't send them into a potential massacre."

Phoenix shook his head. "We have to be seen to be doing something. People know the risks. If they show up, they're prepared to take them."

"We can't best them on strength, not of gifts or numbers. The Menagerie have the boots and their own guards. People could die."

"What other option do we have? We can't just sit and agree."

Nia folded her arms and looked away, but the dregs of the crowd were leaving and Molly didn't have any of the inner circle safeties with her Daisy glamour that she used to have as herself.

She stormed out of the gym and down the lane.

If I can get Sammy to the library, to Milo and Ace, they'll keep her safe.

As she passed her workshop she slowed her step. Getting Sammy to the library would be as big a trial as fighting, even more so. She knocked three times on the door and opened it with her key, not bothering to announce herself as she whirled in.

"That was quick," Sammy announced, not looking up from the book she was reading.

Molly nodded as she grabbed their coats and threw Sammy's at her, then pointed at the bag of belongings she'd insisted Sammy keep ready just in case. She didn't trade much in luck, but for once Sammy was still dressed for outdoors rather than for bed.

"Time to go."

Sammy sat up. "What? Where? Why?"

"It's a precaution, but I promised... I promised her I'd keep you safe."

"Safe where?" Sammy demanded.

"Library. I know you're not Milo's biggest fan, but Ace is fun. He's nice. You'll like him."

She prepared herself for a fight, exhausted at the mere thought.

"Okay."

"I need you to understand-" Molly's brain glitched. "What?"

Sammy shrugged. "It's for my safety, right? I don't know what exactly is happening, but I know when to do what I'm told."

She grabbed her coat from Molly's unresisting fingers, hauled it on, then stood ready with her bag in hand.

"That's literally the opposite of everything you've ever done!"

Sammy managed a tiny, weary smile.

"Yeah well, it's what she asked you to do. Are we going or what?"

Molly opened the door with an unsteady hand, her thoughts frazzled and uneasy. The levels were still quaking gently, not enough to cause damage anymore but enough to be a continual warning.

She lifted her other hand to her throat but of course her neck chain was safe in her privy pouch, too obvious a sign of who she was if she wore it visibly. It had the little silver charm Sammy had gifted her for last Yuletide, her workshop key, and the acorn and bit of moor grass cast in resin that Talie had given her. The only part of her past life she couldn't bear to hide away was the small red *Akiai* charm in the shape of a heart that Talie had given her, still firmly in place as a ring on her right thumb.

The main lane was heaving with nervous energy, and several groups had clustered under lamps muttering among themselves. Molly noticed others boarding up their windows, and shops that were always open had already shut their doors.

"Wow," Sammy muttered. "It's something big, isn't it?"

Molly nodded. "Less I say the better."

They dodged through the throngs of people until they reached the library doors, and Molly braced herself for what might lie inside. She hauled one of the hefty doors open and chivvied Sammy inside as both of them almost collided with Ace.

"I was just coming to find you." He locked the doors behind them and swept them toward the reception desk. "I went to that meeting, but apparently Daisy was already there."

He leaned back against the counter, his broad arms folded across his chest.

Molly hesitated. "I'm meant to be Daisy."

"You're meant to be at home," Milo chimed in from behind the counter. "Luckily Ace thought fast enough to be someone else, but it could have jeopardised everyone."

Molly couldn't find it in her to be sorry, but she

managed a somewhat contrite shrug and a slight hanging of her head.

"Oh don't sulk," Milo huffed.

"What's done is done," Ace added. "You're both safe, which is what matters. Whatever Phoenix and his lot have planned, the library will withstand it."

Molly scowled. "And the people that don't? The shops that will lose livelihoods and entire families if they're destroyed? I should be out there helping-"

"Like it or not, you're part of the royal fam-"

"Don't. I'm not. I refuse. I abdicate or whatever."

Ace's lips twitched. "Abdicate all you like, you're just proving how like them you really are. Either way, it still remains that we can't let you go running into an unknown situation-"

"But-"

"-without protection." He held up a hand to silence her. "Whatever you may think of us, we do care."

Sammy gasped softly, her head lifted to see past the library's main desk, and Molly followed her gaze. The front doors were locked, but swathes of people were emerging from the depths of the library. She didn't recognise any of them but there were so many that she couldn't count them, all adults of varying ages.

"Wait..."

She moved to stand in front of Sammy.

Ace smiled. "Demi can't be seen to interfere, but a lot of us have never been very good at listening. It took a lot of arranging, but if we can keep the peace when the fighting breaks out or start getting people to safety if needed then we will."

Astonished, Molly shoved her hands in her pockets.

"How will we get them all down without being seen?" she asked. "Never mind that, how did you get them all in here? Are they locals? Nobles? What are we doing?"

"No 'we'," Milo insisted. "You stay here. They are all trained and qualified to undertake these things, and know how to integrate with different locations."

"No, I'm going and you can't stop me."

Ace gave Milo a weary look. "How about we go and observe. It's not far and I can have her back if anything kicks off."

Milo shut the book in front of him with a smart snap.

"You're far too indulgent," he grumbled. "Which then means I have to go along with it too. Fine, but the first sign of trouble and we're out of here."

Molly grimaced at Sammy, guessing what would come next.

"Both of you stay together," Ace insisted.

Sammy's jaw dropped. "You're not making me stay here?"

"We need you and Molly together."

"Easier to keep you out of trouble that way," Milo muttered.

Ace grinned and lifted a hand to his mouth. A piercing whistle shattered the hum of chatter and the gaggle of unfamiliar faces turned toward him.

"Right, peacekeeping duties only," he announced. "Any injured get them out of the fray, any scared or lost faces the same. Steer clear of any fighting."

A communal groan echoed at that, but the crowd washed toward the doors like a wave and Ace hurried to unlock them again. Molly followed close behind him with Sammy at her side and Milo grumbling under his breath behind them.

"There's no way they won't see us coming," Molly murmured.

The lanes were deserted already, and no doubt the word had spread like fire after the meeting, but the odd curtain twitched as they passed.

"That's not what we need to worry-"

Ace's voice was drowned out by an almighty roar further down the lane. A cacophonous bang shook the foundations of the citadel, the gentle quake escalating to a rattle strong enough to send signboards and various other outside items skidding across the lane.

Molly eyed Sammy, close enough to Milo that he could grab her and drag her back to the library. As the crowd surged forward and the curve of the lane leading to the Menagerie doors came into view, she ducked and shot forward.

"Don't you dare!" Ace grabbed her wrist and hauled her back. "They know what they're doing. You can't take her down on your own. Be smart."

Molly stood with her heart pounding. Ace was stronger than she could ever beat by force, so she succumbed to letting him lead her to the fringe of the fight with the overpowering aura of Milo's worry shaking at her back.

As they reached the edge of the crowd, the sizzle and crash of gifts welled up and an almighty rumbling shook the ground beneath them.

A deafening crack tore through the air.

The crowd stilled, gifts dissipating against wardings as everyone turned toward the nearest stretch of glass that contained their levels of the tower.

A fissure rippled through the glass and the realm hung on a droplet of utter stillness. Then the glass exploded, splintering outward. Molly stumbled as the rumbling increased and the level beneath them swayed.

"She's bringing down the entire tower!" someone bellowed.

Her panic squeezed her breathless as she took a step forward.

"Molly, don't," Ace warned.

She dropped her weight down to a crouch and tore her wrist free, then twisted away from him before he could catch her. Half the crowd surged up toward them as she darted away, and the other half scattered downward, yells and screams echoing in all directions.

People hurried out of their homes while others staring in horror. Molly couldn't remember anyone ever having a safety plan for if the citadel ever shattered but carts were already being loaded.

She ducked past people fleeing and ran toward the Menagerie's entrance. A huge pane of glass dashed down a short distance away and she dodged to throw her warding over the people beneath it, straining against the effort. She could feel the pulse of other wardings around her, but none she recognised.

I only ever learned to merge with hers.

She shook the thought away and stared desperately at the chaos as it flowed around her.

"What do we do?" one woman asked nearby.

Molly had no idea but up ahead the enormous iron doors of the Menagerie were shut. The foundations of the warehouses and homes on the glass-side of the level were shuddering still but the core-side where the Menagerie was stood firm and untouched, as if warded against the damage.

"The core," she muttered, then lifted her voice to be heard. "Head for core spaces! The libraries, the warehouses. Get yourself into one of those."

For whatever reason, Celeste was only attacking the glass-side, whether to keep the Menagerie protected or because it was the limit of her power, Molly couldn't guess. She focused inward and let her sunshine gift warm her bones as Ace skidded to a halt beside her.

"Enough," he shouted. "It's not safe out here for you, especially now!"

"If I turn myself in, this stops!" she insisted.

He grimaced. "Sorry in advance then."

A strong arm banded around her waist from behind. Even as she opened her mouth to protest, the citadel shifted and dribbled to a mass of swirling purple-grey. Dark limbs grew around her and a blast of freezing air hit her face.

The ground shifted and she stumbled to right her balance as her foot sank ankle-deep in something pale and soft. She'd heard rumour of snow before and even seen a hint of it through the citadel glass a few times, but she hadn't expected it to be freezing cold or able to soak right through her climbing shoes.

She twisted as Milo let go of her and eyed the mass of trees shadowed against the nighttime darkness. Sammy stood beside her with a hand to her mouth, but Molly looked to the lights up ahead and the echo of the citadel tower still breaking in distant cracks and rumbles.

She shivered against the cold and focused on the climbing burn of fury heating her limbs instead.

"How could you?" She turned on Milo. "We need to go back in and help everyone!"

He blinked back at her, apparently happy to berate her for mishandling books but uneasy in the face of her rage outside his safe zone.

"I will be back in a second," he said. "Please don't go anywhere."

Then he vanished like an orb-cast, leaving them alone and defenceless in a forest outside the citadel.

CHAPTER FOUR

"What was that?" Sammy asked.

Molly stared around at the wind whipping through the trees, the only light to see by coming from a large pale yellow moon above and from the citadel still shaking ominously in the distance.

"That was realm-skipping," she muttered. "Don't know how he did it, maybe because the glass shattered."

She vaguely remembered him saying he could skip at will, but she assumed that was within the citadel's limits. The wards alone should have prevented anyone going in and out on foot, let alone skipping by choice.

Molly took a couple of steps forward but the snow clung to her feet, zapping at the lingering dregs of energy she had.

"You're glowing," Sammy announced.

"Yeah, well, I'm mad. Really, really mad. I can't leave you here alone, I can't get back to the citadel in time to stop it from crashing, and I don't even know if the nobles or the boots would even let me pass through."

Sammy frowned. "Why do you want to get back in?"

"People are going to get injured! If Celeste has me back,

she'll stop the chaos, at least enough for Phoenix to arrange to get people out."

"Phoenix doesn't sound like the type of person to want people out of the citadel though."

Molly lifted both hands and knuckled her temples in an attempt to cling onto her temper. With a spike of her connection, her shoulders lengthened and the telltale cold trickle of her glamour lifting rippled over her skin.

She glanced down at her hands, recognisable as her own by the sudden reappearance of several scars and calluses from working in the workshop for so long. Then she lifted a hand and pulled a loose strand of hair in front of her face, the chestnut gleam of Daisy's hair now her own muted blonde curls that she was used to.

She sucked in a breath and hunched her shoulders against the wave of exhaustion threatening to pummel her into the snow.

"Phoenix is ruthless," she agreed. "But surely even he can't expect people to risk their lives simply to stay part of the citadel's body-count. If he does, then he's as bad as she is because it should be a choice."

She flinched as someone appeared beside her out of thin air, her relief see-sawing when more started to arrive.

Molly blinked away the sudden burn of relief in her eyes as Lord Kainen of the Illusion Court came to a halt in front of them. He had thrown a leather jacket over a dark t-shirt but one leg of his black trousers was hiked halfway up his calf, as if he'd not finished pulling them on. Given the ruffled brown hair, he'd been called from his bed.

"Milo gave us a heads up," he announced.

Molly tensed as the Holly Queen of Faerie strode toward them with her arms clamped around her middle to ward off the cold. She didn't look like a queen at all in jeans and a hoodie, with messy black curls and pale skin, but her blue eyes were sharp and alert.

"Demi, what's the plan?" Kainen asked.

"Not a clue." Demi sighed. "Marthe's on her way to set up camp. She's on loan from the Oak Court at Taz's request, and her own apparently, and the Oak Queen is absolutely fuming so that's something else I have to sort later."

Molly had been told to call them by name rather than title before, but she still had some reservations about that. As the sound of rumbling from the citadel grew louder, she pushed past the doubt.

"I need you to take me back in," she insisted. "There are people who won't know where to go, or won't be able to get out. We don't even know if the noble levels are affected, and someone will need to force them to open their doors for people."

Kainen shook his head. "They won't do that Rumours have been circulating through the nobility for a while now that the citadel isn't going to be safe much longer, or prosperous. They're all moving their assets to Gallows Oak."

Molly had no idea what or where that was, but the callousness of it horrified her. She wrapped an arm around her middle and anchored her other hand around the charms hanging at her throat.

"Then we need to get them into the core spaces. The

library is huge, and the Menagerie wasn't shaking so I bet Celeste hasn't targeted the core itself."

A resounding crash echoed through the night, then the distant rumbling ceased. Silence roared in its wake and Molly tried to assess the distance between them and the citadel.

I can sneak in by stealth and take an Arumpii up the levels if the ground is steady.

Before she could ask if they would at least vouch to look after Sammy, the shadows roiled nearby and Reyan arrived. Kainen reached out a hand for her as she tucked her blonde hair into a ponytail, but she at least had thought to bring a puffy black coat. Molly eyed it with a tinge of envy as she shivered in hers.

"The lower levels are in ruins," Reyan said. "The core of the citadel holding but several levels further up are in rubble. There are huge gaps in the ground, and of course the nobles have all fled. There was a cascade of animals fleeing down, buildings crashed in, it's basically only a structure in a few places-"

Molly let her stealth gift cloak around her and inched past them. Even as she dodged Sammy, Demi's gaze narrowed. She lifted a hand and Molly hit an invisible warding.

"No you don't," Demi said. "I understand you wanting to go in there, but people are going to need you here."

Molly reined her stealth gift back and faced the queen of Faerie with a glare.

"What people could possibly need me out here?"

Demi pointed over her shoulder without even looking

back.

"Those ones."

A stream of lights bobbed from the base of the citadel, the front of them now halfway through the trees. Molly had misjudged the distance in her panic but the trail of people heading straight for them were moving wide and slow.

"I've had Milo and Ace ready to get anyone out who needed it," Demi added. "We had to ensure there was a contingency plan in place but I'm not allowed to interfere. Now those people are outside the citadel walls, they fall under my rule."

Molly stared as a host of Fae realm-skipped into the clearing like well-practiced magic, along with bundles of canvas, foldable tables, and huge barrels. The silence gave way to the industrious clang of hammers and saws, and Molly yearned to grab something to fix and join in.

"What about the people still stuck in there?" She sagged, exhausted. "Celeste and Marcus will put the wards back up. I'm not even sure what she achieved by breaking the glass, but she won't need that to lock the citadel down again."

"She wants chaos," Kainen said.

Demi nodded. "She's running a dangerous balancing act between keeping the nobles on side so they support her and keeping the citadel functioning enough to have power to offer them. Clearing out some of the people will damage production and industry and make everyone more reliant on her. Easier to control that way."

"But she ruined the lower levels," Molly said. "You said yourself the nobles are leaving for somewhere else."

"Now, let's not have any of this fussing."

Molly recognised the voice, but she hadn't had time to give any thought to who it belonged to for a while. Marthe, head housekeeper at the Oak Queen's court, bustled past Kainen like he was a stray bit of curtain in her path.

Her pale hair was pulled back into a neat bun and she looked no less determined for the simple sweatshirt and jeans she was wearing, a far cry from the smart outfits Molly had seen her in at the court before.

She tensed as Marthe barrelled to a stop in front of her with a disapproving frown on her face.

"You need fresh clothes. And a bath," Marthe insisted. "I knew the moment I saw you. Like the queen in her younger years, but slightly darker of hair."

Molly froze as Marthe settled a hand on her cheek, then tutted.

"Too cold."

"I'm fine," she mumbled. "I need to help everyone else. There'll be people who are injured and maybe even animals that need sorting. It's snowing and we've got nowhere to live."

Marthe only huffed and snapped her fingers to summon a bundle of fabric into her arms.

"It's better to do as she says," Demi said. "Queens and nobles and Fae and fairies I can argue with. Marthe, not so much. Perhaps if we give Molly a warm coat and some proper, worn-in snow boots, then she can make sure everything we're setting up for the citadel's people will be enough."

Marthe gave Demi a judgemental once-over, but after a

moment she nodded and clicked her fingers again for a pair of boots.

"As you wish, your majesty."

Demi winced as Marthe bundled the mass of pink cloth into Molly's arms, dropped the boots in the snow beside her feet and set off like a determined bee toward the nearest tent. Even in the few minutes they'd been talking, Fae had arrived in droves with boxes, crates and bags. Canvas tents were going up everywhere and a burst of light flared among the trees as someone cast Faelight around.

"You are so in trouble," Kainen said with a grin.

Demi nodded. "Yeah, great. If it was Taz saying it, Marthe would just smile and pat him on the head."

"She wouldn't listen to him though, to be fair," Reyan added.

"True." Demi's gloominess brightened at that. "Right, Molly. Formalities need to be done so let's get them over with. Are you claiming these people as officially yours? If you do, that means you're responsible for them and claiming part of Faerie under your royal title as Princess."

Molly stared back at her as horror twisted in her chest.

"I- what? No! I mean-"

"No, okay good." Demi glanced around. "That makes things much simpler. Otherwise you'd have to challenge me for the right of it, and that takes time we don't have. Are you in any way planning some kind of coup on the queen of Faerie-"

"That should probably be 'queens of Faerie', to be safe," Reyan suggested.

"Argh, fine. Are you planning any kind of coup on the

queens of Faerie that might affect my ability to offer aid and sanctuary to these people, Molly?"

"No!"

"Great. Everyone's on the same side, job done, someone tell Milo I've done it. Let's go."

Molly stared as Demi stalked off toward the first wave of people stumbling into the camp. Ace was at the front with Milo at his side, and Molly recognised Taz instantly as he broke the line to reach Demi's side the moment he saw her.

"She's not a very traditional queen," Kainen explained. "But it works. Most of the time. We'll need to count how many heads we have and how many injured. We've healers coming from various courts as well as a few offers to run a canteen. It won't be a long-term solution, but we can work on absorbing numbers into various realms over the coming days."

Reyan sighed. "Do we at least get our own tent?"

"What do you take me for? Meri's already had one set up for us in the court enclosure." He glanced at Molly. "You are technically the only standing grandchild of the oak line, so Marthe's no doubt set one up for you too."

He flinched as Marthe appeared beside him as if summoned.

"Marthe has set up two," she announced archly. "I assumed you would like privacy."

Molly bit her lip. "You okay with your own tent, Sammy? Or do you want to bunk in with me?"

"I don't mind." Sammy hesitated. "My own would be nice."

"Then that is what we will do," Marthe said.

Molly glanced at the citadel again, four towers standing tall and lit against the night, with the fifth glowing less brightly and missing several chunks.

Why? Why destroy it? Why go for such senseless violence?

"I'm going to see what needs to be done," she said. "I need the distraction."

Marthe sniffed. "One hour. Then bath and bed. You'll be able to help much more in the daylight tomorrow if you're well-rested."

"And well-washed?" Kainen offered.

"That too. One hour. Sammy is it? Follow me."

Sammy gave Molly a doubtful look as Marthe walked away and Demi reappeared beside them.

"I can help if you need me," she offered.

Molly bit her lip, then turned to Demi. "Is it safe?"

"Safe?" Demi frowned. "Marthe? I can vouch for her, if that's what you mean. None of us are here to trick anyone, only to help where we can."

She lifted her arm up between them and pulled back her sleeve. A bracelet of wire and rainbow beads lay around her wrist, and Molly let that be reassurance enough. It was the secret sign carried by those in the queen's confidence, and identical to the one she wore and had seen Milo and Ace wear too.

"Sorry, I just…"

Demi waved her hand. "I get it, don't worry. I'm the queen of Faerie, and Marthe can be trusted with you and with Sammy. Go get some rest, both of you."

It was basically a royal order, but Molly only gave Sammy a nod and watched as Sammy followed Marthe toward a large cluster of tents with an abundance of different coloured ropes and awnings.

"Those are the court colours," Kainen explained. "Ours is silver and dark grey with lilac, if you need to find us. Most of the court lords and ladies will be in attendance by tomorrow for a bit, but they're all friends of ours so don't worry if you go astray. Maybe be cautious with the pink and green, red and black one though. They might have brought the biting plant thing."

"Don't let Arthur hear you call her 'biting plant thing'," Reyan muttered with a smile.

Molly wiped a hand over her face and squared her shoulders. She might have people she knew needing her help. She couldn't do anything about the citadel itself, or the people no doubt now stuck warded inside it again, or even the whims and vigour of royalty, but she could help people that needed it.

CHAPTER FIVE

"You've barely slept."

Marthe's disappointed tone filtered through Molly's hazy consciousness the next morning. She hadn't slept beyond the odd fitful dream and sat watching dawn break over the ruined tower of the citadel. The makeshift camp around her looked gloomy in the morning light, a landscape of dull white snow and spindly trees, with endless flanks of canvas lined by a collection of colourful ribbons in the centre. That was the nobility section, but the camp spread out between the trees further than she could see. Several people were still working through the night, but she needed to take a break and get her raging mind under control before jumping back in.

Fae had been pouring in from the citadel all night so she dodged between checking newcomers for people she knew and helping random people find beds and blankets and passing out food. She had finally succumbed to Marthe's insistence that she sleep after several hours at work, seconds away from frustrated tears.

We don't even know where all these supplies are coming from, not in terms of who will owe who what after this.

"Was the tent at least to your liking?" Marthe prodded.

Molly nodded. "Far better than anything I'm used to."

It was true, although she guessed anyone else Marthe might have set up tents for wouldn't have had the absolute abundance of gold and pink bedding she had in hers. There was also a large mirror painted gold with a pink trim, which Aurora had perched herself happily on for the night, a wash-stand, and a finely carved and immaculately polished wooden table with two accompanying chairs.

And the wardrobe. She didn't even want to face the enormous wooden monstrosity that had invaded an entire corner of the tent, along with a privacy screen and a large wooden bath insulated with a soft, waterproof canvas.

"Well, I'm sure you'll tire soon enough," Marthe said. "Don't forget, the wardrobe will give you whatever clothes or accessories you ask for, so pick something warm. Now, do you have any preferences for breakfast? I know you're going to say you're not hungry-"

"Eggs are always good. *Offke* too, by the vat-load. I usually have a meat pocket."

A sob bubbled up but she choked it back down. She hadn't found Merry the night before, her friend who ran the food stall on the park level near her workshop.

"Oh my dear." Marthe tutted. "I'll do my best. You need to eat. Keep your strength up."

Molly pressed the heels of her hands to her eyes to hold in the sudden burning as Marthe hurried away.

First Talie. Now this. She sucked in a shaky breath. *I need to help as much as I can.*

If she went in search of the royals, maybe asked Taz or

Kainen to get her a place at a court, they would. She had royal blood and while it didn't mean anything to her, it did to them. Marthe would all but crown her on the spot if she mentioned it, and she could even secure Sammy's entire future like Talie had asked her to.

Can't bring her back though.

She huffed through the rising panic clawing at her throat and stabbing in her chest until she could force it all down again. Unwilling to let the entire camp see her cry, she ducked back inside her tent. With her hands over her face, she regained control of her breathing.

"Marthe suggested I bring you food."

She lifted her head as Kainen waltzed into the tent without knocking.

"I might have been changing," she muttered.

He pulled a face. "Well do it behind the screen next time then. Here, Marthe said I was to make sure you drink this as well."

He held out a cup. Molly took it and peered inside at the murky purple liquid.

"This isn't *offke*."

"Nope. Tonic of some kind. Taz and Demi swear by it."

Molly lifted the cup to her lips then stilled. Kainen caught the hesitation and his expression softened.

"Want me to have a bit first?" he asked.

She hesitated, frozen by what that might imply, and what truths it might hold.

"Celeste… she had Ru pretend… anyone can glamour, right? Most people can."

Kainen nodded. "They can, but they can't lie. I'm

Kainen Hemlock, Lord of the Illusion Court, always have been and I've no need or intention to hurt you. Happy to drink a bit, then if Marthe's somehow poisoned it I can take umbrage with the royal court."

Molly held the cup out and he swiped it, taking a big gulp.

"Doesn't taste all that great but it has good after-effects." He handed it back.

Molly drained the lot, then Kainen clicked his fingers and another cup appeared.

"Same with this one, still me, still nothing wrong with it. Just *offke*." He took a sip. "Marthe made me promise not to give you this until you had the tonic."

Molly took the cup and gulped half of it down without even hesitating, closing her eyes as the familiar taste jolted her senses into action.

"That's better. Marthe is basically in charge of everyone, isn't she?"

Kainen grinned. "In the oak court? Absolutely. In my court she wouldn't be, or any of the other courts, but she's raised all the little oak line babies, including Taz, and she kind of sees Demi as like an extension of that. Rumour has it she does a stitch and bitch session with the actual natural embodiment of Faerie once a month but nobody's ever been able to prove it."

Molly finished her cup and grabbed the plate of egg with what looked like an attempt at a meat pocket on the side.

"Takes a lot of practice to get the melty cheese right," she muttered.

"When you're done with that, you're to come and meet the rest of our group. Then plans need to be made."

Molly inhaled the food without even noticing the taste, then took the plate to the wash-stand. Before she could even begin to dip it in the water, a loud gasp made her jump.

"No! Absolutely not. We don't wash plates in our washing water!"

Marthe snatched the plate out of Molly's hands as though it had mortally offended her.

"Well... where am I meant to wash it then?" Molly asked.

"Leave dirty things on the table, or the chair for clothing, and I will see them clean."

"I can't even wash my own stuff?"

They stared at each other until Marthe's eyes narrowed.

"You have much more important things to be doing than washing dishes. There are Fae still unsure of what is to be done and lots more to do. Demi is asking everyone to convene for a meeting too, so best not be late."

Molly hesitated, torn between the irrepressible urge to be belligerent and the knowledge that there were more important things to be doing than dishes.

"It'd only take me a minute to wash the plate though," she tried. "Worst case I can tip the water out after and refill it from somewhere. I probably could have done it in the time it took to have this conversation."

"Yes, dear, so how about you don't waste any more time and get going on the important things, yes?"

Molly's brain glitched. "Er... I guess."

"Excellent. You follow Lord Kainen and he'll show you to the queen's quarters."

Molly let herself not only be chivvied out of her tent, but also into a thick winter coat with a fleece-trimmed hood and sturdy boots that were somehow already worn-in, all in gold and pink.

As she crunched through the snow beside Kainen, she sighed.

"I got totally manipulated, didn't I?"

He nodded happily. "Yep. Meri does the same to me to be fair, that's my version of Marthe. Demi has Milo for that, and Ace."

He continued on but Molly's steps faltered as they approached the section of tents with green, red and icy silver ribbons all over it.

Her insides guttered so sharply she almost doubled over and a shocked gasp puffed from her lips. Kainen turned back, saw her, then followed her line of sight.

"Ah, Molly." His expression turned ashen. "I didn't think to warn you, sorry. Come and meet Hutch, Harvey's twin."

Echoes of memory screamed back around her, the slash and zing of gifts, the Menagerie entrance hall, and Harvey racing toward her then going rigid in her arms as Celeste slaughtered him with a smile on her face, like he meant nothing.

"I don't... I can't..."

She shook her head and took a step back as the man who looked exactly like Harvey, except for a shock of bright green hair, saw them and approached.

"Hey, Molly, isn't it?" The voice was identical and all the worse for being gentle, like she was a deer about to run. "Don't worry, please. It's been an absolutely cruddy time but none of us blame you."

Molly stood frozen as he stopped in front of her, Kainen forming a triangle beside them as tears sprang to her eyes.

"I never wanted him to," she whispered. "With Baby Aurora and everything."

Hutch nodded. "I know. We can't blame each other for the casualties of war. You didn't kill him, and he knew exactly what risks he was taking when he decided to take them."

"We all do," Kainen agreed. "We take them anyway because it's the right thing to do."

"Exactly. Focus on blaming the cause of all the rot, not yourself."

Molly wiped her eyes with her hand, not entirely convinced about the state of the tissue Kainen unearthed helpfully from his pocket.

"There's some sense in that. I'll do everything I can to bring her down. All of them."

Hutch nodded. "Me too. Beryl will be arriving soon as well and she'll be happy to see you. Don't make the mistake of hiding in your grief either. I tried but too many people came to drag me out again."

"I'll try to remember that."

"Good. It's a bit weird though, seeing you after hearing about you from everyone. Put your hair up and a coat on you, and I could have almost sworn you were Taz from the back."

"Er… I'm not sure what to do with that."

He shrugged. "Neither am I, but we keep trying anyway. Meeting's been postponed for an hour by the way."

"Great," Kainen groaned. "That means I'm going to get jumped for court paperwork if I go anywhere near my tent. Can I come with you instead?"

Molly slipped into stealth mode and stepped away from them. Hutch's words revolved around her head like a taunt. She looked like Taz. She looked like Celeste. She looked like the Oak Queen in younger years.

She looked like her stupid bloodline.

If I didn't exist, none of this would have happened. Talie would never have been forced to tail me and she wouldn't have died trying to save the fairies because I asked her to.

It didn't matter that Celeste had chosen Talie, or that if Molly hadn't been born another child would have in her place.

She stormed into her tent with her determination rising. She couldn't change who she was in terms of blood family, but she could take some control over her own self.

The wardrobe doors flew open expectantly as she charged toward them and stood with her hands on her hips.

"Hi. Can I have some hair dye please?"

There was the possibility of glamouring too, but that seemed too easily fixed, too Fae. It was also exhausting and she wanted to avoid glamours where she could. She thought of going with dark hair, but thoughts and whispers of the past dug in deep enough to hurt and she forced that idea aside.

"Red hair dye, please." She turned away, then rotated back around. "Bright." She bit her lip. "But natural looking if you can."

A small red tube tumbled out from somewhere near the back of the wardrobe and landed on the boards under her boots. She ducked to swipe it up.

"Any instructions?" she asked hopefully. A small paper pamphlet flew out at her, then a pair of thin gloves. "Thank you."

She walked away and skimmed through the paper as the wardrobe closed its doors with a smart 'click'.

Simple enough, slather on, comb through, wait and wash out.

The dark red goop smelled strongly of sour berries, but she pulled on the gloves and set to work lathering it through her hair.

The determination lasted all of five minutes. She paced the tent and dithered over whether to wash it out early in the hope it hadn't had time to work, but the thought of ending up with pink hair and looking like most of her new clothes if she didn't go through with it frightened her away from the wash-stand each time.

Ten minutes passed according to the ornate wooden clock on the bedside table, carved of course with acorns and oak leaves all over it. She sat down. Stood up. Sat down.

"Nope."

She shot up and hurried over to the wash-stand. Doubting the water would even be enough to wash the dye out thoroughly, she doubled over and dunked her head in.

"Come on, come out, come out," she muttered.

The sound of the tent flap tapping open barely even registered.

"I- oh, Princess, I almost didn't recognise you."

Molly froze at the sound of a feminine voice, and at the honorific being used so naturally. Nobody had called her princess yet, not Kainen or Demi or Taz.

Only Talie.

It sounded so wrong from someone else's mouth, but panic about her hair pulsed strongly as she lifted her head to the rim of the wash-bowl, along with a burning dose of utter mortification.

"Kind of the point," she muttered. "Regretting it already."

She swiped her hair back into the bowl and wiggled in a hopeless attempt to swish the dye out, but the water was looking suspiciously not red still.

The hazy outline of a woman appeared a suitably respectful distance away.

"I can help if you want?"

Molly turned her head. "You know a lot about hair?"

The young woman must have been about her age, tall with a cascade of sunny blonde curls. For a second, Molly wondered if she was some errant relative sent to befriend her, but anyone offering to help her with the mess she'd created was tempting, relative or not.

"Enough." The woman shrugged. "It looks bad now but once you dry it the colour will look more settled. Probably. Are you happy for me to give it a quick rub through to be safe?"

Molly nodded. Her neck felt stretched beyond belief, her back muscles screaming with tightness, but the thought of having to glamour herself back to blonde to hide the disaster made her want to cry.

"Okay."

Molly held herself tense over the bowl as firm fingers ruffled through her hair, rubbing and detangling with little splashes of water. She had no idea how the water stayed warm so long, no doubt more of Marthe's seemingly boundless Fae magic, but it was a blessing all the same.

"Right, that should do you. Up you get and I can brush it out for you."

Molly grabbed her hair in two hands and straightened up with a grunt, her heart sinking at the bright red strands hooked over her fingers. When the woman pointed to the chair at the vanity table, Molly sat obediently.

"Shouldn't take long. I'm Solaine, by the way."

Solaine grabbed a towel and started gently ruffling Molly's hair with it.

"Pretty name. You're not related to me, are you?"

"Thanks, and no, absolutely not. Lord Kainen sent me to tell you that the meeting will start when you're ready. So the colour looks like it's taken well. It'll be a burnished auburn once dried."

"Anything that isn't blonde." Molly hesitated. "No offense."

Solaine laughed. "None taken. We all want a change sometimes. It can be liberating. Red will suit your complexion, but then blonde did as well. Sunshine or fire, both work."

Molly might have preened just a little at the compliment any other time, but the grief crept around her as silence descended. She sank into the soothing sensation of Solaine brushing out her now burnished auburn waves and let her thoughts drift. She would find out what the royals planned to do first, then if they weren't able to help fix the citadel and get Celeste out, she would find a way to do it herself.

She flinched as the tent flap flipped open and Marthe bustled in.

"They're calling for you- oh." The atmosphere turned icy, right down to the temperature in the air. "Who are you and what have you done to the princess's *hair*?"

Molly sighed. "I dyed it myself. Solaine was helping me brush it out."

"I… see." Marthe didn't say a word for several moments. "I may have to alter the shades of everything in your wardrobe then. No matter. They're waiting for you."

Molly got to her feet and pulled her still damp hair back from her face with her old hair ribbon. It was green and one of the ones that Talie had gifted her once for Yuletide. It was the most irresponsible thing, but shortly after the first fight at the Menagerie, she'd crept into the workshop, just once. She took her best mini tools with her, a change of clothes that she felt most comfortable in, her pillow and the bundle of hair ribbons.

She tied her hair in a haphazard bow, glad she'd thought to shove a couple of spares in her pocket. The green wasn't her favourite, that one had been lost in the Menagerie, but she still had two left, two tiny strands of Talie to cling onto.

"Here, let me."

She stood as Solaine deftly scraped her hair back, clawing her fingers gently here and there until she knotted the ribbon to make a ponytail and finished with a much neater bow than Molly had ever managed. Molly risked a glance at Marthe, who was still blocking the exit and sending arctic mother-hen vibes.

"Who are you, exactly?" Marthe asked.

Solaine shrugged. "I'm a nobody. Came out of the citadel like the rest. I was asked by Lord Kainen to come and fetch the princess, then the princess asked me to help with her hair, then you came in and here we are."

"Hmm. If you say so. Come along, Princess."

Molly grimaced. "You call Demi and Taz by their names. Can't you do the same for me?"

"Not around her majesty the Oak Queen, no. But here? If you wish. Now let's go, Molinia."

Molly flinched. "No. Not Molinia. That's not my name. My name is Molly."

Marthe closed her eyes momentarily in torment.

"Molly then. It doesn't do to keep a queen waiting, even one as progressive as Demi."

Molly gave Solaine a weary grimace of gratitude and slunk after Marthe.

If I have to, I'm going to start pulling rank if only to get a bit of orbing peace.

CHAPTER SIX

Molly stood in the warmest of warm coats, with the sturdiest of winter boots, as well as a hat, a scarf and a pair of thick gloves, all muted pink with hints of gold. That she could tolerate because they were practical at least, but she'd almost thrown a tantrum when winter goggles were mentioned.

With balmy Fae heating in the queen's tent, which had an entire sectioned off bedroom and an enormous exotic tree Molly didn't recognise, she felt ridiculous. She pulled off the puffy coat and used it as a cushion on one of the many wooden chairs while the nobles assembled around her. Taz smiled at her, but it was still weird to think of him as family so she only grimaced one back and turned her gaze to her hands. She twisted the *Akiai* charm around on her finger as Milo and Ace stamped in, puffing against the cold.

"Right, let's get this started," Demi announced.

She hadn't changed overnight into anything queenly, but Milo had slipped a circlet of silver onto her chaotic curls when she wasn't looking. Somehow, the casualness of it all gave Molly a reassuring jolt of strength.

Kainen slumped into the seat beside her and opened a small cloth bag. Molly eyed the round red sweet he pulled out, but he popped it in his mouth and crunched it a bit before offering her the bag.

"Sticky Saps," he said.

She nodded. "We have these. Had."

"Have, keep positive. Demi, what's the plan?"

Demi sighed. "It's tricky. We're offering refuge to anyone who needs it under protection of the crown, but we can't interfere with anything to do with the citadel. The covenant covers all five towers, so unless I'm asked to get involved, I can't."

Molly sagged, disappointment stabbing at her chest.

"So, there's nothing we can do?"

"There's a lot we can do," Taz said gently. "We can offer everyone places in other realms. We can send word to the citadel and offer aid for rebuilding."

Molly couldn't imagine Phoenix accepting outside aid, let alone Celeste.

"They'll be fighting it out between them still," she said.

Demi nodded. "Most likely. Our first step will be to ensure all Fae leaving the citadel are accounted for and don't get lost in the woods. We have that covered, but after that we need to be considering we can't keep this camp going indefinitely."

"So, we start making lists of available realms and locations?" Taz asked.

Molly wiped a hand over her face.

"Nobody will want to leave," she insisted. "We're stubborn, born and raised on having to stand for ourselves.

They'll be more likely to march back into the ruin than be marched elsewhere."

Demi nodded and hoisted herself up to sit cross-legged on her desk, which caused Milo to hiss in annoyance as she disturbed a bunch of paperwork piled behind her.

"I'm sure, but we need to make the offer. It's their choice. I also want to keep everyone involved in the options. It's not my decision, or the crown's or the courts. Or the citadel's."

Molly managed to hold the piercing, electric blue gaze for a couple of seconds, amazed that Demi was giving up the opportunity to gain from the situation so easily.

She could pull rank anytime she likes but she's actually offering everyone a choice.

"I can talk to people if you need me to," she offered. "I recognise some that have come through the camp since."

"The nobles will also be massing any moment, bear that in mind," Kainen warned.

Demi groaned. "Any chance to be part of a spectacle. Well, perhaps that's a good thing. They can earn their keep for a change and start volunteering their bountiful lands for anyone who does want to leave and start afresh."

"I'm not having that conversation," Taz said with a snort.

Kainen grinned. "Me either. I'd even take guard duty over that."

"There's guard duty?" Molly asked.

"Of a sort. Mainly keeping an eye out for beasties from the woods. We know so little about this realm."

Molly stood. She needed space to think and she could

watch for beasties easily enough. It was better than waiting around doing nothing.

"I can take a turn on guard," she suggested.

All eyes turned to her, then each other.

"We wouldn't expect you to do that," Demi said, her tone uneasy.

Molly grabbed her coat and folded her arms around it.

"Why not?"

"Well…"

She waited, her heart dropping.

They don't even trust me.

"We need to keep you safe," Kainen said.

"I can keep myself safe," she muttered. "I don't need protecting from invisible woodland animals."

"All the same, we've got plenty on guard," Demi added.

Taz nodded. "More than enough. Why not see if there's anything Marthe needs help with?"

Molly stared around at each of them, including Ace and Milo who were both looking anywhere but at her. The tiny flicker of belonging that she'd refused to admit to guttered in her chest and snuffed out.

I'm just a bauble, a part of the royal bloodline.

She couldn't blame them for it. In any traditional sense she should have been raised in a palace and taught all sorts with all kinds of gifts and wealth at her disposal. But she would refuse any crown or title before she ever let herself succumb to being used.

With her chin level, she stalked out of the tent and hauled her coat on. The fringe of the camp overlooked the ruined tower and the sight of it chilled far deeper than the biting wind.

Somewhere inside the ruins, Celeste would be cosy as anything, no doubt with Ru slaving away behind her. Marcus would be machinating in his office. Phoenix was probably safely sequestered in the tunnels winding through the citadel's infrastructure. All while the rest of the citadel were struggling to survive. She'd counted heads hundreds of times throughout the night as she worked, but so many would still be trying to recover and survive still inside.

"Room for one more?"

She turned her head to find Solaine a few steps behind her in a thin black overcoat and ragged boots. She shrugged.

"Room for several more, technically."

"I can go, if you prefer?"

Molly sighed. "No, it's fine. I could do with a distraction anyway. You didn't… is there anyone…"

She couldn't finish the question, but Solaine stood at her side and shook her head.

"Not many to miss me, or for me to miss. I've spoken to some of the Fae out here though and apparently someone told people to get to the core spaces. News spread fast and most of them ended up in the library of all places."

Molly's mind darted back to the woman she'd given that very idea to.

Probably nothing to do with me, but at least most are safe.

Before she could say as much, Solaine pressed a finger to her lips and pointed with her other hand to the trees nearby. Milo and Ace stamped out of the shadows, their footfalls heavy in the snow.

"It's not sensible," Ace grumbled. "I know it's a loss, but better the books… actually no, better I don't finish that."

"You were going to say, 'better the books than the Fae', weren't you. Don't you think I know that? But it wouldn't be difficult for me to liberate the most valuable."

Ace sighed. "It's crossing the line and you know it. No, not even crossing, it's obliterating the line. No."

Both lifted their heads as they realised they were being overheard.

"You have a way to get in?" Molly asked. "Back into the citadel, I mean?"

She didn't mention his realm-skipping abilities in front of Solaine but the implication was there all the same.

Milo glanced at Ace. "It doesn't matter *apparently*."

Molly thought of what Solaine had said, that most were safe in the library. No doubt the mere thought of it would send Milo screaming back in to rescue the books from everyone he deemed unworthy.

If it saves people, what's the harm?

She shrugged. "It does actually. Rumour has it most of the Fae who got stuck in the citadel are now using the library for sanctuary. Go in, bring a person out but on the condition they carry a book with them."

Milo's eyes lit up. "Oh, that's a brilliant idea!"

"It is." Ace groaned. "But I'm not going to be the one telling Demi."

"I will, the moment she's done with her paperwork." He rubbed his hands together and breathed on them to ward off the cold.

"She does a lot of paperwork," Molly said.

He nodded. "She has to. She jokes that I'm always hounding her, but I know she doesn't really mean it."

The moment Milo glanced toward the camp, Ace pulled a face. Molly stifled a laugh, still not prepared for the all-encompassing swoop of sorrow that dragged it back down.

Talie's barely been gone any time at all and I'm here laughing and joking.

"She was so annoyed about that human-Faerie treaty you drew up though," Ace said.

Milo frowned. "It seemed like a good idea at the time."

"Humans?" Molly's jaw dropped. "Actual humans? What are they like?"

"Well, Demi is one, at least in part. She grew up in the human world."

"Is it true they can lie?" Solaine asked, her amber eyes wide.

"They can and do often. They also have all sorts of weird and terrifying things there, but oh the books." Milo's eyes glazed over.

Ace sighed. "Off he goes. I'm part-human too, and it's not so different to Faerie really. Both are made of the same base elements but we can gift and they can lie."

"What kind of base elements?" Solaine asked.

Milo blinked. "Oh. So, if you have a particle in a vacuum, it behaves differently than not in a vacuum. It's like they have this thing called a slit experiment, where the particles behave differently when seen as opposed to not seen. Faerie and the human world have lots of similarities and core base things, but then differences have kind of grown and evolved in the cracks."

"Nope, don't get it." Molly shook her head.

"Matter is what it is." Milo tried again. "Like dirt, or leaves, or water. Whether in the Faerie realm, the human world, or who knows what goes beyond them. Here in our realms, without Faerie there would just be the raw chaos of the nether. Faerie is the magic's balance, the order that stops trees becoming teapots and all sorts. In the human world however, they have to rely on their humanity."

"Humanity?"

"Like Faenity, but for humans," Ace chimed in.

Molly grimaced. "But there are hardly any with proper Faenity, especially these days. Everyone just runs around taking advantage of each other."

"The human world is apparently much the same," Milo said. "Lots of wars. Demi says there are good humans out there though. Still, the nether, or matter, gives power to all, but here Faerie is essentially like the protection warding around us all, channelling it."

"Is that the same as this well of power under the citadel that everyone's been after?" Solaine asked. She frowned when everyone turned to look at her. "What? Fae gossip. Rumours are everywhere, at least in the citadel. People know there's something under the core."

Milo grimaced and blew on his hands again.

"We think it's to do with the Omens," he said. "Ancient entities spawned from the depths of the nether. Some sources suggest they manifested to balance the wickedness of Fae, but the citadel was built long ago over the well of power they sprang from. They'll be swelling against the constraints of Faerie, needing to grow and likely using Fae to do it. They feed off belief as much as the nether, conduits that desire to grow strong."

"Sounds delightful," Solaine muttered.

"Very not delightful, in my opinion," he said. "There was one inscription though from the time of their imprisonment: circles of three contain all that be, with Fae iron from point to point."

The mention of Omens tickled something in Molly's memory but she couldn't place it. Either way, none of it sounded good.

"So, there's some ancient well of power stopping the citadel from being wicked?" she asked. "How in the name of Faerie has it coped with Celeste for so long?"

Before Milo could answer, Kainen appeared out of thin air and clapped his hands on Milo's shoulders.

"Don't keep doing that!" Milo huffed. "I swear I will hit you with a book next time. That's about the extent of it though, Molly. Think of it like the earth. There are pockets beneath holes in the ground where rainwater collects, and in those pockets, high moisture gathers and things begin to evolve and breed."

"Sounds like a standard weekend at court," Kainen joked.

Milo sniffed. "Your court maybe. Faerie is like the grass and earth, and the nether is the rain. The nether pools in various dips and furrows of Faerie, and where there is excess power, it must be balanced. The well has probably been drawing Fae to its power for several ages without them really knowing why."

"So, the power is the Omens themselves?" Solaine asked.

He shook his head. "The nether is the power technically, but the Omens are like children of it. How tangible they are, we don't know. Perhaps they've manifested as creatures or simply spectral wisps of magic, but either way stopping the Omens will still leave the well there."

"Breeding and evolving," Kainen said, his tone far less amused than before.

"Exactly." Milo pulled a small bag from his pocket. "Well done, have a Sticky Sap."

Kainen grinned. "I know you're being sarcastic, but thanks."

"Those are my favourite," Molly added hopefully.

Milo passed the bag around and Molly crunched her sweet as her attention drifted back to the citadel.

I'm still surprised I didn't see Ru lurking about. He wouldn't have known who to glamour into to trick me I don't think. Sammy was safe in the house the whole time, and it's not like he can glamour as Talie.

Again the gut-wrenching grief hit her and she inhaled a sharp, icy breath to force it back down. Clenching her fists in her pockets, she fixed her attention back on the others.

"Well, Demi's in a delightful mood," Kainen grumbled. "She's had to handle the Bank of Faerie, who are basically screwed on insurance policies and looking for someone to blame. She mentioned handing Taz over as the culprit and having done with it."

Milo's eyes widened. "Oh orbs. I'd better go and

smooth things over. I'll tell her your idea Molly, it's a very good one."

Molly shrugged even though Milo was already steaming off toward the camp with Ace striding alongside him.

"You might as well go and get warm, both of you," Kainen offered. "If I send you back to Marthe any more an icicle, Molly, she'll be cursing people next."

"Not yet. I need more alone time before I have to face people."

He sighed. "Okay, but next time it'll be her dragging you by your feet."

Molly didn't answer as he set off toward the camp after the others.

"Not a big fan of people?" Solaine asked.

"Not always. It's fine, but social situations are always loud and everyone wants to hear themselves talk. I never know when to speak up so I don't at all, then I end up getting talked at the whole time. I guess that sounds really horrible of me."

"No, I get it. I'm not known for being a people person either. We can sit and be grouchy together."

Molly clenched her fists tighter against the twisting in her gut, memories and ghosts of the past threatening to choke her.

"Yeah, sure."

"Rumour has it the queen is apparently determined to hold a dance for morale," Solaine added.

Molly nodded, her mind still far away as she stared at the citadel. She couldn't imagine how Demi would put a dance past people who'd just lost their home. Probably send Kainen to charm them into it.

"Would you want to go?"

Molly froze. "Go?"

"To the dance yeah, if there is one."

"I-" She hesitated. "I'll probably be expected to. Semi-unfortunate familial connections and all that."

"I mean would you want to go with me."

Molly's face flushed hot despite the chilly air and she fixed her gaze firmly on the citadel.

"Sorry, I can't. I'm still not over someone else. It wouldn't be fair and I don't want to lead you on. Unless you meant as friends, I mean, you probably did, so we can all go."

Her insides crunched with embarrassment as Solaine sighed.

"Can't blame a girl for trying. I'm going to sneak off and get us some snacks. Back in five."

She was off before Molly could burble any more inane apologies.

I guess that could have gone worse. She probably just wants some kind of advancement for herself now that I'm all fancy and titled anyway. As long as Sammy never finds out I just got asked out, we can forget it ever happened.

She wiped a hand over her face and walked to the shallow edge of the lake. The pearlescent ice, solid in places and broken to the water below in others, rippled with each plink and plunk of the rain droplets.

We didn't even get to bring her home. She rubbed her neck as the familiar anguish weighed her down. *I didn't get* to say goodbye, or promise her I'd do my best for Sammy. She died in pain because of me.

When footsteps squelched behind her a while later, she sniffed and wiped savagely at her tears and the rain water that made a mess across her face. She stayed in place as the footsteps stopped right behind her, Solaine's she assumed, not willing to turn until she had her expression under control.

"That was quick," she said.

"Actually, it felt like a lifetime."

Molly froze, icy horror and sheer bewilderment keeping her captive as that wholly familiar voice came again.

"Hello, Princess."

CHAPTER SEVEN

TALIE

Coming back from the dead, socially anyway, hadn't been on Talie's daily to do list. Escaping the Menagerie after the big fight wasn't all that difficult in the chaos, but the few weeks afterwards were fraught with uncertainty. Then the citadel came tumbling down and she barely made it out unscathed, but it was worth reaching the camp to see Molly again and find out Sammy was safe.

Now that she was in Molly's life again, albeit as someone else, she was finding it difficult to admit who she was.

Maybe the Solaine glamour is over the top, but still.

She walked toward the camp, reassured that while Molly was clearly not happy, she was at least safe. The trees were lined with suspiciously casual Fae lounging against trees, smoking pipes or playing cards, and she'd have put any money she might have made on those being secret guards of the queen's.

Molly hadn't mentioned her as Talie yet, not in terms of

missing her or wondering where she was, but she secretly hoped that Molly's sadness was at least a tiny bit due to her absence.

She and Sammy have no idea where I am, although I'm guessing Kainen told them I was in the Menagerie with him during the fight.

"Ah, there you are."

Talie slowed and wrangled her tense shoulders down away from her ears. She wasn't exactly on overly friendly terms with the Lord of the Illusion Court as herself, but as Solaine she was just another citizen of the citadel needing sanctuary.

She turned to face him, unsure if she should bob her head or not. She hadn't remembered to when he collared her to go and get Molly before, the same day she found Molly dying her hair red of all things, but it was a blessing sent from Faerie that he'd chosen her out of everyone. Even to be that close, it took all of her effort not to drop the glamour and admit who she really was. She didn't even know really why she hadn't, but somehow talking to Molly incognito gave her a brief space of peace.

She needed to tell Molly the truth but it would be best to find the right moment first. Maybe take another day to let things settle.

Meanwhile, Lord Kainen was frowning at her in a surprisingly similar way the old woman in Molly's tent had. He folded his arms over his chest and looked her up and down as a tingle of something trickled over her skin. She didn't even have time to ward as a sour taste tanged on her tongue.

"Who are you?" he asked.

She froze. "I… I'm one of the people from the citadel."

He lifted an eyebrow and her insides plummeted.

He knows. She gulped. *How am I going to explain this?*

"What's your name then?" he demanded.

"Talie."

It tumbled off her tongue and she recognised the same sour taste that she'd had once before when Molly compelled her.

Kainen nodded. "I know. I have certain skills as lord of my court, being able to see through glamours being one of them."

"You've known who I am this whole time?" She couldn't keep the utter indignance from her tone, even though he was far superior to her in terms of both power and title.

"I told you when I gifted you the ability to glamour that certain people could see through it, didn't I?"

He didn't look impressed, his lips pressed thin and his brow narrowed. She half expected that sour taste again, but he didn't even bother to ask her any more questions. Anxiety squished in her chest and she glanced over her shoulder, but Molly was still staring out over the water at the citadel beyond.

"This isn't anything awful," she insisted. "It's really not."

Still he didn't say anything and the truth tumbled out.

"When you and your friend disappeared to save the fairies in the Menagerie, I got caught by Molly's friend. He and I… well, he was on Celeste's side originally but he said he'd pretend to be me to get Molly away from Celeste safely while I helped get the fairies out."

"And you believed him?"

She hesitated. "I wasn't sure, but Molly would have wanted me to sort the fairies out first, and I know she had others protecting her outside. It's not like I can rival the king consort of Faerie in power."

Kainen's lips might have twitched ever so slightly.

"By time I got out of the Menagerie, the fight was over," she continued. "I knew I'd be a target the moment Celeste was out, so I made up a new glamour, something completely different."

He snorted. "Different, sure. You look like a weird hybrid of Molly and yourself."

She hadn't even bothered to look in a mirror beyond the quickest check in the citadel glass occasionally to make sure the glamour was still holding, but she guessed it wasn't meant to be a compliment.

"I figured you lot had taken Molly out of the citadel but when I went back by the workshop, I saw Sammy going in with Daisy." She fought the urge to pull a face. "I know you said she was one of yours, but I couldn't risk showing who I was. Ru said there was a price on my head set by her mother too which might endanger them, so I kept watch instead while trying to find a way out. Then the tower came down and did it for me."

"She thinks you're dead."

It took a second for Kainen's words to hit.

"She what? Why?!"

"You haven't heard?" He frowned. "Celeste killed you.

Except you're here, so it sounds like she killed this friend of Molly's instead."

Talie choked over a horrified breath and looked behind her at Molly still holding her solitary vigil by the lake.

"She thinks I'm dead?"

"We all did, your sister included. Molly was glamouring as Daisy in the citadel after the fight, then it came down and here we are. I won't ask, but you need to drop the glamour and tell her you're alive. Any longer and she might not forgive you. She's had Celeste toying with her mind through glamours, and she's already doubting who everyone is."

"Maybe... maybe it's better I don't then, if she's already fragile. She and Ru were best friends for a long time and I don't want to make it worse by telling her he's dead instead of me."

She didn't mean it, but panic was charging through her head.

"Very noble." Kainen's tone was drenched in mockery. "She obviously cares a lot about you so I imagine she'll get over it, but not if you continue lying to her now."

"We barely know each-" She couldn't finish without lying. "We haven't known each other that long, not really, and she cares about everyone. I doubt she's... I mean..."

Kainen's lips lifted and his arms dropped to his sides.

"She almost burned the Menagerie to the ground when you 'died', and her mother with it. Just lit up like a fierce summer morning. Even I struggled to keep it contained, and I'm not exactly a beginner when it comes to wielding shadows."

Talie bit her lip and turned to look at Molly again.

She's going to hate me.

"Go, do it now," Kainen insisted. "She might be angry a while but she'll understand eventually."

"Maybe she needs more time though."

"Surely it's better to take the consequences for tricking them for a day than continue it and have them not trust you?"

"I know and I will tell her." Talie hesitated. "But I can wait for the right time at least, when she's not so fragile."

Kainen sighed. "Coward. It's better not to hide behind glamours and masks too long or you start to forget who you really are. Those kinds of pretences become lies you tell yourself, and even those can twist your mind."

"A noble sentiment."

"I thought so." He shoved a hand in the pocket of his leather jacket then held it out to her, palm up. "Take this. We need to ensure everyone is reachable."

Talie took the dark green orb lying on his palm and slipped it into her jacket pocket. She was walking a dangerous line by talking to a noble like an equal, let alone backchatting him. Rejecting a demand would likely get her exposed before she even had a chance to tell Molly her side of things.

"Now go put Molly out of her misery," he added.

Talie rolled her tongue across the roof of her mouth, searching for that sour taste, but he apparently wasn't going to force her to do it. He walked away without another word and she stared at Molly with her nerves pounding in her ears.

He had a point about not dragging it out, and if she wanted any chance of being in Molly's life she had to do it honestly. After a deep breath of chilly air, she let the glamour drop.

Her extra curves dropped away and she eased into her familiar limbs with a quiet groan of relief. As the cold trickle of the glamour washed away, she pulled a strand of hair between her fingers to watch it turn from blonde to dark.

This is going to be bad. She shoved her hands in the pockets of her threadbare coat and covered the short distance back to Molly. *Orbs, I didn't even get her the snacks I said I would.*

A sense of swelling hysteria beat wildly in her chest and the urge to laugh bubbled up at the worst possible moment.

"That was quick," Molly said, and Talie heard the lifelessness in her tone.

Might as well do this my way and screw it up utterly.

"Actually, it felt like a lifetime."

Molly stiffened. Her shoulders tensed and her ridiculously puffy pink coat rustled quietly as she started shaking. When she didn't answer, Talie threw a last shot in.

"Hello, Princess."

Molly twisted around, her eyes stormy and swimming with the remnants of shed tears. Even with tiredness fading her usually rosy skin and her hair a mad twist of auburn when it should have been blonde, Molly looked every bit as beautiful as she had the day she fell out of the rafters in the citadel warehouse.

"You… You…" She looked like a glitching orb-cast as her mouth flapped over words. "*You.*"

Talie shrank further inside her coat. She needed the extra layer of armour, even though getting rid of her Solaine glamour felt like shedding several layers of baggage.

"Yeah, me. I have some explaining to do."

Molly stumbled past her so that she had the safety of the camp at her back and Talie had the vastness of the lake at hers.

Yeah, this is bad. Talie couldn't fight past the sheer panic that cascaded over her exhausted limbs. *I barely glamoured for longer than a day. This can be fixed.*

"Whoever you are, it won't work," Molly snapped, her voice climbing higher. "Talie's… that's a sick thing to do, glamouring as her. Who are you?"

Talie froze. In all her imaginings of the moment she revealed who she was, she hadn't considered Molly might not believe it. She hadn't even thought to ward around Molly and that strain of sourness wisped over her tongue again.

"It's me, Talie." She searched frantically for proof. "I gave you the moor grass around your neck, and the acorn. I'm the one who wiped your mind the night your guardians died, and we shared bottles of *Beast* on that glass-front beam you like so much. We got trapped in a rubbish tunnel together, and you gave me a dagger for Yuletide. I gave you hair ribbons. You're wearing one right now."

She had no idea if it would work, but Molly's expression guttered to pure anguish, her mouth moving over several sounds before she choked out a single word.

"*How?*"

"It's a long story, but I'll do my best." She hesitated. "You might want to sit down."

Molly's arms folded across her middle, a sure sign she was about to put up the realm's biggest defensive wall. She didn't say a word, so Talie had to dive in without a single hope.

"There's so much confusion now," she started. "I'm not sure how much you even know since you ended up in the Menagerie."

"I know you were pretending to be that maid, Lia, while I was in there. You left me the orb, then I heard your voice."

Molly's tone was like granite, even though she couldn't hide the panicked hurt swimming in her stormy eyes. Talie ignored the twist of anguish at being the cause of Molly's pain and soldiered on.

"I was Lia but I escaped to get help. Then I went into the core with Kainen and Milo to free as many fairies as we could. They did most of it, but then Ru found me."

"Ru..." Molly's tone turned frail.

Talie grimaced. "It was his idea but I didn't stop to argue with him or anything. He insisted he would glamour as me then go out and show Celeste a quick slip of it. In that moment, I asked what would you want me to do, come find you or focus on freeing the fairies?"

"Fairies, obviously. But-"

"Yeah, thought so. Anyway, Ru glamoured as me and took my place. He said something about it being his penance for betraying you, for not seeing that you were right all along. He told me to get you out once the fairies were free and hide because Celeste put a price on my head to lure you back."

"She already had me there so why would she have needed to target you? She wouldn't have bothered."

Good, if she's starting to bite, it means she's angry instead of hurt. Talie wiped a hand over her face. *Let her be angry.*

"Well, that's what he told me." She shrugged to hide a violent shiver as the cold burrowed through her coat. "He said I was a danger to both you and Sammy. Then the entire place started to shake from the fighting. Kainen and Milo were too far in the core's labyrinth for me to find, but I got myself out through the service quarters and that window you used to get us in."

Molly doubled over, a low groan wailing out of her.

"He knew," she mumbled. "He knew Celeste wouldn't have spared him, glamoured as you or not. She guessed he was loyal to me over her, and he knew it when he… that means he's… but you're not…"

Talie fought every instinct to take the couple of steps that would bring her to Molly's side. She couldn't offer any comfort that Molly would want to receive.

"I kept an eye on Sammy but she was staying with that other woman, or so I thought. I didn't dare show myself, not until I found a way to get Sammy out, or to figure out where you were."

Molly groaned again. "That was me. Daisy, me, one and the same. Oh orbs, this whole time…"

Talie bit her lip when Molly's breathing became ragged.

"When the citadel tower came down, I was fighting to get to Sammy," she continued. "Then that bloke from the library with the big shoulders appeared and whisked you into thin air before I could. I had to get myself out on a passing cart, and even then I nearly went splat twice when the cart overturned and a piece of stone almost fell on it."

Molly whimpered, still doubled over. Talie flexed her fingers and clenched them into tight fists to keep from reaching out as words tumbled from Molly's lips.

"Why? Why reveal who you are now? Why spend all this time pretending to be someone else? I've- Sammy has been out of her mind with grief!"

The last part dialled the volume up a hundred-fold and startled the birds from the trees. Even then, Molly stayed hunched over, as though even looking at Talie's face might break her.

"I had to glamour as Lia to get myself out through the halls, but then I realised I couldn't be her without people asking questions, so I invented someone entirely new to get out here as. Then I walked into your tent and you were busy with your hair. I didn't want to dump it on you then, and you've been busy, and it's not really felt like the right time to drop a glamour and shout 'surprise!'."

"And now?" Molly hissed. "Why not just drop the glamour after my hair was done, or even today?"

Talie grimaced. "It was easier to be someone else for a bit. It's barely been more than a day." She panicked as Molly's mouth dropped open in wordless fury. "I wouldn't have continued it, but Kainen collared me just now before

I could figure out how to tell you. Said he could see through my glamour the whole time."

She shuddered as the memory of Kainen's words echoed in her head again.

"Surely it's better to take the consequences for tricking them for a day than continue it and have them not trust you?"

No doubt he was lurking somewhere nearby, or one of them would be. Kainen was fond of Molly but all the royals and nobles seemed to be conveniently appearing whenever she was in any potential vulnerable situation. Like that old woman who kept glowering as if she could see right through to the soul and judge accordingly.

"I can't believe this," Molly mumbled. "I think I'm going to be sick."

Talie nodded. "Fair. I'll take whatever hate and punishment you want to give me. I know I more than deserve it. I know I'll have to see Sammy and deal with her hating me too. I just… I used the Solaine glamour to get myself out of the citadel and into the camp to be safe. Then it was freeing to not be myself for a bit. When you smiled at me, I sort of lost my head and kept it going. It was easy to be Solaine but the glamour was getting wearing."

She tensed as Molly took a step toward her. Hope fluttered in her chest, even though Molly's face was twisted with fury.

"How awful for you."

Talie shuffled a step back until her heel hit the bank of the lake.

"The name was thought out though," she tried.

"I so don't care."

"It loosely translates into sunshine and lo- *aaah!*"

She flailed as Molly's hands landed on her shoulders. Her foot slithered on the snow-covered ground and her arms flew out wide as she hit a conveniently placed patch of water. Icy chills shocked the breath out of her, but the river wasn't all that deep by the bank, which Molly must have known.

I really hope she knew that.

Talie forced herself to her feet and up onto the sheet of ice. She hauled herself on her hands and knees to the edge of the bank with her teeth chattering and pulled herself out onto the snow with several unladylike grunts.

With even more effort, she forced her gaze to lift and meet the sheer fury of Molly's.

"I deserved that," she muttered. "Still wasn't expecting it."

She froze, as did Molly, as another unexpected yet familiar sound shattered her eardrums.

"WHAT THE F-"

CHAPTER EIGHT

MOLLY

Molly stared as Sammy stormed toward them. Her insides felt scraped raw and her vision kept wavering as though she was blinking away a film of sleep. She wanted to be sick, to tear her hair out, to scream and cry. So she pushed Talie in the river instead.

Bewildering enough that Talie was standing in front of her, dark hair tucked loose behind her ears and her eyes ringed with dark shadows. Her clothing was torn in several places and Molly had managed to hang onto some of what Talie told her, but with her pulse crashing she couldn't do anything more than stare as her Fae connection bubbled and her sunshine gift bloomed over her skin.

She took a healthy step back with her sunshine sizzling the snow under her feet as Sammy charged past her and threw her arms around Talie's neck. Her sobs cascaded through the air until Sammy pulled herself free seconds later.

"Where have you been?" Sammy demanded. "We've been worried sick! We thought you were dead!"

Talie grimaced. "I know I've got a lot of exp-"

Molly gasped as Sammy's fist landed square in Talie's stomach. Before she could intervene, although how she had absolutely no clue, Sammy whirled around and stormed off back toward the camp.

"Should have expected that," Talie wheezed, doubled over with one hand clamped to her side.

Molly forced her expression to shutter before Talie saw any hint of emotion there.

I don't even know if she's really her.

The thought slammed through her mind again, of Ru or Celeste or even Phoenix or Marcus back to torment her more, word-tangling truths into lies through some arcane sorcery she didn't know of. She wrapped her protection warding tight around her and glowered at Talie.

"You need to tell your story to the others. They'll decide what's going to happen."

They'll be able to tell if you're really you.

Talie nodded, her expression rueful as she wrung out the ends of her coat.

"I will. If you show me who to speak to, I'll tell them everything."

Molly turned on her heel and set off. She forced aside the worry that Talie looked thin inside her coat, her eyes ringed with darkness and her skin dull. The urge to insist that Talie at least change into dry clothing before she caught a cold surged up, but she shoved it back down and powered through the camp toward the royal tents.

Demi raised her head and lifted a wary eyebrow as Molly walked in without asking. When Talie followed her in, Demi frowned.

"What's going on?"

Molly folded her arms and gave Talie her best no-nonsense look, but Demi spoke again before Talie could.

"We know you've been among us under a glamour, Kainen guessed as much, but you need to tell us your side before we start slinging accusations."

Talie nodded. "Fair enough, your majesty."

Molly noted the slight wince Demi made at the honorific, but she sat on the edge of her desk and fell silent.

They listened as Talie explained freeing the fairies in the labyrinth, about losing sight of Kainen and Milo, and meeting Ru. Molly winced when the realisation sank in, but she pinned her lips between her teeth and kept silent as Talie explained about the shaking and the servants hall, and that everyone was gone when she emerged, and the lanes around the Menagerie were in chaos.

Molly managed not to make a single sound or movement when Talie detailed her escape and the near brushes she'd had with overturned carts and falling debris.

Celeste killed Ru. I can't blame Talie for that. It's exactly the kind of thing he'd do, assume Celeste wouldn't harm him if he showed her who he was.

"Why not announce yourself immediately?" Demi asked, her tone wary.

Talie hesitated. "It felt safe to be someone else for a while. I barely made it out of the citadel when it came down. Had to grab a falling cart, almost got hit by a bunch of rubble, fell a couple of levels through a gaping hole in the floor. I was already in the glamour when I got here."

Molly clung to the charms hanging around her neck with tight fingers as Demi frowned deeper.

"Well, you've been missed. You should have reported in. I may need to get you to swear to it now, as you're not exactly giving us much to go on."

"Okay." She shrugged. "My name is Talie. Apparently it's short for Thalia, but nobody's ever called me that. I was dumped at one of the kids' homes on the upper levels of the citadel and I've never known who my parents are. Happens to a lot of kids up there. How much more do you need?"

Demi frowned. "A bit more. What's your role in all of this?"

"There's a swear-block on me for part of it, but I was picked and given a mind-wipe gift, and made to use it on people. I was told to be part of the resistance and I've monitored Molly since before she knew who I was. Didn't ever expect her to crash into my life though, she did that herself."

Molly fought the sheer waves of relief and hysteria that made her want to laugh. Or scream, she couldn't be sure.

"You were Lia too, Kainen said you were," she mumbled.

Talie turned to look at her but she couldn't bear it and dropped her gaze to Demi's desk instead.

"It was the safest way to get in and keep an eye on you. He asked me what I'd be willing to do so I made up Lia, got myself into the laundry service at the Menagerie. I couldn't risk letting you know who I was, not until I had a proper way out for you."

Molly shook her head, all the more muddled for Talie's presence and the constant stream of revelations she could barely even keep up with let alone process.

"Where are your allegiances now?" Demi prompted.

Molly rubbed a hand over her neck in a pointless attempt to settle the fizzles bouncing around in her chest.

"I want to keep Sammy safe," Talie said. "That's always been why I do what I do. I don't have any allegiances other than that. Only…"

She hesitated, her gaze flicking sideways. Molly flinched as their eyes met and she looked away.

If she really was thinking of me, she wouldn't have faked who she was, not after everything Celeste did to me, Ru's fake kiss, all of that.

She couldn't even remember what parts of that Talie knew, or which parts of the past were truth and which were deception.

Demi sighed. "You're on probation then. Any more deceit and you're on your own. Sammy gets to choose now too, and she's welcome to stay with us if she wants."

"Thank you." Talie bowed her head. "I get if people don't want me around, but as long as everyone is safe that's what matters."

Demi snorted. "No need to be so noble about it. You're still a member of the citadel and we're not kicking you out just yet. Get some sleep both of you. Tomorrow we need to be focusing yet again on what to do next."

Molly didn't wait around. She hurried out of the tent and across the snowy ground, hoping she was imagining the steady footsteps crunching behind her.

"Molly..."

"Don't speak to me," she shouted back.

"I get you're angry, but-"

She slammed her hands over her ears.

"Not listening, go away."

She stormed into her tent and let the flap drop, wishing it was a proper door she could slam.

"That was smooth."

She jolted in alarm to find Kainen already lounging on the edge of her bed.

"Go away."

"She really is sorry," he said.

"Out, now." She pointed to the exit. "Or I'll tell Milo you want to help him update his archives."

Kainen grinned. "He'd never believe you, not in a million years. He wouldn't trust me anywhere near them even if I offered myself."

Molly couldn't think of any other retort or idle threat to throw back at him as he got up and sauntered to the exit.

"Oh, I gave her an orb by the way," he added.

"What? Who?" She could easily guess who but her heart wouldn't stop pounding and her mind seemed to be three steps behind.

"Talie."

"Why should I care?"

Wickedness shone in his eyes as he passed her and turned back at the tent flap. She folded her arms and glowered at him, but that only made his smirk wider.

"Because I had it programmed to call yours every hour. First call should be in about ten minutes or so."

"You what?!" She stared at him in horror.

"Yep, proximity trigger. Marvellous what the brains can do with these orbs now. It'll go off every hour unless you're in the same room. When you find it in you to forgive her for wanting to be someone else for like *a day*, then I'll have the setting removed."

She stared after him in horror as he lifted the tent flap and ducked under it.

"But… that's blackmail!"

CHAPTER NINE

TALIE

Talie skulked along the fringes of the camp with her hands shoved in her coat pockets. Molly wasn't willing to look at her but at least she was shouting now, unlike Sammy who had taken a very uncharacteristic vow of silence and disappeared. Talie lifted her head in time to see Kainen emerge from Molly's tent, but he saw her before she could blend into the trees fringing the camp.

"She'll think she needs some time to cool off," he announced. "I wouldn't listen though if I were you."

Talie sighed. She got the distinct vibe that he meant well, but he didn't understand Molly like she did. Push too hard and she would storm off the opposite way.

"She won't forgive me and I don't blame her," she said. "I not only survived so the friend she had for years could die in my place, but then I stayed missing and came back pretending to be someone else. I'm surprised all she did was push me in a lake."

His lips lifted and he gave her a once over.

"I thought you looked a bit soggy. Aren't you worried

about your sister as well?"

Something crashed from the nearby cluster of tents and cheering echoed through the air. Several Fae nearby turned their heads toward the noise but Talie looked toward Molly's tent instead.

"Sammy will come around," she said. "She'll delight in bringing this up every single time she wants to get her way, but she'll always be around to do it. It's how we are."

"But not Molly?"

"No. Even if she does forgive me, she deserves people around her she can trust. People who are strong so she doesn't have to be."

"I wouldn't exactly call you weak. Not many Fae would go into a fortress of royalty in a glamour to look after a friend."

She guessed it was meant to be a compliment, but that automatically set her nerves jangling.

"I'll always do everything I can to make sure she's safe, but I'm not sure I deserve to be a part of her life. I should probably do the right thing and leave her be. That, and I need to find somewhere to sleep."

Kainen glanced around. "No friends willing to give you space?"

"None out here, not that I've seen. They're all likely still in the citadel helping Phoenix."

"And your sister…"

"Will either refuse to let me inside or shout at me all night, and I'm getting a headache just being myself again."

"I couldn't possibly comment." He grinned. "But trust is a very fragile thing, especially now. Can I give you a piece of advice?"

Talie snorted. "No offense, I know you're some fancy lord and all that, but you have done literally nothing except give advice since we met."

He shrugged and glanced back at the camp, his breath puffing on the chilly air.

"One more for old time's sake then. Let Molly decide who she thinks is worthy. Don't be so arrogant that you try to decide that for her. It'd be an insult. Oh and grovel. A lot."

Talie scowled and kicked out at a drift of snow. A huge clump of it sailed into a hole in her boot and she winced as the cold bit at her toes.

"I don't grovel."

Kainen shrugged. "Neither did I once. I learned pretty quick. Even if you're only in her life to be a friend, that's got to be better than not being in it at all. There are some flowers still growing by the lake a bit further down by the way, fairly nice ones."

He wandered off and Talie slouched in the direction of the lake.

It had seemed harmless to stay as Solaine when she first walked into Molly's tent. Her bones still felt like they were rattling from the mad dash out of the citadel, she hadn't slept properly and her mind was like sour soup, but even seeing Molly for a moment was enough.

It's for the best to keep my distance from her for now.

In time she could explain that she had no idea Ru would die when she agreed to let him take her place, and that she hid herself away for weeks because she didn't realise Molly was Daisy, or that she'd been lingering in hopes of seeing her while trying to find Sammy a safe way out.

Or that the couple of brief days as Solaine had given her a false, heady freedom where she could pretend to be someone worthy for a while.

She flinched as her hip warmed. Seconds passed in confusion, until she remembered the orb Kainen had given her. She pulled it out of her pocket and her heart gave a dangerous thud as Molly's name scrolled across the surface.

She's calling me. Wait, no...

The name was scrolling from right to left, which only meant one thing.

"How in the name of Faerie am I calling her?!" she gasped, fumbling to end the orb call.

She shoved the infernal thing back into her pocket and set off toward the camp, clumps of snow flying up as she broke into a jog.

I can explain it was an accident and insist I'll be giving her space. I can shout it through the tent flap so she doesn't have to see me.

She slowed on approach to Molly's tent and her trepidation doubled to a pounding in her chest. Molly and Sammy stood close together, their faces shadowed from view. Molly looked up and her hesitant expression clamped down into a fearsome glower, which would have been intimidating if it weren't for the adorable scrunch of her nose.

Sammy went one further and gave Talie a feral glare before turning on her heel and stalking off. Talie frowned to see her heading away through the tents as if she knew the paths between well already.

"Is it safe for her to go wondering around at night?" she asked.

The words leapt from her mouth on instinct, but she groaned inwardly as Molly's shoulders shot up even higher.

"You think I'd be that careless with her after everything?" she snapped. "She has her own tent nearby."

Talie nodded. *Good. Snapping is good. Better than her breaking down in tears.*

"I didn't mean to call you just now," she explained. "That's all I came to say. I think Kainen gave me a glitchy orb. I'll give you space too. I know you hate me and I don't blame you, what with all the grief and everything. Not that I'm saying you care enough to grieve or anything, but you know. Anyway, I'll keep my distance."

Her ears burned with growing mortification and she took a step back, her lips pinned together to avoid anymore nonsense spewing out.

Molly shrugged but the movement was uncoordinated, and her cheeks were pink as she stared rigidly toward the rest of the camp.

"Where are you sleeping?" she asked. "So I know where to avoid."

Ouch.

Talie hesitated as snow started swirling down around them. She hadn't slept, not since leaving the citadel. The first night she'd worked through to help people fit into tents and make beds, anything she could to keep herself moving. Then Kainen had collared her to fetch Molly, seemingly at random but now she knew exactly why. It felt like fate at the time, but apparently a court lord just wanted to play her guardian angel, or Molly's, for some worrying reason. Since then she'd found a few minutes to rest sitting by various fires, and had a quick bite to eat in passing when she remembered, but no actual sleep.

"I've made do where I can," she embellished. "It's fine."

"Oh."

"Don't worry about me, Princess."

The words were out before she could stop them but Molly only turned away.

"I won't."

She stalked into her tent without a look back and Talie sagged as the snow grew thicker, a whirling onslaught that bit right through to the bone.

She looked longingly at Molly's tent once more, remembering how blissfully heated it was, and turned to assess the rest of the camp. She needed to find somewhere but unless she took the hit and went in search of Sammy, it was going to be a painful night.

Somehow I don't think his lordship's kindness will extend to me curling up on his floor.

As she started toward the makeshift kitchens with barely enough energy left to lift her feet, a chilling scream tore out of Molly's tent.

Panic ripped at her insides and set her blood pounding as she drew the thin dagger Molly had gifted her from its wrist strap. She charged through the flap, blade raised, adrenalin hitting her system fast.

Molly stood on her bed with a huge book in both hands, her terrified gaze fixed on the wooden boards that made up the flooring.

"Get it out!" she begged.

Talie eyed the pigeon pecking lazily at tiny crumbs with absolutely no concern for the quivering girl standing on the bed. She lowered her arm and sheathed her dagger.

"It's just a pigeon."

"It still has claws that can tear a chunk out of you!" Molly snapped.

"So what do you expect me to do?" She fought the rising urge to grin. "Risk getting chunks torn out of me by this savage leviathan?"

Even as she said it, she grabbed a pair of trousers from a nearby chair and herded the poor bird toward the exit.

"I can't believe you're mocking me. Fear of birds is a completely legitimate phobia."

Talie nodded as the bird made it outside unscathed.

"Yes, Princess. I don't see how you can be fine with Aurora but scared of a mere pigeon, that's all."

She looked around but couldn't see any sign of Molly's pet bird, pet being a relative term considering Aurora had chosen Molly rather than the other way around. The large mirror in the far corner was far too clean and polished for bird use and she wondered if something had happened to Aurora in the escape from the citadel.

"Aurora didn't give me a choice, you know that." Molly's tone had turned snippy now that the 'danger' was gone. "Birds are still birds with talons and sharp beaks."

Talie bit her lip hard to stifle the grin brewing and

walked back to fold the trousers over the chair.

"Where is she?" she asked.

Molly shrugged. "Out hunting I'd imagine. I saw her last night but every time she's in here, Marthe has it clean again by time I get back. Anyway, that's not the point. Aurora is… different. Normal birds like pigeons still can't be trusted not to attack."

"Poor pigeon." Talie sighed. "Maybe it has a nest I can hole up in for the night before it eats me."

She was pushing it, but Kainen had insisted she do exactly that and she wasn't going to disobey a direct order. Not one that seemed to be working in her favour anyway. She turned her head and thought for a second that there was the tiniest quiver of a smile on Molly's face.

I won't be able to live with myself if I don't at least try to earn her trust back. I owe her that much, if only to protect her from random and mostly non-existent pigeon attacks.

"You didn't bother to find a tent or a bunk, did you," Molly muttered.

"I was too busy pitching in where I could at the time, but it's fine. I'm sure I'll figure something out."

"Ask Kainen. He definitely seems to be your number one fan."

Talie frowned. "Meaning?"

Molly clambered down from the bed and started fussing with the ridiculous mound of pillows and blankets. Talie had never seen so many, and she madly wondered what it would be like to dive into them as Molly huffed loudly.

"Meaning, the orb he gave you is cursed to ring mine

every hour unless we're in the same room."

Talie's mind stalled. "It what? But why?"

That explained the unexpected orb call hers had made, but she couldn't exactly march up to a court lord uninvited and start screaming questions at him.

"His idea of a joke probably." Molly gave a jerky shrug. "It'll keep me up but I have no intention of answering."

Talie fought the smile tugging at her lips. Molly looked so sulky and vulnerable with her mad red hair all messy and her gaze fixed on her fingers as they tugged the same pillow back and forth across the bed.

"You look like you need a good sleep," she announced. "I'll leave you be. You sure you don't have any idea where I could bunk down?"

"Wherever you can find."

It was the vaguest suggestion she was likely to get, filled with potential, but Molly wasn't overtly telling her to leave.

Talie took a deep breath and shrugged off her coat.

Here goes nothing.

CHAPTER TEN

MOLLY

Molly pressed a hand to her chest to calm the pounding. Even when she was beyond furious, she couldn't throw off the urge to keep trading insults like they were still friends, which wouldn't do either of them any good.

Something rustled and she lifted her head to find Talie pulling her coat off.

"Er... what are you doing?"

Talie arched her brow. "Going to bed wherever I can find."

"I didn't mean in here!"

"Where else am I meant to sleep? Sammy will shout at me until she faints if I go ask to bunk in with her. That's really more if a morning pastime, and I can't exactly go snuggle up with your new royal friends when they're all giving me such dirty looks."

"That's no more than you deserve," Molly muttered. "No way are you sharing my bed."

Talie shrugged. "Wasn't expecting to."

Molly stared in horror as Talie dropped sit on the bare

wood near the entrance, folded her coat around herself as both a blanket and a sleeping mat and faced the wall.

I can't make her sleep out in the snow.

She had the option of calling Marthe who would likely have a new tent rustled up in seconds, and probably set up almost as quickly, but explaining why wasn't top of her evening to-do list.

With Talie resolutely turned away from her, she couldn't see any other choice.

It's not like we're sharing a bed or anything, and tomorrow she can find somewhere else.

She extinguished the light from the orb on her bedside table and plunged them into darkness. When Talie didn't make a sound, Molly climbed into bed and burrowed into the voluminous soft warmth.

Talie was alive and Ru was dead. Her heart sank. It had been his choice to obey Celeste, to betray their friendship which he had lied about at Celeste's bidding for most if not all of it, but in the end he saved Talie and took her place. She'd never be able to ask him why either, never know if in seeing her fight so hard to spare Talie's life once before, he did the one thing he could to secure it for her.

Talie didn't exactly lie to me either. She risked her life, everything, to come into the Menagerie as Lia, and she's only been Solaine for a day.

Molly pinched between her eyes and forced her mind to wade back through those awful days. She'd been tricking Talie as Daisy originally for her own safety, but Talie had entered the Menagerie as Lia for her. There was still the time in between the fight and the citadel crumbling unaccounted for, but she was safe.

She's safe. Alive. She pressed her finger and thumb harder against her eyes as the tears leaked free and a ball of unspent grief swelled in her chest. *Even if she is working for Phoenix still, she went to Kainen and the others to help me. She doesn't have a choice in any of this but she chose to try and save me anyway.*

The thoughts whirled around each other but she needed sleep and a clear head before attempting to sort them. Wiping her eyes on one of the many pillows, she took a couple of long breaths and tried to unknot her tense muscles. None of that stopped the recurring thought that Talie was alive and sleeping almost in reaching distance.

Molly let her Fae connection flare and the subtle curling warmth of her sunlight gift sensed a wholly natural chill elsewhere. If she listened, she could hear the slightest rustle of Talie's coat as she shivered. The tent was heated but the flap would let in draughts, and it was a bitterly cold night outside.

Furious with herself for being so soft-hearted, she sat up and dragged a huge wedge of blanket into the middle of the bed.

"You stay on your side, got it?" she said.

There was silence for a long moment.

"What?" Talie's voice was almost inaudible.

"Your side of the bed. Sammy will forgive you eventually, and she probably won't appreciate having to nurse you if you get sick from freezing on the floor."

She expected some glib retort, or maybe even some weak attempt at a refusal drenched in pride first, but Talie hesitated for all of a second. The sound of fabric shifting filled the air, along with the thud of boots hitting the floor, then Talie clambered between the sheets.

"Orbs alive, how many pillows are there?"

Molly scowled into the darkness. "No talking. Go to sleep and stay on your side."

Perhaps Talie didn't dare push it by retorting, or maybe she was too entranced by the many soft blankets. Either way, Molly could *feel* her smile somehow, and that alone irritated her enough to focus on the one sensation rather than the cascade of many that had dogged her sleep for weeks.

Bad enough I have a girl in my bed, but it's one I'm untameably furious with.

The thought lulled her into sleep but each time her consciousness dipped, she resurfaced to check that Talie really was still alive beside her.

I can't hold any of this against her, not really, but I can't pretend everything's fine either.

Her sunlight grumbled awake and warmed gently inside her bones, giving enough illumination that she could see the tiny frown on Talie's sleeping face.

She's alive and safe though. I have to take that for the blessing it is and work through the rest.

She turned on her side and shut her eyes firmly.

Either way, Sammy's going to be unbearable for days.

That alone was enough to lull her into a proper sleep, a restful one without nightmares. By the time she woke again, it was a hazy dawning of consciousness rather than the jolt she'd been experiencing for a while.

Without opening her eyes, she turned from her side onto her back and froze at the subtle sense of something extra.

Why is there a hand on my ribs? Oh orbs.

She contemplated trying to fall back to sleep, but Talie's fingers pressing her bare skin where her top had ridden up were branding more wakefulness into her than an entire vat of *offke*.

She considered pretending to sleep and rolling away. That could work. With her eyes shut tight, she twisted onto her side. Talie's hand slithered away.

Molly let her limbs relax again but the relief died when Talie's entire arm surfaced instead, wrapping around her middle and closing the tiny gap between them.

There wasn't a single doubt that Talie was in the deepest throes of sleep, but getting away from her without waking her now seemed impossible.

Why does this feel so comfortable?

Molly tensed as Talie's breath blew softly over the exposed bit of skin where her neck met her shoulder.

Before she could figure out any reasonable excuse to go on pretending to sleep and make the most of the unexpected comfort, the tent flap slapped open.

"I've decided it's time to tal- oh! Yay! I *KNEW* it!"

Molly winced as Sammy's delighted shriek blasted through the tent. She pretended to flail and wake in confusion rather than outright hysterical laughter as Talie sat up with a start.

"What in the name of Faerie are you doing stamping into other people's tents without warning?" Talie shouted.

Sammy grinned wider. "Molly, tell the person who used

to be my sister that I'm not talking to her, but if she intends to explain where she's been all this time and why, then I might consider hearing her out."

"No, tell her yourself," Molly grumbled.

"I'll bring you breakfast?"

She groaned. "Fine, but this is the last time!"

Sammy's laughter echoed behind her as she left the tent. Molly pulled her knees to her chest and wrapped her arms around her legs as Talie sat cross-legged with her forearms on her knees.

"She's got you round her little finger," Talie said.

Molly shrugged. "Same with everyone else. At least I get breakfast out of it."

"Thank you for looking out for her."

"As if I wouldn't." She hesitated. "I considered it briefly, pretending to leave her to see if it brought you back from the dead. Wasn't expecting it to happen for real though, or for free."

Talie kept her gaze welded to her lap. "Did you get my letter? Did it at least explain some bits of the past?"

"Yeah."

"And you're wearing that." Her gaze dropped the *Akiai* charm circling Molly's thumb.

Molly ran her forefinger over it. "Yeah."

"I'm not forgiven, am I?"

"For what exactly?"

"For letting you think I was dead. For letting him take my place when you and he could have made up."

Molly winced at the thought of Ru. He'd done so much wrong but that couldn't erase all the years she'd believed he was her closest friend.

"It's not my place to forgive you for that," she said carefully. "He made his choice after what he did, for whatever reason."

"He loved you."

Molly remembered a time where she would have swooned to hear that, but now it only made her heart sink.

"When he knew I held the potential for power, sure. He was my friend because of Celeste. His loyalty was always to her. That's not real love."

"And you'd know about that?" Talie asked.

"I don't anymore but it doesn't matter now. You should be focusing on getting Sammy to forgive you anyway, not stressing about me."

"Oh great." Talie snorted. "That'll probably take decades."

Molly fought the urge to smile, even as her body warmed and the tiniest hint of sunshine illuminated the otherwise gloomy tent. Talie had deceived her but not to take advantage of her.

I'm not even in a position to be demanding anything from her anyway. We're friends, kind of. She might not even see us as friends since we were thrown together. It's not like we're...

She acted on pure impulse and leaned across the bed, ignoring Talie's startled flinching. Nose to nose, Molly stared right into the wide hazel eyes with their circle of gold around the edges that reflected her own radiating glow.

"Get Sammy to forgive you, then we'll talk." She slid

off the bed to grab her coat and shove her bare feet into her snow boots. "Lie to me again, or try to trick me with glamours or any of that, and I'll end this myself."

Striding out of the tent, her heart lifted as she heard Talie chuckle. There was still so much that needed to be cleared before forgiveness was possible, but they had time. Before any of that, Talie had to win Sammy over and Molly had to find somewhere else to change and get Marthe to bring her fresh clothes.

CHAPTER ELEVEN

TALIE

"How many times are you going to make me say I'm sorry?"

Sammy tilted her head, then gave Talie a sulky expression with her nose all wrinkled. The entire day had been much of the same, but Molly had told her to get Sammy's forgiveness so that's what she would do. Outside the nobility tents in the bitter, gusting wind and snow wasn't exactly how she'd wanted to do it though, not while she was only wearing a threadbare coat.

Sammy on the other hand had a warm snow-coat on similar to Molly's, along with fresh new boots on her feet. She looked like she at least was over the shock already and having a brilliant time at camp.

Talie sighed. "Fine, I'm sorry. I won't explain why again because I've already told you three times, but I was doing what I thought was safest for you. And for Molly."

She added the last bit against her better judgement, but it worked because Sammy's expression lessened slightly, desire for gossip lighting in her eyes.

"Why didn't you knock when Molly was out though? There were so many days you could have seen her leave as Daisy and knock for me."

Talie sighed. "I thought about it, but then what could I have done? Where would I have taken you to? Phoenix might have found us somewhere else but the Menagerie were hunting Molly, they knew who you are and I was told they'd put a price on my head. For all I knew, you were being watched and I couldn't risk it. I was searching for a way out."

"So, if you'd found one, you'd have grabbed me and off we went? What about Molly?"

Talie hesitated. She hadn't admitted the depth of her alone time to anyone else yet, but getting Sammy on side was the first step she had to take.

"When I wasn't watching you, I was climbing those orbing girders looking for her."

Sammy's eyes widened. "Wow, and you're cruddy with heights."

"Yeah, so come on, how many more apologies do I have to make before you forgive me?"

Sammy pulled a serious face and held up both hands, fingers extended to the sky.

Ten more I'm sorry's.

Talie sighed. "I'm sorry. I'm sorry. I'm sorry. I'm sorry. I'm sorry. I'm sorry. I'm sorry. I'm sorry. I'm sorry. I'm sorry. And one last I'm sorry for the sake of it. Now will you forgive me?"

Sammy folded her arms across her chest and lifted her nose in the air.

"I forgive you," she announced. "Although I think Molly forgave you far too quickly. I would have made you beg much longer if I was her. Wouldn't have jumped straight into bed with you either."

Talie sagged. It had taken her the best part of a day, but finally she was on the right level.

"It wasn't like that," she insisted. "I did rescue her from certain death last night though."

"You did? How?"

"There was a pigeon in her tent."

Sammy squinted. "A pigeo- how is that rescuing her from certain death?!"

Talie laughed, the action so unfamiliar and freeing that it startled her.

"You know she hates birds, so to her it was rescuing. I still have a lot of making up to do."

"A ton. Like seventeen tonnes, at least. We can't all be as forgiving as I am."

"Er… yeah. Very forgiving."

She tensed as Sammy drew closer, but she relaxed into the hug that followed and held on tight.

"Don't do it again," Sammy mumbled into her shoulder. "I'm still grieving and now I have nowhere for it to go, but Ru was Molly's friend for a long time. She's bound to be really mixed up in the head."

"How did you get so wise?"

"Practice. Also, now you're back, can you do my hair properly? Molly sucks at it but I didn't want to upset her."

Talie grinned. "No problem, anything you want. Should I make myself scarce for this meeting do you think?"

"Why?"

"Well, I doubt Molly wants to see me yet, and the royals have made it clear I'm on probation."

"Oh, that." Sammy waved a dismissive hand. "No sense hiding away now. We need Molly to forgive you and that won't happen if she doesn't see you."

"I doubt it's going to be that easy."

Sammy frowned. "You do want her to forgive you, right?"

Talie hesitated. She rarely told Sammy dangerous or logistical things that involved both of them, but now and then she grudgingly let slip the odd bit of personal information. Discussing what was turning out to be a complicated and excruciating crush on royalty was a sacrifice.

It would get me back on her good side if I admitted the truth.

She nodded. "More than anything. She told me this morning that I had to get you to forgive me before she did, so I'm that bit closer at least."

Sammy's lips lifted in a frighteningly bright grin.

"Perfect. I officially forgive you for tricking us and will do everything I can to help you get Molly to forgive you as well."

Talie grimaced. "Okay, but nothing too out there, please."

"As if I would." Sammy paused. "Fine, nothing too dramatic or embarrassing. We don't want to scare her off and she's actually quite sensitive deep down. Let's go."

Talie let Sammy loop their arms together and followed

through the tents toward the queen's fenced off enclosure. She tried to slow down on approach, worry flickering at the thought she might not be welcome, but Sammy steamed through the makeshift rope that fenced the royal tents and bounced right up to Kainen and Molly.

"Are we having those wicked finger sandwich things again?" Sammy asked.

Kainen frowned but there was a knowing glint in his eyes.

"I don't know, should we go and check?"

"Absolutely we should." Sammy beamed. "You two stay and chat or whatever. No throwing things."

Talie stared in horror as the two of them shot off like naughty kids toward the queen's tent, which left her with Molly. Alone.

"That was subtle," Molly muttered.

"She's not known for her subtlety."

"No. She's forgiven you then."

"Yeah, after hours of pleading and explanations. Not that I don't deserve it."

Molly rolled her eyes. "Humility doesn't suit you. Scowling and glowering and lurking in corners is more your style."

Talie's heart leapt but she kept the smile off her face as she shrugged.

"If you want, Princess."

"Stop calling me that."

"It's what you are."

"Yeah, more secrets you didn't share with me."

"Couldn't." Talie grimaced. "Literally couldn't share

them with you."

"Oh, like you 'couldn't' pop out of your hidey hole afterwards to at least let Sammy know you were alive?!"

Okay, so we're doing this.

Talie fought the frustration bubbling up as she glanced around to make sure nobody was watching the showdown, then inhaled a sharp lungful of cold air.

"I couldn't risk it. I spent most of my time after the whole scene at the Menagerie looking for a way out for her, or somewhere to hide that wouldn't have us on the starvation line."

"And you didn't think to even leave a note that you were safe?" Molly slammed her hands on her hips, her eyes flashing with emotion. "Anything that could have told us you weren't dead?"

Talie lifted her hands between them, hoping for a calming gesture and ending up with a frustrated waving instead.

"I didn't know you thought I was dead though! I assumed the royals got you out of the citadel because you were nowhere to be found, and that they left Daisy to look after Sammy. Imagine if I'd revealed myself only for Daisy to turn me in?"

"I was Daisy!"

"Well I didn't know that did I? There was no guarantee it was safe if I showed myself or left a note either. It's not like I can run around relying on fancy friends like yours."

The words shot out like bullets.

Molly veered back as if she'd been slapped, her eyes widening like a starving kitten's.

Talie winced. "I didn't mean-"

"Yeah, you did. I have no intention of relying on them either, or on anyone. Everyone lets you down eventually."

Molly took a step back and her hands dropped to her sides as the queen's tent-flap parted.

"When you're done spatting, everyone's ready to start the meeting," Sammy announced.

Molly stalked away before Talie could even open her mouth, let alone apologise. Fighting the urge to flee into the woods and get eaten by whatever creatures lurked in the depths, she squared her shoulders and followed.

The queen's tent was almost as opulent as someone's normal home, with a separate part entirely for the bed and a huge tree climbing over one side of the canvas. In the higher branches of the tree, a weird scaly green lizard was snoring on its back.

Talie recognised most of the people seated around, from the queen and the king consort to Kainen and the man who'd realm-skipped them into the Menagerie. A couple of them nodded to her or smiled as she squeezed herself onto a wooden chair next to Sammy, but her attention was fixed on Molly seated on the other side of the tent.

The grouchy old woman who seemed to have appointed herself as Molly's full-time servant was fussing around her, and Talie had to squash down an ill-timed smile as Molly pushed the woman's hands away from her hair.

"I'm fine, Marthe, honest," she insisted. "If I get cold, I'll get a coat."

Taz leaned over from his seat beside her and Talie wondered if she still had the privilege of calling the king consort by his name as he'd previously insisted, or whether she was back to titles. Then he whispered to Molly loud enough for the whole tent to hear.

"It's easier to let her fuss, or she'll assume there's something you're not telling her and start insisting on bedtimes."

He yelped as Marthe tapped him on the back of the head as she passed, but it was enough to make Molly smile the tiniest bit as the queen hopped up to sit cross-legged on her enormous fancy desk.

"All assembled?" she asked. "Right Milo, you're up."

Milo held up his hand and projected an orb-cast onto the side of the tent.

"With the tower down, the wards are weakened. Celeste has had to hem herself into the Menagerie from what I've heard, which of course encompasses the core and the labyrinth beneath it."

He took a breath but before he could continue, the shadows roiled in the corner of the tent and a woman materialised from them.

"Ah, good, what we got?" Demi asked.

"That's Reyan," Sammy whispered. "She's Lady of the Illusion Court."

Talie nodded. There was no point reminding Sammy that she'd met Reyan briefly before, not when she wanted to hear what was said next.

"Yeah, not good," Reyan announced. "I managed to get a fair way but the shadows grew hostile after a while. I can confirm though that Celeste is convening around the well of power, and I would assume drawing from it. I didn't linger but there are definitely fairies down there that are… let's just say it doesn't sound pretty."

Talie eyed Molly sitting with her fists clenched beneath her thighs and her face taut in anger. She fought the urge to get up and say some acidic retort, anything that might get Molly to glower or scoff at her instead of swilling in rage. A soft glow illuminated Molly's skin and her lips pressed thin as she closed her eyes, her back going stiff.

"Uh oh," Sammy muttered, already halfway to her feet.

Talie caught her sleeve. "What?"

"The last time she started glowing like that, she almost burned the Menagerie to the ground."

Talie froze as Sammy tore her sleeve free and crossed the room. Nobody else had noticed Molly yet, but Kainen turned his head as Sammy passed and noticed the brightening glow. He grimaced and got to his feet, a swathe of shadows building behind him like a shield to protect the others.

Talie shot up and hurried over before he could do whatever he was planning on doing. Without thinking, she guided Sammy aside and dropped into crouch in front of Molly's chair.

"Molly, I know you hate me right now, so if you need to blast something, aim it at me."

Molly opened her eyes and Talie flinched backwards. Molly's eyes were orbs of glowing white, tiny hints of blinding golden sunshine massing at the edges. Talie gulped down a rising wave of fear.

"Okay, that's kind of cool," she muttered. "Can you still hear me in there?"

The light dimmed slightly.

"Of course I can hear you. I'm fine."

She wasn't, but Talie only shrugged.

"Fair enough. I wouldn't know."

"You would have if you'd stuck around."

Talie nodded. "True. My fault again. Can you turn the glow off at will then?"

"I… most of the time."

Talie resisted the urge to set a hand on Molly's knee, even though her own were aching from crouching already.

"Show me?" It was part demand, part plea.

Molly sucked in a breath and closed her eyes again. Slowly the glow dissipated, but Talie noticed the tiniest of shudders that followed.

"Wow, that's cool," she said.

Molly blinked. "I don't know about that. It has been useful sometimes. Not so much others."

She lifted her head and eyes widened.

"All okay?" Taz asked, his tone far too cheerful.

Molly nodded as her cheeks turned pink. Talie clambered to her feet with a grunt, not entirely surprised when Molly wouldn't look directly at her. Sammy grinning and waggling her eyebrows suggestively as they reclaimed their seats didn't help either.

"Smooth," Sammy whispered.

Talie blinked away the remaining blur from Molly's gift that was still dazzling her vision.

"Hardly," she muttered as Milo cleared his throat to reclaim the tent's attention. "Now quiet and pay attention."

Sammy rolled her eyes but fell silent.

"What we need to bear in mind is that the citadel is still functioning," Milo insisted. "One tower has crumbled, but many of its people are stuck out here and others are stuck inside. Then there's all the books, and Faerie knows how many other libraries there might be in other towers."

Taz nodded. "We need some goodwill from the nobles who are privileged enough to go back and forth, those Celeste might deal with directly."

"She might be sending Marcus out to do her dirty work," Molly said.

"We do have someone still in there though," Kainen added. "She promised to work her way down and get a message out from the terraces."

Talie frowned. "That's risky. Everyone knows even the terraces are monitored for orb-waves."

She bit her lip and wondered if she was still meant to be not seen and not heard, but Demi raised an eyebrow.

"Everyone knows?"

"We get taught it in school," Sammy said.

Kainen and Reyan exchanged a look, then Reyan huffed and dissolved into the shadows.

"Who do you have inside, Kainen?" Demi asked.

He pulled a face. "Glennoria. Not Reyan's biggest fan but she's loyal to our court, sworn to it and currently in the top dog spot among our nobles, so we can trust her as far as we can trust any court Fae."

"Not exactly far though is it," Taz muttered.

Kainen shrugged. "It's what we've got. Reyan's had to go in through the cracks already once, so we'll take what we get and be grateful.”

The warning in his tone was enough to make Taz raise his hands in weary apology. Talie slouched on her seat and a wave of estrangement swept through her chest as the others interacted like one big dysfunctional family. She thought about slipping away, but the tent flap lifted and a vaguely familiar face walked in.

Talie tried to figure out where she’d seen the woman with the bright purple hair before, but Sammy was up on her feet and Molly’s gasp was like a tiny cry. Both crossed the tent in seconds, but while Sammy was smiling, Molly only managed a muttered hello.

Talie bit her lip as the memories settled. She recognised the woman who’d lived next door to Molly’s workshop for a while but couldn’t remember her name as everyone bent over the tiny bundle of cloth in the woman’s arms.

“Orbs, she’s grown!” Sammy exclaimed.

CHAPTER TWELVE

MOLLY

Molly stared at Baby Aurora asleep in Beryl's arms. She didn't look any bigger but Beryl's hair had grown longer and there were lines around her sad brown eyes. Beryl smiled readily enough as Sammy gave an enthusiastic greeting, but it was a knowing smile still dredged with grief.

"Is she bigger?" Molly asked. "She looks bigger already but I can't tell." Memories collided and her gut crunched tight. "I'm sorry, I'm so sor-"

Beryl shook her head. "Don't. I can't go round and round about it. Just give me a hug and hold the baby so I can sit down. None of what happened was your fault, but someone will have to babysit while I go rip the head off the orb-muncher responsible."

The words flowed over Molly's mind like a balm, sweeter than sunshine. The guilt she carried over Harvey's death had nestled deep in the few weeks since it happened, but Beryl not blaming her helped immensely.

"You'll have to get in line," she insisted.

Kainen appeared beside her and peered delicately into the bundle of blankets as Molly took careful hold of them.

"Who's babysitting while you two are going pillaging then?" he asked. "Touch toes not me!"

"Touch toes!" Taz joined in.

Milo was already doubled over with his fingers welded to his toes.

Demi rolled her eyes. "I still can't go in, so I can handle her."

"She's not an opponent." Beryl sniffed. "She doesn't need 'handling', she needs looking after. But I've looked after Leo several times so I guess it's fair payment."

Taz huffed. "When you say looked after-"

"He was fine!"

"He escaped into the training rooms and ate five people's lunches! Then threw them up!"

"Oh don't be such a pageant pet-dad."

Molly laughed. She couldn't help it, unable to catch the bubbling sensation before it burst out of her mouth. The familiar swell of guilt stabbed at her insides, but she pushed it aside as Taz and Beryl gave each other one final, well-practiced glower and slunk away to sit down.

Molly clung to baby Aurora as she went back to her chair, but she didn't comment on Talie tailing after her. There was nowhere near her for Talie to sit, but somehow having her hover nearby, peering down at the baby like she might bite, was comforting.

"So, what's the plan?" Beryl asked.

Demi sighed. "You're all going to hate it, but I think we need to throw a party."

"I love parties!"

"A nobility party."

"Oh, then no thanks."

"We need their goodwill," Demi argued. "Several have left the citadel, but if we show them we're in control outside then they might consider coming to our aid if and when the time comes to fight."

"What about the people here though? The non-noble ones?" Molly asked.

Demi shrugged. "They can join in too. I'm not holding with this whole court hierarchy thing if I don't have to. They're as much a part of the citadel as the nobility, arguably more so."

"Won't it look frivolous if we start holding parties?" Milo asked.

Molly rocked Aurora gently and a tiny smile crept across her face. She'd never thought to ask Beryl if the purple hair was a glamour or not, but the wispy puffs on Aurora's head were golden brown.

As the others looked around at each other, she remembered what her guardian Basil had once told her.

"Cheer the good and outlast the bad," she said. "We celebrate what we can get in the citadel, or our levels do at least. Most folk here will just be glad of the food and the shelter, and a party will be the perfect excuse to bring everyone together so they can see we're united."

Demi's expression grew hesitant.

"And are we? I know you aren't keen on claiming your birthright and we don't want to force anything on you that you don't want."

"You can abdicate if you want," Taz offered. "Right now you're in line, whether Celeste is or not, but you don't have to accept. You'll always be family either way."

"Abdication takes paperwork," Milo muttered. "I've only just finished the red tape from that stunt you pulled."

Molly shrugged, glad of the distraction in her arms.

"I don't want to have to pick sides and I'm not bothered about titles." She sucked in a breath, aware her decision had been made long ago. "She forced my hand. If I'm choosing between a queen who wants nobles to party with normal Fae and a mother who uses fairies as lab experiments, then it's not a choice I need to think about."

Demi nodded. "I'll take that."

"We definitely wouldn't use anyone as experiments," Taz insisted.

"Not when we have you," Beryl added sweetly.

Demi pressed a hand to her forehead with a quiet groan.

"Okay, enough both of you. Taz, go home and check on things. Kainen, can you go and start buttering up the nobility?"

Kainen grimaced. "Urgh. I hate being me."

He disappeared into the shadows a moment later while Milo grabbed Taz and vanished with him. Beryl put her feet up on Taz's empty chair with a satisfied groan, which left Molly with Talie and Sammy, except Sammy was nowhere to be seen.

"She squawked something about dresses," Talie said when she saw Molly looking around.

Molly pulled a face. "I don't have to get all dressed up, do I?"

"Yeah, 'fraid so." Demi sighed. "Me too, which sucks. Marthe will have something ready for you by time we get it arranged. We'll probably need to hold it tomorrow, which is madness, but we want the nobles talking about it to other nobles who'll get it to Celeste's ears. We want her to see this as a win for us and a loss for her, rattle her confidence a bit."

"Who's confidence are we rattling?"

The tent-flap opened and Molly's day improved even further. She had a split second of excitement and jumping to her feet before she remembered the baby in her arms and calmed herself again.

May had her blonde waves pinned up in elaborate curls atop her head and her usually hidden tattoos were on full display, the vines and flowers twisting across her skin. She eyed the baby, then gave Talie's suddenly glowering face a dismissive look.

"Molly, I say this kindly, but since when do you have a baby? I absolutely cannot be a great aunt at my young age."

Beryl showed no signs of getting up so Demi wearily came to take Aurora, and Molly smiled as she crossed the tent to let May fold her into a big hug.

"Hello, auntie," she said.

A not-so-discreet choking noise echoed from Talie's corner and Molly revelled in the wickedness of having an excuse to smile. Her cheeks ached from it after so long spent in sadness.

"Oh orbs alive, do *not* go around calling me auntie." May huffed. "But it's good to see you, baby or no baby. I hear we're having a party?"

Demi nodded as deceptive innocence lit in her bright blue eyes.

"We are and struggling already. I still need to tell Marthe-"

"Oh, leave all that to me." May grinned. "I'll handle Marthe. I'm sure we can whip up a usual guestlist. Most of the nobility are here in some way or the other already, twitching their lace curtains. Apparently some of them are also twitching lace knic-"

"Right, great, thank you," Demi interrupted. "I'll let you plan it on my behalf."

Molly bit her lip, unable to stop her cheeks from splitting. She didn't dare look at Talie but the overly frosty reaction to May's arrival, along with the evident shock when she realised the familial link between them, gave Molly a mad sort of hope.

Perhaps a party is what everyone needs while we figure out what to do.

Demi stood and shuffled expectantly toward the exit.

"As lovely as it is to see everyone, get out. Milo has left me a mountain of paperwork."

May grinned. "This is why I'm so glad I'm not queen. I'll find Marthe."

She left the tent and Molly followed her out, not entirely surprised that Talie was right beside her. Sammy stood lounging nearby and wiggled her eyebrows at them.

"I saw May rush past," she announced. "I wondered if you and her were a thing at first but turns out you're related. That means you're single, right?"

Molly sighed. "You think me and everyone is a thing at

first. No idea why. Don't go getting any ideas at this party either. No doubt I'll be shipped out and paraded around the rest of the nobles."

"I still don't see why a party is necessary," Talie muttered.

Sammy gave her a sharp look. "Because it's important to present a united front. Nobody's going to ask you to dance or anything, don't worry."

Talie folded her arms across her chest and looked away with a huff, but Molly caught the subtle flicker of emotion crossing her face.

"This is why it's hard to love her," Sammy added. "She makes you so mad, but then she does that face."

"What face?" Talie demanded, her lips pressing thin.

"Don't be mean." Molly joined in. "But I know the face you mean. The scrunchy one like she wants to punch you but knows she can't."

Talie's eyes widened, a hint of raw vulnerability lurking in the golden brown depths.

"Exactly," Sammy exclaimed. "Then her eyes go all shiny."

"And you feel bad for upsetting her."

"But at least we both admit we love her." Sammy grinned wickedly. "That's progress. Of course, I love her like a sister, whereas you..."

"Wait, I didn't- you said- stop word-tangling me into things!"

Sammy's smile was nothing short of fiendish as she hurried away.

"I have things to be doing," she announced over her

shoulder. "Make love not war."

Molly stared after her, panic and mortification mingling into a lethal cocktail.

"I didn't..." She could barely look Talie in the face as her cheeks burned. "I didn't."

"Sammy's Sammy. I know better than to read anything into it, don't worry." Talie glanced down at her mucky clothes and holey boots. "Hardly a fit choice for a princess anyway, am I?"

Molly shrugged. Seeing May, being forgiven by Beryl, and having had time to let the truth sink in that Talie was alive, it made her feel stronger than she had in a long time.

"Wait until you're all done up for the party then," she suggested.

"As if I have a dress," Talie scoffed. "No, I'll be skulking elsewhere."

Molly saw Marthe approaching and grinned.

"Marthe! Talie doesn't have a dress for the party. Can I give her mine? I'm guessing I'll have to wear one, but can I give it away?"

"Absolutely not! We have plenty of spares."

"I really don't need a dress. I'm not even going," Talie protested.

Marthe rolled up her sleeves and lifted a hand.

"You have somewhere better to be?"

"Literally anywhere else. I don't dress up."

Marthe snapped her fingers and a pile of fancy fabrics in all sorts of colours appeared in her arms a second later.

"First time for everything. We can either do it in the warmth and privacy of your tent or out here in the cold kicking and screaming."

"I… it's…" Talie's mouth flapped over countless unvoiced arguments. "I don't even have a tent!"

"You don't? Oh dear. You'll need to borrow Molly's then. Out here or in there. Your choice. I'd go for the tent though. The nobility aren't known for their when it comes to a woman's modesty. Or her virtue for that matter."

Talie eyed Molly. "Is she serious?"

"She is." Marthe pointed to the tent with a defined jab of her finger. "In. Now."

Molly couldn't hide her giggles as Talie gave her a furious look and marched toward the tent, but she hurried after them to give Talie a tiny measure of help.

"Marthe?" she called out.

"Yes, dear?"

"Nothing too flouncy or she'll never forgive me."

Marthe smiled. "Of course not, but where's the harm in having a little fun first?"

She set off after Talie and Molly thought of the privacy screen in the tent.

No way am I missing this.

For the first time in a long while, her laughter echoed freely through the freezing air.

CHAPTER THIRTEEN

TALIE

"She's beautiful, look!" Sammy breathed, her brown eyes sparkling with delight.

Talie watched Molly standing a fair distance away in a beautiful silver gown that shimmered in the Faelight. While nobles and citadel Fae alike were wary about the idea of a party with each other, May, Marthe and Kainen had moved through the masses planning and cajoling and charming until the central space of the camp was a vision. Colourful streamers hung from the trees that were lined with glowing orbs of Faelight and a wooden dance floor had been set down with tables and chairs around the edges.

Talie glanced down at the dress Marthe had finally conceded to, a long slip of soft dark blue fabric with a flared skirt and sleeves stiff enough to hide a blade under.

She could barely believe that she'd spent the previous day and night being forced into several dresses, which she tolerated purely because it made Molly laugh, then a relaxed evening playing games with Sammy. Marthe had even managed to dredge up a less fancy bed for her, and nobody mentioned it being put in Molly's tent, all too busy with party planning. As the party opened though and Fae began to filter in around the fringes, she stood staring at Molly and wishing she could be anywhere else.

Molly had re-dyed her hair back to blonde and it glowed like starlight against the silver dress as she chatted with Kainen and Taz, her face alive with smiles and laughter.

"She looks like a princess," she grumbled.

Sammy nodded. "Exactly!"

"Exactly. Right down to that ridiculous piece of metal in her hair."

It was sacrilege to call the delicate ice pink and silver tiara Molly wore a 'ridiculous piece of metal', but she couldn't shake her sour mood.

Sammy placed her hands on her hips, her nails painted a glittery gold to match her sparkly halter-neck dress.

"And that's bad why?"

Talie had any number of glib retorts to hand, but one look at Molly with her hair spilling over her shoulders like a cloak of pure sunshine and the truth tripped off her tongue.

"She's always been beautiful, but now others are going to realise it too."

Sammy sighed. "Then you need to make a move fast."

"Oh sure, make a move like I actually have a shot."

"You do have a shot, more than most." Sammy prodded her shoulder with a determined finger. "She actually likes you, Faerie knows why."

"Nice, thanks, but she's a princess. A literal bloodline royal. What am I?"

She flinched as Sammy's face appeared inches from her own with the scary, wide-eyed, 'I mean business' glower.

"You're an idiot if you don't at least try. Ask her to dance, or someone else will. She's already been propositioned by some lord named William during the party set-up earlier, but he insisted she could call him Billy. He looked totally smitten and she was giggling along. Don't let her think you're not interested, that's all."

Sammy stalked away and left Talie reeling in hot-chested jealousy.

William, what kind of name is that for a Fae lord? She scoffed to herself. *I bet he doesn't even come from a decent court.*

She had no idea if nobles were often called William or what courts there were, let alone which courts were decent and which weren't. One thing she did know was that she wasn't from any court at all.

Molly lifted her head then, her chat with Kainen and Taz finished, and looked Talie's way. Instead of keeping eye contact, Talie glanced down at her borrowed gown again. Someone, Marthe she guessed, had left three pairs of tights in different shades on her bed alongside the dress, but she couldn't fathom why she would want to wrangle herself into them.

A pant suit would have been better. At least nobody's complained about me wearing my boots yet.

She tugged at the fitted bodice, finding it hard to get a full breath in as Molly breezed past her toward another group of Fae from the citadel. Mentally hooked on a string, Talie followed her.

She recognised a couple of the people in the group Molly joined as them and settled herself at Molly's side.

"Well, it's not a party in the park, but it'll do," one man said.

A quick glance around the clearing, from the long table groaning with mouthwatering food to the dance floor and the hastily provided wooden chairs that didn't quite match each other, and the divide between nobility and normal couldn't have been clearer. The nobles were sparkling in jewels and cloaked in finery, whereas the Fae from the citadel hadn't done much more than brush hair or find a slightly cleaner outfit.

None of us have anything left.

Molly smiled. "No, it's not. I keep wanting to ask about people we left behind but I'm almost afraid of the answer."

"Well, Merry went for Butch of course, not that he probably needed it. He'd survive a realm falling on his head. I heard from Sav that they ended up in the library though."

"Thank Faerie." Molly pressed a hand to her chest. "I keep looking for her in the crowd here."

The man sighed. "Ah, she's tough. Fern too, saw her gathering several up in that cart of hers then getting a bunch of kids to push it going up the lanes."

"That's a relief," Talie admitted.

"They'll be fine," he insisted. "We're more worried about what's to happen next. Are we going into the citadel to claim it back, and if so with what strengths? If not, what are we left with?"

"The citadel will never recognise a crown as our

leader," another man grumbled.

Talie recognised him from some levels up because he often came into the gym when she was there, but they'd never had any need to talk to each other. He glanced Molly's way and Talie stiffened as Molly kept her chin level and held his gaze.

"You might be one of us in some ways," he added. "But your new title won't make any sway with most."

Molly shrugged. "I don't expect it to. I know better than that and I don't want a title. I can't help who I was born to, but I can trade and contribute as easily as any other Fae from the upper levels."

"Good enough for me." The first man grinned. "So, we're not to go around calling you 'Princess' now then?"

Molly frowned. "Not unless you want me to glower at you. It's an inconvenient extra, nothing else. I'm still me and I still know the best end of a hammer."

"Good. I have a couple of pesanas in my pocket and my kid's busted another pair of glasses."

"Again?!"

Talie let their conversation flow over her. Molly looked happier than she had in days, her shoulders relaxed and her expressions easy. She could let that be enough.

A few of their group straightened up and the jovial expressions shadowed away from their faces.

"We thought we'd come and join you," Kainen announced. "This is Lord Ungent from the Fauna Court, and Lord Tyren from the Court of Revels."

Talie's mind switched off as he continued introducing the group with him, a mass of finely dressed people who looked uneasy at being out of their gilded halls. She watched Molly instead, amused that everyone had to bow and greet Molly like she was one of them.

I'll try not to mock her too much about that.

The band started up a lively tune, and apparently the queen wasn't planning on doing any kind of introduction as several people headed straight for the wooden square of dance floor set in the snow.

Talie tensed as one of the nobles, older than Kainen by the look of him, turned so that his shoulder was separating her and Molly from the rest of the group. Talie raised a warding over both herself and Molly, ready to draw the blade hidden under her sleeve.

"Would you like to step away from all this noise and nonsense, Princess?" the lord, whose name she couldn't remember, suggested.

Molly hesitated and Talie scowled. Molly's title didn't sound right from anyone's mouth but hers.

"She's fifteen, creep," she muttered.

The lordly eyebrows shot up into the ridiculously side-swept hairline.

"Excuse me?"

Talie nodded. "Excused."

Molly stifled an ill-timed snort of laughter as Kainen appeared beside them, charm itself oozing from his smooth smile.

"Is there a problem, Lord Ungent?" he asked, his tone far too silky to be anything other than a potential threat.

"More like Lord Pun-" Talie huffed as Molly clamped a hand over her mouth and pulled her away.

She stumbled happily through the snow with Molly's hand still over her mouth until they were a suitably discreet distance away.

"Are you trying to start a diplomatic incident?!" Molly hissed.

"Come on. He was pushing thirty at least. Total predator, he only wants you for political reasons."

"Obviously, but we have to play nice."

"Why?"

"Because- Because Demi said so."

Talie shrugged. "Well, better you than me because here comes another one."

A more age-appropriate young man with ridiculously flouncy lace sleeves approached and bowed low.

"Princess, may I have this dance?" he asked.

Talie eyed Kainen and he gave her a nod. Like she was somehow in control of who Molly chose to dance with.

He knows I'd decapitate anyone who tried anything.

Molly managed an awkward smile at the young man and accepted the hand he held out to her, leaving Talie to watch as what felt like part of her chest whirled away toward the dancefloor. She stalked after them to hover at the edge and observe while trying not to laugh. The boy was more determined in showing off than anything else, arms flinging and feet tapping with a flourish. As they waltzed near and twirled past, Molly caught Talie's eye.

"*Help!*" she mouthed.

Talie eyed the man's hands at a respectful enough position, one on the waist the other holding Molly's hand.

She still wanted to cut them both off.

The moment the song slowed, she stamped across the dancefloor and rounded the oaf as he bowed to Molly again.

"Another?" he asked, already reaching for her hand.

Talie batted his fingers away. "She's all booked up."

His face dropped in pure outrage as chatter filled the space between songs.

"Excuse me?" he huffed.

Talie nodded. "Exactly, you're excused."

The retort had worked well on stunning the previous suitor before, but as she turned away a heavy hand landed on her shoulder to pull her back.

She ducked her hand down and whirled around, her dagger under his chin before he could speak.

"Uh, uh, bodyguard?" He managed a weak smile. "Whatever offence caused, Princess, I meant none."

"Talie, let him go."

The amusement in Molly's voice was everything. Talie retracted the blade with an icy smile as the man lifted a hand to his neck.

"You should keep your dogs better trained, Princess," he muttered.

Talie ignored him. She'd heard far worse aimed at her many times before, but Molly's eyes narrowed and her lips pressed thin.

"Call her that again."

He hesitated. "I meant no-"

"Call her that again, I dare you."

Well aware the next song hadn't started yet and people were turning to stare, Talie settled a hand on Molly's arm.

Molly shook it off as the idiot bowed his head, but his expression was mutinous beneath the apologetic mask.

"Forgive me, Princess. I meant no offense to you."

"No, just to someone who doesn't benefit you," Molly snapped. "Learn better manners."

As she stalked off the dance floor, Talie resisted the urge to rub salt in the idiot's wound and hurried after her.

Kainen held his cup up in mock salute as they passed.

"Was he important?" Molly asked.

Kainen gasped. "Aren't all Fae important, Princess?"

"You know what I mean."

"Not especially." He shrugged. "I can have a word with the court he belongs to if you like."

"No, don't. I'll be back in a minute."

He straightened up as if to follow, even though Talie hadn't sheathed her dagger yet and was more than prepared to defend her.

"Where are we going?" he asked.

Molly frowned. "I am going back to my tent."

"Why?"

"Because."

"Because why though?"

She threw her hands up in frustration.

"Because the princess needs a wee, is that okay with you!"

He grinned. "Delightful, off you go."

He gave Talie a wicked look, cackling when she replied with a very specific hand gesture and set off after Molly.

This party is turning out much better than I expected.

CHAPTER FOURTEEN

MOLLY

Molly stormed into her tent, well aware Talie was behind her but not in the mood for a scene or any kind of glib retort about her dancing.

"Sammy told me you have an admirer," Talie announced. "Not that one I hope, although apparently you have plenty."

She frowned. "Huh?"

"Yeah, she said he introduced himself as William earlier but that you can call him 'Billy'. Said he seemed totally smitten and you were giggling along with him."

Molly stilled. Her irritation capsized and sank as she realised what Talie was talking about. She bit her lip to hold in a burst of laughter. Whatever Sammy had told her, Talie assumed Billy was some kind of romantic interest. Wickedness surfaced and she shrugged.

"Oh, he was very sweet. Insisted on telling me about his fancy family home."

"One of your noble types then."

"Yeah, heir to a distant title somewhere. He'll make

someone very lucky one day."

Talie had her back turned to pull off her boots so Molly couldn't see her face, but the rigid stance spoke volumes.

"How... convenient."

"Convenient?" Molly pretended to frown even though Talie couldn't see her face. "Convenient how?"

"Well here you are all royal and there he is, a viable lord."

Molly snorted and laughter bubbled out. She choked it back down in time to manage a bemused frown as Talie swing around to face her.

"Me?" she asked, feigning confusion. "Why on earth would you assume he'd marry me?"

Talie scowled. "Sammy said he's cute, you've said he's sweet and from a titled family, what more is there?"

Molly eyed her nails with a lofty sigh.

"A lot. Not least the fact that he's only six. Not my type either."

She glanced up to see Talie with her mouth hanging open, and it was every bit as satisfying as she'd expected.

"You and Sammy are going to kill me one day," Talie muttered.

Molly flinched. A cascade of emotions hit her chest and she sucked in a sharp breath at the pain.

Talie's expression shattered and she lifted her hands in frantic apology.

"I didn't mean that," she insisted. "Sorry. I'll try to choose my words better."

Molly wiped a hand over her face. She'd danced. She'd chatted. She'd caused a scene, although that was Talie's doing. She'd had two and a half cups of *Beast Lite*, two of which were before the party started. Her skin was aching like gift exhaustion and her head felt too heavy for her neck.

Party over.

She lifted a heavy hand and pulled the strategic network of pins from her hair, tossing them onto the wash-stand.

"I haven't been able to sleep," she admitted. "I keep seeing you dead in my dreams. Now it's not you, but it still is in my head sometimes, and I feel so orbing guilty that I'm happier about you being alive than I am sad about finding out Ru is dead."

She folded her arms around her middle, not even able to find the resolve to pull away when Talie crossed the tent and wrapped tight arms around her, one at her back and the other holding her shoulders.

The tears leaked free and she let them as heartbroken sobs vibrated her entire body.

"I can't say anything to make it better," Talie murmured. "But I can be here. I'm here. Wasn't ever great at words anyway."

Molly choked over a laugh, her face welded to Talie's shoulder. She barely noticed the soft, tentative kiss Talie dropped to her temple, nothing more than a simple reassurance.

"You were Lia, you said?" she asked.

Talie nodded, her chin tucked above Molly's head. "Yeah. Are you okay to hear this? We can wait."

"I need to know. I need it straight in my head. I can't get over it if I don't fully understand it."

"Okay. Let me get you into bed then first."

Molly pulled back to look up at her, but Talie laughed.

"Not like that, Princess, orbs alive. You've got snacks on the table there, and enough *offke* to melt the snow outside. We're going to sit and talk, drink and eat, yeah?"

Molly nodded and stepped back.

"Okay."

She grabbed her comfortable purple pyjamas from the bed and changed behind the screen, the faint flicker of amusement lighting in her chest as Talie did the same and reappeared in matching dark blue ones.

"Marthe," she said by way of explanation.

Molly stifled a smile as Talie put snacks and drinks on a tray and ferried it across to the bed.

"You can sit," she offered when Talie hovered. "I know you don't bite. Well, except for that once in the Menagerie. That I know of."

Talie sighed. "Biting is the last resort, always. You think I want people's disgusting skin in my mouth? Urgh."

They sat cross-legged opposite each other with the tray between them, and Molly served them both when Talie hesitated again. Then she drained half a cup of *offke*, shoved a Sticky Sap sweet in her mouth, and took a deep breath.

"Okay, tell me."

Talie clasped her hands in her lap and fixed her gaze downwards.

"I followed you after that time at the gym, or followed Daisy anyway. I wanted to see where you went."

"You didn't trust her? Daisy I mean?"

"Of course not. Then I saw her get taken and I figured someone should at least tell your friends, even if I didn't like her. Turns out it was you the whole time. They promised to keep Sammy safe if I went in glamoured to see what was going on. Something about them already crossing the line of some covenant."

Molly placed her empty cup on the tray and clasped her hands in her lap. She wanted more than anything to reach out, but they needed the past hanging between them fully aired before she could make that final decision to trust.

"So in I went as Lia," Talie continued. "You seemed to be holding your own fine, but then she tortured you."

Molly shuddered. Darkness edged at the corner of her vision, memories dancing forward, but she blinked hard and shook them aside.

"You tried to get me that stuff for my hands."

Talie sighed. "Yeah, that wasn't my smartest moment. I nearly had to explain why I wanted to trade for it, but I couldn't bear seeing you in pain. Then I dropped it like an idiot anyway and the whole thing got worse, so I broke out to get help. I barely had time to ask them before you were ringing the orb and you sounded so frail. Taz and Kainen were out the door in seconds, then Milo showed up. Taz went in for you while Kainen, Milo and I went through the service halls for the fairies."

"Celeste can't know about what Milo can do at least," Molly mumbled. "It gives us an edge."

She lifted her knees to her chest and wrapped her arms around them. Her back ached and she wanted sleep, but already her mind was clicking parts of a plan into place.

Talie sighed. "After that, I've already told you. I lurked around watching Sammy, but Ru told me Celeste had put a price on my head so I had to do it with a glamour and I almost got caught twice by Menagerie people. If I'd known you were there as well I'd have shown myself, but I didn't trust Daisy. Far too smiley."

Molly chuckled sadly. "Thanks, I think. She was Ace first, when we met her, but then me afterwards."

"Well, no more Lia, or Solaine, or Daisy."

Molly looked up, her heart beginning to pound as she caught Talie's eye.

"You said Solaine meant something, the name."

Talie hesitated. "Yeah, sunshine in love. Or sunshine and love, maybe. It was a translation in an old book I read ages ago in the library."

She can't mean what it sounds like she means.

"Strange choice," she tried.

Talie shrugged, a soft smile lifting the corners of her lips that were now only inches away.

"Not strange at all when you think about it, Princess."

Molly bit her lip. She'd had the account from Talie and believed her, but the admission about the name and the sheer depth of the risks Talie had taken for her were daunting.

I've barely even spared a thought for Ru, and he was as manipulated by Celeste as everyone else around her was.

"Do you want to go back out to the party?" Talie asked softly. "Not that I want to get dressed again, but I don't know if you'll get in trouble for disappearing."

"Orbs no. Kainen knows where I am and I bet Marthe

and the others will be keeping an eye out as well. I'm exhausted. I want to sleep for a week."

"Then that's what you can do. I'll keep everyone away."

Talie clambered off the bed before Molly could find anything to say. In a few deft moves, she had the bed clear and their snacks tidied away on the table. Molly watched her climb into her own bed in the corner of the tent, even after she extinguished the lamps.

"You said once you used to read the stories in the library," she said.

The sounds of Talie settling under her covers echoed, then stillness. She wondered if Talie had heard her but she couldn't bring herself to ask again. It's not like she wanted Talie to tell her a story or anything.

"I don't remember a lot of them." Talie cleared her throat. "But in a Faerie that once was…"

CHAPTER FIFTEEN

TALIE

Talie opened her eyes with the weirdest sensation in her gut. It was like warmth, except it buzzed. She glanced around at the tent, then at Molly gently glowing in the bed nearby. In sleep she had no frown on her face, but the rest of her was slumped around a pillow with one leg hanging off the edge of the bed in the most un-princess-like pose ever.

Talie stifled a smile and clambered out of her covers. She kept an eye on Molly as she tiptoed to wash and change, but being able to explain herself properly to Molly after the party made all the difference.

There's still the citadel to sort out, and Faerie knows what's going on while we're out here.

The usual sinking resignation she might have felt seemed unreachable somehow, and she emerged from behind the screen to find Molly sitting up in bed.

"Morning, Princess. You glow in your sleep."

Molly wiped the grit from her eyes and yawned.

"First I've heard of it."

Talie approached the side of the bed and hovered until Molly stood up.

"Surprised Sammy hasn't interrogated you about it. She's a light sleeper."

Molly disappeared behind the privacy screen.

"She never said anything. Maybe I haven't been shining much recently. What's your plan today?"

Talie shrugged. "Don't have one. What's yours?"

Molly reappeared in a fresh green sweatshirt and jeans. As she lifted her hands to tie back her hair, Talie unashamedly ogled the brief glimpse of bare stomach on show.

"Avoid getting sucked into nobility disputes." Molly sighed and sank onto the edge of the bed to pull on her snow boots. "Dodge sycophantic lords and ladies hoping for favour, and think of a way to get a proper meat pocket."

She pulled a face and Talie laughed, the sound bubbling out so suddenly it startled both of them. Talie held still as their eyes locked and suddenly Molly was right in front of her.

"Thank you for being honest with me yesterday," she said.

Talie shrugged. "I won't word-tangle to you unless I can't help it."

"Which is word-tangling in itself."

"Fair, but I mean it. I'm always going to be honest with you unless there's something physically preventing me."

Again Molly caught her gaze, the deep blue a faint hue of turquoise as her eyes shone in the tent's Faelight. Talie slid her clammy palms over her hips.

"Did you know your eyes have rings of gold on the edges?" Molly asked, her cheeks turning pink instantly. "That's not- I should..."

Talie reached out and grabbed Molly's hand before she could flee. Knotting their fingers together, she wiped her thumb back and forth over Molly's knuckles.

"And yours have hints of green."

She took comfort and confidence from Molly being as anxious as she was and lifted a hand to Molly's chin. Molly blinked as she levelled their eyes, then leaned close enough to feel soft puffs of breath on her lips.

A loud, insistent tapping halted both of them when they were barely a whisper apart. They held still, nose to nose.

"Pretend we're not here," Talie whispered. "We have more important things to do."

Molly shivered. "Fae have excellent hearing."

"We do." Kainen's gleeful tone slipped through the tent a moment later. "You've been summoned, your most magnanimous highness of important things. You too, Molly. The queen demands your presence, so maybe brush your hair first."

Molly sagged and Talie forced herself to take a step away.

"You should go," she grumbled. "No doubt they want you before this big communal meeting thing."

She dropped Molly's hand and stayed where she was as Molly gave her a shy, almost rueful smile and left the tent. Then she flopped backward onto Molly's bed, threw an arm over her face and laughed in disbelief.

It's madness. She's royalty. She could have anyone in

Faerie. A strain of heated jealousy bubbled up but she let the morning sweep it away again. *Unless I really am delusional, she was going to let me kiss her.*

The sour voices she usually lived with threatened to creep back into her mind but she shoved them firmly aside and strode toward the privacy screen. With the unexpected spare time to herself, it wouldn't hurt to try and get as clean as possible. Just in case.

Fae trickery had the air in the tent at a constant warmth but the occasional snap from the frosty air outside swirled in as she washed and dressed in warm clothing from Molly's cavernous wardrobe. She stopped short of using Molly's toothbrush and opted for her finger instead.

If I'm doing this, I have to go all in. She wiped her mouth and grimaced at her reflection in the mirror. *Might not be forever, but even a second would be worth the risks.*

The tent flap swept aside as she moved toward it.

"Oh." Marthe gave Talie a stern once-over. "I thought nobody was in here."

"I'm on my way out," Talie muttered.

"You didn't use the princess's toothbrush, I hope?"

Talie folded her arms across her chest. "No, I didn't."

"Good. If you're to be hanging around, I'll ensure there are spares available. Are you?"

"Am I?"

"Hanging around." Marthe gave the messy bedcovers on both beds a pointed look.

Talie shrugged. "That's up to Molly."

"Hmm. Perhaps a portable washbag then. I need to get her some spare things as well. She used the last toothbrush to clean some kind of contraption and ended up getting a sweet stuck to it."

"Sticky Saps," Talie confirmed. "They're her favourite."

Marthe reached out a hand and clicked her fingers. A moment later, a small cloth bag dropped onto her palm.

"You'll be going to this meeting, yes?" she asked. Talie nodded. "Good. Give her these then. Sticky Saps aren't good for the teeth but she deserves something nice."

Talie crossed the short distance between them and took the bag.

"Thanks, I will."

Marthe gave her another once-over, eyes narrowed.

"Hmm. Should you need anything domestic, you can let me know."

Talie nodded, uneasy at the deep perusal Marthe was still giving her. She escaped the tent and strode through the camp toward the meeting ground. Several nobles were already milling around and while the dance floor was still in place, the tables and mess had been cleared already as if by magic.

She cast a wary glance around and spied Molly and Sammy already seated. Her pulse sped up as she approached but determination pushed her forward. Molly sat on the end of a short row of chairs and there was a spare chair on Sammy's other side, but Talie stopped in front of them instead of taking it.

"You're in my seat," she announced.

Sammy pulled a face. "Says who? What makes this your seat?"

"It's next to Molly, so that makes it mine. Move."

Even Sammy sat utterly stunned into silence for several seconds, while Molly's cheeks turned pink and she glowered back, flustered and terrible at hiding it. Then Sammy gleefully vacated the chair with a huge grin and Talie flopped onto it.

"Claiming chairs now?" Molly asked faintly.

Talie nodded. "Someone's got to keep an eye on you, Princess."

"Don't I even get a choice about it?"

"Yeah. You can choose to say no and break my heart. Sweet?"

Molly stared at the bag Talie held out, the tiny furrow of her brow twitching as she calculated the odds and potential pitfalls of accepting it.

She can say no, but she probably will break my heart at this rate.

Talie pushed the sickening possibility down and tried not to focus on her hand shaking slightly around the sweet bag. When Molly called her a bad word under her breath a few moments later and took a sweet, Talie did her best not to fall off her chair from sheer relief.

"Right, let's get this going." Demi approached the gathering. "Welcome everyone, nobles and locals alike."

Around the edge of the wooden floor and the royal enclosure, nobles had flocked to the court camp side and Fae from the citadel were clustered in between the tents on the other. Talie didn't miss the wary looks passing between the two sides, but she had to admire Demi's resolve as she ploughed on.

Even when May crossed the divide in full view of everyone and set up her own chair on Molly's other side, the unspoken hostilities between the two sides hung in the air.

Demi turned to Milo as he hurried up beside her to whisper something in her ear.

"Are we fighting then?" Sammy asked. "Is that what this is about?"

Talie shrugged. "Not sure what the plan is. If we are fighting, we'll need a better plan than 'let's get this going'."

"It'll be a difficult task," May agreed. "Getting into the citadel is one thing, but if it's true that Celeste has confined herself behind extra wards, storming the place won't make much impact other than create more chaos."

"Will we need some kind of armour then?" Sammy suggested.

May laughed. "Oh no darling. Fae tried armour during the last age and it was extremely inconvenient. Got the idea from some ghastly human tales, then so many perished stuck in their little metal suits when the gifts started flying. Best stick to your warding, I would."

May stood and walked across to where Reyan and Milo were now having a furiously hissed conversation with Demi beneath a subtle dome of protection with a faint rainbow sheen. Taz slumped in the seat May had left a second later with Kainen hovering beside him.

"May's taking this whole thing way too seriously." Taz grinned. "A bit of freedom and she suddenly thinks she's past a hundred with all the airs and graces of wisdom."

"Wisdom knows better than to have airs and graces," Molly added philosophically. She glanced quickly at Talie. "Wisdom knows to carry weapons."

Talie smiled and slipped back her sleeve to show the hilt of the dagger Molly had given her, along with the wrist strap that held it there.

"Still got your gift, Princess, don't worry."

Molly snorted. "I noticed. You held it to that man's throat last night easily enough."

"Don't like being touched."

She waited for some retort but Molly only smirked knowingly, which unsettled her enough to make her cheeks smart.

"Are you blushing?!" Sammy asked gleefully.

"Don't be mad." She couldn't lie. "Go away."

Sammy cackled and launched out of her seat with the mention of finding some kind of snack while the meeting stalled.

"You two work well together," Kainen announced far too innocently.

"You do." Taz agreed. "Are you two anchored, or maybe you have a mind-link of some kind?"

Talie gaped at them. The mere idea that Molly or anyone might be able to see inside her mind was a frightening thing.

"Of course not." Molly hesitated. "Wait, is that actually a possible thing?"

"I don't think she'd want to be able to read my mind," Talie added.

"I don't think anyone would."

"Ouch, Princess, but fair."

Taz laughed. "If you say so. Demi's going to have to do the diplomatic thing and insist we know what we're doing, but the real discussions will happen after."

"Do we know what we're doing?" Talie asked doubtfully.

He shrugged. "We usually wing it. Oh, confab over."

He stood and Kainen flopped into the empty seat as Molly sighed.

"It's like musical chairs," she grumbled. "I'm exhausted and nothing's happened yet. I miss the days of fixing things and being left alone."

Talie smiled. The urge to make some kind of suggestive joke filled her head, but instead she reached into her pocket and pulled out a small wooden box with the lid detached, and a small parcel of taped-up screws. She held it out to Molly, who stared at it.

"Traded for it," she explained. "Something for you to fiddle with."

Molly's eyes lit up, and it was worth the two hours early morning guard duty Talie had offered to take from someone before the party as a trade to get the box. Molly grabbed it with a gleeful smile, pulled some tiny tools from somewhere inside her coat and was lost to her craft.

In the centre of the dancefloor, Demi cleared her throat to gain the crowd's attention again.

"Welcome everyone," she began. "As we all know, the citadel is no longer safe. We've reached out since to other towers asking if they'd consider letting people take refuge, but the answer has been a resounding no."

Muttering started across the crowd and Talie frowned. She or anyone from their tower could have told them that.

"What is the plan then?" A man called out. "Do we even have one?"

Demi surveyed the crowd, from the cluster of nobles to the sea of others.

"Due to a covenant between the citadel and the royalty of Faerie, there's nothing we can do ourselves to intercede, however-"

"What good is royalty then?" someone hollered.

Talie sort of agreed with them, but she did it silently in her head. Beside her, Molly's hands slowed over the box she was almost done fixing, her head cocked and her attention on the crowd noise.

"The safest thing for us to do is find everyone sanctuary in other realms of Faerie," Demi insisted. "We have protection with various courts-"

"I'm not going to some far-flung realm!"

"We've got family in there!"

"What's the point of having royalty and nobility if they can't even pull rank?!"

Talie tensed and one hand slipped to her blade as Molly stood up, her shoulders straight and her eyes narrowed.

"What if they do?" Molly raised her voice over the clamour, but barely anyone heard her.

Talie lifted her hand to her mouth and whistled. Loudly. Silence filtered like a wave through the crowd seconds later as all heads turned toward them.

"Go on," Talie muttered.

"What if they do?" Molly repeated. "What if the royal

family charges in, knocks the citadel wards down and starts telling everyone what's going to happen. Would people be fine with that? No, you'd say they were taking over, interfering."

Talie eyed the crowd. Most were grim or disagreeable still, but while they were listening they weren't arguing.

"We can't get everyone back into the citadel right now," Molly continued. "But that doesn't mean it can't happen at some point. Everyone deserves a choice. Either we continue to live in camps here and find ways to hunt in the forest when the queen's charity has to dry up, or we accept the refuge offered to us."

"But what about everyone still inside?" someone asked.

Molly hesitated. "We don't have the answers right now, and I'm not going to word-tangle any fancy promises. If there's a way to either get them out to safety or make it safe for everyone to go back in, then personally I'll take it, but right now the queen has been really generous. If she says she has realms for people who just want a safe place to live, then I believe her."

Talie bit her lip, a sliver of her attention still wary on the crowd even as she gazed up at Molly.

Spoken like a proper princess from all the stories.

Looking at Molly with her ponytail tumbling down her back like a golden veil, her gaze firm even as her fingers trembled slightly at her sides, she was what a royal should have been.

As the meeting descended into muttering by the normal Fae and nobles alike, Talie sensed a presence hovering. She turned her head to find Kainen grinning at her.

"Want to make some mischief?" he asked.

She shrugged. "Maybe. What kind?"

He moved to the seat beside her. "I have a gift for you."

"Why?"

"What do you mean why?"

"Why are you so determined to give me stuff?" she demanded.

He hesitated and let his gaze flick meaningfully to Molly.

"Because it's fun."

Translation: because it'll help you protect her better.

"What kind of gift?"

"Silence would do," Molly muttered. "Or some sense."

Talie smiled. "Nice, Princess, really nice."

"No fun in me telling you, but it won't harm you," Kainen said. "Want it, or not?"

As Demi tried to call for the attention of the crowd again, Talie hesitated.

Kainen had given her the ability to hold a glamour, and Molly clearly trusted him and his friends. If it was some kind of trick at her expense, a gift was still a gift.

She nodded. "Go on then."

He held his hand out so she had to extend hers, and she waited while he lifted her fingers to his lips for the briefest of kisses.

"I gift you the ability to make it rain, to control the water in your immediate vicinity and evaporate it when needed."

Molly's head shot up. Talie blinked in astonishment at Kainen, then looked to Molly for reassurance. A glamour gift was one thing. She could already glamour so it was something she was used to. Water was… water. It came out of vents, although in the vast land outside the citadel, it was everywhere.

A subtle tingling started in her fingers and radiated like a cool wave through her body right down to the bone.

"Oh orbs, I can feel the snow." She lifted her head. "The trees are drenched in it. It's like tiny little specks in the air all around us."

She flinched as her new gift chilled through her skin, not icy but still cold enough to be noticed. Droplets of water beaded on her hands and underneath her clothes.

"Focus on calming it," Kainen suggested. "Isolate it to one part of your body."

"How?"

He frowned. "What do you mean how? The usual way you isolate gifts."

"I've never had to isolate gifts before!" she hissed. "I've never had any!"

The alarm on his face would have been comical in any other situation, but she couldn't even take comfort from Molly beside her as the snow beneath her feet began to grow soft. The holes in her boots were taking in water alarmingly fast, and an ominous rumble overhead had everyone looking up at the suddenly dark grey sky.

"Okay, this is fine," Kainen muttered.

Talie winced as the gift grew inside her, a swelling sensation that felt a lot like yearning which seemed to be calling all the water in the nearby area toward her. Fast.

A few shouts went up as the trees were drained and the snow underfoot began to melt. With the camp on a hill and the trees on the higher side, the growing water level was heading straight for them.

"Okay, maybe not fine." Kainen dodged in front of Talie so she was staring at him, frozen with horror. "To isolate your gift, imagine all that energy travelling through you to one point in your body. Pick one, like your hands."

Talie stared at her hands. "What if I end up draining the lake?"

"Yeah, that's not helpful. Your gift responds to your thoughts, your will. Do not think about draining the lake."

"Now it's all I can think about!"

Kainen stumbled out of view as Molly shouldered him aside and waded through ankle-deep water. Talie had no idea how or when the water had reached her ankles, so terrified that she was apparently the one causing it. All around them the nobles fled to their tents and others set about rescuing what little they could.

"Focus on me," Molly said softly. "Where can you feel the gift? Hands, head, chest?"

"All over."

"Okay, close your eyes. Now visualise the feeling like droplets running out of your head to your neck, your shoulder, just keep bringing the focus back."

Talie did as she was told and imagined the water all around her trickling toward her hand.

"I… think it's working."

"Great, keep going. Let it dribble down into your hands, and up from your feet. Isolate it to your hands and imagine it going to sleep."

"Water doesn't sleep."

"No, but the gift kind of does. Out of thought, out of action."

Talie snorted hysterically but did as she was told.

"Is it working?" she asked.

"Looks like it. Um… just keep working on it for now. Kainen, you can deal with Reyan because she's headed this way and I don't think it's me she's scowling at."

CHAPTER SIXTEEN

MOLLY

Molly watched as Reyan paced around the Court of Illusions tent while Kainen stood against the dark oak desk in the centre, surrounded by leather chairs and purple fabric as he tried and failed to look meek.

"It's not like I did anything that awful," he said reproachfully.

Reyan rounded on him, shadows curling around her shoulders and twisting through her blonde hair as she shoved her hands against his chest.

"No, you just gave someone a gift that almost washed out the entire camp without any thought for training them for it first!"

Molly groaned quietly as Demi and Taz swept into the tent without knocking.

"What's all the shouting?" Demi asked.

"Kainen, in his infinite 'I can do whatever I like' idiocy, has gifted Talie with the ability to make it rain," Reyan said. "A lot. Apparently, that deluge that almost washed away three tents was not a natural habit of this realm."

"What?!"

"Oh keep your crown on. We can't send them in completely unprepared," Kainen huffed.

"I wasn't planning to," Demi said, her eyes flashing icy. "You can't just run around gifting people at the drop of a hat!"

Kainen hesitated, confusion scrawled across his face.

"Isn't that kind of the point of being nobility though? Otherwise it's just paperwork and court feuds."

"You're allowed to gift within reason, but you're not Santa!"

Kainen eyed Taz. "That's the big bearded one from the human Yuletide tales?"

"Yep." Taz grinned. "I love it when I'm not the one in trouble."

"Send us where?" Talie asked.

All eyes turned to her and she leaned forward with her shoulders hunching in anticipation.

"You can refuse," Demi began. "Nobody will make you or think any less of you, but we need someone who knows the layout of the citadel to go inside."

Molly frowned. "And you want us to go? Surely any of you would be a better choice."

"We tried," Taz explained. "The wards Celeste has raised reinforced the covenant set in place to stop any royal interference."

"As it turns out, because the courts report to the royals, they can't interfere either," Demi added. When Taz opened his mouth, she shot him a glare. "And you're not abdicating again so shut it."

Taz rolled his eyes. "Yes, your majesty. Again, you can say no, both of you. The plan would be to get inside the Menagerie with Milo's help and map a way through the core. We're hoping we can rattle Celeste from the outside enough for her to challenge us, then she's incited the war and we can respond in kind, but she knows that so it'll take some doing."

Molly glanced at Talie, who folded her arms across her chest and slouched back in her seat.

"You want us to waltz into the Menagerie," she stated. "Past *her* and all her guards, to map an absolute labyrinth which tunnels far beneath the citadel. Why?"

Demi sighed. "Because we need to know what's down there. It may be the Omens, or something entirely other. We have nobody else to ask that we can trust, because all the FDPs work for me in some capacity, and allegiances run deeper than employment in many other areas."

Molly wiped a hand over her face.

"I've already said I want to get even with her. She's powerful though, no doubt draining from that well of power everyone keeps avoiding talking about."

"If there is an actual well of power down there, we need to know."

Molly nodded. "And if she'll still be using fairies, or possibly even Fae from the citadel, to run her gift experiments. We can't let her go on doing that. When do I need to leave?"

"Steady on, Princess," Talie muttered. "There's no merit to running in to play hero."

Molly frowned and folded her arms across her chest,

astonished that Talie wasn't the first to insist on raging back inside.

"I'm not running in to play anything. You want her to continue stripping the place and using people like resources? This has nothing to do with being a hero."

Talie frowned and they stared each other out.

"I had a very dim view of heroism when I joined Arcanium," Demi admitted.

Molly pulled her attention away from Talie, stung by her sudden dismissive attitude.

Taz nodded. "I think we all did. It's easy to say 'save the fairies' and not think about the trolls in the outer realms, or the rights of Fae who are still under the boots of nobles who have traditional values."

"Not so easy to fix it," Demi added. "Those who benefit from power won't give it up, and they will lie, steal, trick and manipulate the truth to keep it."

"So you either play nice and try to guide people slowly the right way-"

"Assuming you're arrogant enough to believe you know what the right way is in the first place."

"-or you match their energy and bulldoze them in the name of the 'greater good'."

"So, what can anyone do?" Molly asked.

Demi smiled. "One step at a time. Find like-minded people. Have the tough discussions."

"Above all, be kind," Kainen said. "It's so easy to get angry and start a war, but it's better to remember they're also people and you don't want to be like them."

"No, you just run around gifting everyone," Reyan

muttered, although she was trying her hardest not to smile as he blew her a kiss.

"Control is a funny thing," he continued. "First they control base resources, food, heating, shelter, and so on. Then they start to control functional resources like transport and access to knowledge. What comes after they run out of tangible resources? What's left to control after that?"

"People," Taz suggested.

Demi nodded. "Control the resources and you can control the people, but what if someone else offers them freedom, or better resources?"

"Everyone leaves," Molly said.

"So when there's no people, there's no labour to keep the resources cycling. What noble wants to farm their own land and grow their own food, write their own books and create their own art?"

"I tried to grow tomatoes," Kainen offered. "Eight have turned pink so far and there are three more still ripening."

Molly couldn't bring herself to smile at him, her mind whirling full of potential plans and the unspent fury driving them.

"They keep us trapped behind walls of glass," she seethed. "They use poverty and fear to control us because we can't escape. That's why it's hard to get a library card in the citadel, and why we only get a handful of orb channels."

Milo nodded. "Knowledge is currency. Fae think it's strength, or morality, or trickery, but without knowing things you're always at a disadvantage."

"So many levels weren't allowed cards to the library," Molly said sadly.

Talie sighed. "And why do you think that is? It's not an access issue. It's not even a security issue. It's a control tactic to keep people from asking difficult questions. Phoenix always said she wanted to keep the reins close to her chest so nobody else had a chance to steer things."

Milo scowled and clutched the books in his arms tighter, as if he could protect the information inside through sheer muscle alone.

"There are no punishments severe enough for denying people access to knowledge. I was horrified to see how restrictive she had the library. Monitored and guarded, absolutely, but everyone should be able to enter."

"Celeste always did have weird views about traditions," Taz said. "I was young when she left, but she would always go on about ancient stories full of heroes invading and conquering places in the name of righteousness or some nonsense."

"She had every intention of turning Molly into her chosen heroine," Talie muttered.

Molly frowned. "And Phoenix didn't? He might not be the one tearing the citadel down but you know as well as I do he'd happily use me to play poster girl if it suited him. He as good as asked me to."

"There's no such thing as one hero, or a 'chosen one'." Demi shook her head. "We make choices every day, all of us. Do you think I would have survived without Taz, or Ace, or Milo? We aren't important because we're special, none of us, but because of those who are special to us."

Molly frowned. "The rest of us maybe, but you're a literal queen chosen by Faerie itself."

"So? It's a job and a crown and an obligation. It'd mean nothing if I couldn't use it to help people."

"So disgustingly noble," Kainen said cheerfully. "It pays to be though, in the end. No pandering to vanity."

Reyan snorted. "Your wardrobe would say otherwise."

"Vanity is the mask of a very fragile ego," he insisted, conveniently ignoring her. "I should know, it used to be mine for a long time. The obsession with being perceived is always a clear tell, but strip away the stuff, the glamour, the pretence, and what do we have? No moral foundation. Even the morals are purely performative."

"So, figure out their vanity? What's Celeste's?" Molly asked.

"Her vanity sounds like it pivots on her proximity to power. She needs to be both feared and adored, but above all she needs to be in control. That'll be what this whole gift extraction thing is about. She needs something to trade on to keep her power strong."

"Gift extraction is a perilous business," Milo insisted with a shudder. "Nasty. All this talk of soul severing, and who actually uses nightshade in any kind of potion known to fairy, Fae or beast?"

"It's not that much nightshade, actually," Talie muttered.

Milo's gaze narrowed. "How would you know?"

Talie hesitated as all gazes swung her way.

"Because I was sent looking for stuff on it. 'Twelve parts yew to one part nightshade, twice swill with oia residue, distil once and steep for three days.' That's what it said."

Milo frowned, but Molly spoke before he could.

"It's three parts nightshade, isn't it?"

Talie shook her head. "Pretty sure it's one."

"No, it's three. I had to memorise it."

"Memorise what?"

"When Celeste sent me to the Oak Queen's court, she had me look in a book."

Demi grabbed one of the books from her desk and opened it as Milo's head snapped up.

"Which book?" he demanded.

"Uh, something of Perils and Poisons, I think? Potions and Poisons? Perils and Potions? I can't remember now. But it definitely said three for nightshade."

"Potions and Poisons Most Foul?"

Molly nodded. "That's it!"

Milo's eyes widened like a kicked puppy's.

"Demi, they do have it!" he whined. "They didn't mention that on the ledger either! I need to insist we have a copy immediately. "

"Er… sure. Can you remember the whole thing, Molly? About the nightshade?"

"The infusion is to be brewed twelve parts yew and three parts nightshade," Molly recited. "Then swill it with oia residue, distil once and steep for three days. Then brew it one last time with two parts infusion to one part coalbane."

Demi shot to her feet and Milo lunged to catch the book she dropped with a fearsome scream. She ignored him, her eyes wide.

"Coalbane? That's… outlawed, illegal," she said. "Anyone found producing it is straight off to the Forever mountains."

Milo nodded. "I did read something during my time in the citadel's library. Gift extraction apparently has something to do with the Omens, at least originally, and it sounds like they're not to be messed with."

"Remind the class what these Omens are?" Kainen asked.

"The Omens are entities that sprang from the nether-"

"Like the *Maladorac*?" Reyan asked.

"Sort of, but not quite so innate or ancient."

"The Apocalyptians then?"

Milo shook his head. "No, again those were bound in Fae form in a way. The Omens are merely entities, imagine them like gifts that have no host, able to roam at will. There were said to be three, freedom, eternity and power. With freedom came chaos, with eternity there was eventual stagnation, and as always power grows entitlement. They are manifestations of the nether's power."

"And as we know, it's the nether that feeds Fae gifts," Demi added. "So these Omens are bound to be excessively powerful and probably unwieldable."

"Yay us," Taz muttered.

"Well, in a way the Omens can be balanced if harnessed right. Freedom can offer variety and choice. Eternity is supposed to be an education, a long life to earn knowledge. As for power, with true control of the mind and soul, raw power can be harnessed to do great things."

"Yeah, but this is Fae we're talking about," Reyan said.

Milo pulled a face. "Yeah… The texts I found say they did some real damage a couple of ages ago, almost wiped out a couple of realms. Then some Fae found a way to contain the power in a well and create the citadel as a sort of Faerie ring around it out of ancient stone."

Molly's gut went into freefall at the realisation.

"The tower coming down…" Demi murmured.

Molly grimaced. "The Omens could leak out."

"We have to consider that is a very real possibility," Milo agreed, his tone grim. "The wards might be up to stop Fae going in and out, but it's the stone that kept the Omens in, and if huge parts of that have been obliterated, who knows?"

Molly wiped a hand over her face, her pulse thundering almost as fast as her mind.

"If I hadn't told her about the coalbane before, she might not have attacked the citadel so soon," she admitted. "I need to end this and now."

Taz sighed. "Coalbane is hard to make, but if anyone could do it then I bet the artificers of the citadel could. They're rumoured to have gatekept all sorts of arcane lore that even the books at Arcanium or the courts haven't recorded. We need to tread really carefully. No unauthorised excursions inside the citadel until we know what's going on."

Milo snapped the book shut and stalked out, muttering under his breath.

Demi winced. "He's not happy I've forbidden him from going back to the library."

"Well, why don't you?" Molly asked. "He can sort himself out quick enough, and if there is information in there about the Omens, or the well of power or whatever, then he's the safest person to find it surely?"

Demi nodded and settled back on her desk.

"He did mention your idea about him bringing people out, but we're already backlogging with the ones we already have out here. It takes time to find them new places to go where they won't just end up being reliant on the goodwill of others, and several of them are insisting they'd rather take their chances going back in."

Molly frowned. "So, the best bet for everyone is to get Celeste out and the wards open so everyone can return and rebuild."

"That's about the extent of it, yes. We'll need a couple of days to think about how best to keep you safe, and again you don't have to do this."

Molly stood with a groan. Her back ached, her head ached, and she knew if she begged an afternoon to herself nobody would deny her.

The levels are never going to get along," she said. "The only thing that keeps them from fighting the nobles is trade, necessity, need. Someone needs to go into the citadel and get Celeste out, then the citadel can be opened up and everyone gets to choose. No more glass cage. But I need some time to think about it, some peace and quiet."

Demi nodded. "Fair. Have a think and let us know as soon as you can."

Molly left the tent with Talie stomping behind her, the thud of her boots on the wooden board of the tent turning to crunches as they walked across the snow.

"You're not seriously thinking about going back in there?" Talie asked. "Remember what she did to you?"

Irritated by the sour mood, Molly scowled back at her.

"Vividly, thanks. If there's a way to get rid of her then I'm taking it. We have Milo to get us in and out, and once we know what's down there, we know how best to combat it. If nobody else can get in or out but me, what else can I do?"

She spied Sammy steaming toward them and increased the pace. As lovely as Sammy was, she didn't equal peace and quiet.

"Well we can't waltz in there on our own," Talie hissed. "These things take planning. It's absolute madn- will you stop walking away from me!"

"I'm doing this, alone if I have to," Molly insisted.

"I'll… I'll… I'll take all your screws so you can't fix anything!"

Molly whirled around and almost choked on a mouthful of loose hair that had slipped from her hair ribbon.

"I haven't got a home left let alone any screws," she snapped. "*That's* the whole orbing point of getting the citadel back!"

Talie pressed both hands to her head and Molly stormed away, Sammy's amused voice floating behind her.

"Smooth. Really smooth."

CHAPTER SEVENTEEN

TALIE

Talie sat on Molly's bed for hours with her knees clutched to her chest. The meeting that morning and Molly's irritation seemed a long time ago, but Molly was out somewhere doing something and Talie couldn't find her. Even Sammy had made a couple of friends who served at one of the courts and was happy to spend time with them for the evening instead.

Talie lifted her hand to watch the tiny drips of condensation beading on her fingertips. She'd spent the afternoon and evening trying to practice controlling her rain gift, but it seemed to be linked to her mood. Being without Molly and not knowing where she was threatened to make the whole tent soggy.

Footsteps crunched outside the tent and Talie lifted her head hopefully.

Hope. When have I ever dared have hope before?

She crossed her legs on the bed and pushed aside the unsettling swoop of anticipation that buzzed through her chest as Molly walked in.

The moment the tent flap was down, a cheery smile drained from Molly's face. Talie's insides squeezed tight but Molly hadn't even seen her yet. She cleared her throat and Molly jumped.

"What are you doing sitting there in the dark?" she asked.

Talie shrugged. "Waiting."

"For?"

You. She hesitated. *I can't say that.*

"What else is there to do?" she sighed. "I even tried to find Sammy but she seems happy hanging around with some friends she's made. Either way, she's safe here and I'm going into the citadel with you."

Molly pulled her puffy coat off and threw it over the nearest chair where it slithered quickly to the floor. She stared at it, then shrugged and left it there.

"Going where with me?" she asked.

"The citadel. Whatever mad plan you're going with." Talie hesitated as Molly's skin began to glow and warm the damp space. "Sammy's safe here, I can trust that, and if we get the citadel back then we can all go home."

Molly pulled off her sweatshirt and grabbed her pyjamas. As she disappeared behind the screen, wild thoughts filled Talie's head that they might say she wasn't allowed to go.

"Are you sure?" Molly emerged again.

Talie nodded. "You need someone to watch your back, do the fighting."

"I can fight fine by myself."

"You don't move your feet and you never watch your

sides when someone's attacking."

She twisted so they could face each other in time to see a magnificent scowl cross Molly's face.

"I do so," she muttered.

"Okay, Princess, if you say so. You still need someone to watch your back though."

Molly hesitated and her gaze flicked to Talie's bed in the corner.

"It might be dangerous," she said. "Demi's insisting that we do it in tiny bits but that'll take an age. I understand if you want to stay here with Sammy and take the luxury that comes with it."

Talie smoothed her fingertips over the soft fabric of Molly's bedcovers.

"She's fine here with or without me. I'd probably just get in the way. It's nice to have this luxury for a bit but right now I'm just doing my best not to rain on it."

Molly smiled and a flicker of pure sunlight spilled between them.

"Everyone tells me not to see the gifts as separate from yourself," she said. "It responds to your will. If you want it to be dormant, you have to speak to it."

"You want me to speak to it?"

Molly pulled a face. "It works for me."

"You're glowing now."

"I'm choosing to. Think happy thoughts."

Talie smiled. "I don't have many happy thoughts to think of."

"None?" Molly leaned forward. "None at all?"

Talie closed her eyes and thought of the citadel, her

home and the gym. They were there waiting for her, assuming they were still standing, but the thought of going back to Phoenix and his weird little side missions he sent her on didn't exactly scream 'happy'.

Molly's fingers slid over her damp ones and Talie latched onto the warmth.

She thought of Molly instead and focused on the waterlogged sensation climbing over her arms. Her gift sulked at the mere touch of Molly's heat, but she would master it or die trying.

Can't believe I'm doing this. Hello, rain. We need to stop being so rainy.

She took a deep breath and imagined a soft, warm towel catching the water. The gift shuddered in horror.

"Keep going," Molly said softly. "What happens to rain when it stops?"

"Not a clue. Didn't spend much time in school. Preferred the gym or the library."

"It dries into the air. Imagine it drying and hydrating into dry things, like a parched flower that needs water, or a jug that's empty."

Talie scrunched her face tight and fought the urge to snap back. She could sense the gift itself around her in the damp air and the cold drips clinging to the tent poles.

I must be getting the water from somewhere. It can't just magically materialise.

She cupped her hands in front of her and willed the water to gather. It struggled but the more she insisted, the closer the droplets came.

"Wow," Molly whispered. "How are you doing that?"

Talie had no idea, or what it looked like, but the rivulets of water from around the tent dribbled over her fingers. She focused until her body ached worse than days of fighting in the ring.

"I'll get a bowl," Molly said. "You can pour the water into it. This is so cool."

Talie clung to her handful of water with her eyes welded shut. There were tiny echoes everywhere, like whispers except of knowing instead of sound or sight. She could sense the droplets, and in time she might even learn to channel some and not others, but now hanging onto them was more than she felt able to do. She bit her lip as something thudded in the cradle of her crossed legs.

"Drop the water in the bowl," Molly insisted. "The tent's bone dry now."

Talie couldn't open her eyes even when she tried, or get her mind to communicate to her fingers, her muscles shaking from effort. Soft hands surrounded hers and parted them. The water sloshed out with a splatter and she winced as the gift seemed to drag part of her with it.

"Easy," Molly murmured, her voice like an anchor. "Lie down. You might have done too much too quickly."

Talie couldn't coordinate herself but for once she let herself be led as Molly tipped her sideways and straightened her limbs. A soft cocoon of blankets wrapped around her and she managed to lick her parched lips.

"Ow."

"You dried yourself out. I'm just going to put some moisturiser on you, okay? Just the crusty bits."

Talie snorted. "Crusty bits, nice. You give the best

compliments, Princess."

She didn't even have the energy to tense as Molly swept something cool over her face, then something solid and soothing over her lips. The bed dipped sometime later and Talie's mind lifted from sweetly blissful oblivion.

"I'll be going into the citadel in a couple of days," Molly announced.

Talie frowned. She tried to open her eyes but they still wouldn't budge.

"*We* will be going in a couple of days," she insisted.

"Because I need someone to watch my back?"

"Yeah, that. What exactly is the plan? We go in, walk around and hope if we find her we're strong enough to stop her?"

The bedcovers rustled as Molly lay beside her, a soft warmth emanating across the tiny slip of air between them.

"Nothing so dramatic. The core is huge. I've been given a summoning link with Milo, so we're going to test that tomorrow. We go in, he leaves. I call him. If he hears me, we know it can get through the wards. Then we begin to map the core."

"Exciting."

"Hopefully not." Molly yawned. "I'm not saying I won't take the chance if I get it after everything she's done, but we can't risk any more danger to people still inside."

Talie smiled and managed to open her eyes, although the lids felt crusty and caked as if she'd slept for a week. The tent was in darkness but the tiniest hint of a glow flickered beside her. She rolled onto her side and stared at the outline of Molly's face.

"No risks then," she murmured.

Molly mumbled something incoherent and immediately her breathing deepened. With her limbs still aching, Talie pushed aside the habit urging her to get up and move about. She inched closer to Molly instead.

I need to be strong enough to protect her and that requires rest.

She froze as Molly wriggled closer in her sleep. A moment later, an arm pressed against her chest and Molly's face landed right into the crook of her neck.

"Orbs," she muttered under her breath. "If Marthe catches us I'm worse than dead."

Molly didn't answer, but since she was glowing softly still, Talie inched a gentle arm around her with the covers between them and closed her eyes.

I still don't deserve her, but maybe I can take a tiny bit of the illusion to keep for now.

CHAPTER EIGHTEEN

TALIE

"We're going to be playing this very carefully."

Talie stood two mornings later watching Demi stride back and forth in the royal tent. Molly was off doing something unconfirmed, which Talie didn't like one bit, but she was finding it scarily easy to sleep in Molly's bed and Molly had snuck out without waking her.

"We'll be fine," she insisted. "No heroics, in and out."

"Said the priestess to-*mmph*-" Kainen spluttered as Reyan covered his mouth with her hand.

"We don't have the wayfinder either," Reyan said. "It seems to go haywire when it gets close."

Demi nodded. "We run the test first. Milo should be here soon and he'll take you and Molly in. Stay exactly where you are and call for him, so we can be sure you can communicate out."

"What if we can't?" Talie asked. "What if we have contact then lose it?"

Kainen grinned. "I have a contingency, don't worry.

Someone who's going to watch over you both."

The shadows shifted. Talie took a healthy step back, then another.

"That's a snake," she announced.

Kainen laid a hand on the leviathan curling the tip of its shining black tail around his ankle. The thickest part of the creature was wider than his body, and when it reared up with a soft hiss, it topped his height by over a head.

"This is Betty."

Talie struggled to keep a straight face.

"The giant fanged serpent is called Betty," she clarified. "The creature that could crush the bones of a grown man, is called Betty."

"Yup. She's the unofficial mascot of the Illusion Court, but she only really answers to Reyan. She kind of humours me on occasion too."

Talie tensed as Molly entered the tent with Milo. Molly's eyes grew wide the moment she saw Betty, and Talie waited for some kind of flinching or shrieking, similar to the reaction Molly had to the pigeon some days before.

"Aww!" Molly's eyes lit up. "Who's this? Hello. She's so cute!"

She swept past to greet Betty with a hand outstretched, but Talie reached out automatically and caught her around the waist to hold her back.

"No! You don't just approach giant animals like they're fluffy pets!"

Molly frowned. "That's rude. She can't help being scaly, or big. She's beautiful."

"Of course," Talie muttered, letting her go. "Birds you're afraid of but creatures that can strip your bones like a stickpop, no problem."

Molly didn't answer as Betty flicked a tongue in the air near her hand and dissipated into a small curl of shadow.

"She'll be going with you," Kainen explained. "She can track you through the shadow and if something goes wrong, she'll be able to let us know."

Molly flinched as Aurora fluttered down onto her shoulder and gave Betty a warning click of her beak. Talie agreed with her and dug out a piece of crumbled biscuit she'd stashed there for emergencies, earning herself a soft crooning noise as Aurora took the offering happily.

Princess can have the snake, I'll take the bird any day.

She eyed the wisp of shadow Kainen handed over to Molly, with instructions to keep her in the dark of a pocket and not to worry if she disappeared on them occasionally.

As Taz and May strode in, Talie's gaze dropped immediately to the absolute beauty laying across Taz's outstretched palms.

"Take this," he said.

Talie gazed at the glint of the sword he held out, a beautiful silvery blade with a hilt made of polished and muted metals. The ornate curl on the handle looked more like a prop sword or something from a book, but she could see the impeccable craftsmanship on it. Then she realised Taz wasn't holding it out to Molly.

Her jaw dropped as Taz gave it another little shake in her direction.

"Um... what?"

"Take it. Use it to keep you both safe."

"Is that..." Kainen frowned. "That's Kingkiller."

Molly snorted hysterically. "Who names these things?"

Taz ignored them, his gaze firmly on Talie.

"Stories have power, and they've been told about this sword," he said, smiling enough to lessen the tension with a wicked gleam in his turquoise eyes. "It killed the old king at the battle of Arcanium but it knows its allegiance well enough. The hilt has been modified as well, so you can check that out when you get a chance. No offense, Molly, but out of the two of you, Talie's probably the safest to wield it."

"Yeah, no, not arguing with that." Molly grinned. "Do daggers get ridiculous names too? Wait, can it hear me?"

He rolled his eyes. "Don't be dim, but yeah, why shouldn't daggers have names? Size doesn't mean everything."

"Tell yourself that a lot do you, brother?" May asked sweetly.

Demi pressed her fingertips either side of her nose and sighed loudly.

"Faerie save me," she muttered.

May grinned. "As it happens, I have a few meagre gifts of my own to bestow."

She held out a hand to Molly and unfurled her fingers to reveal three small hairpins.

"Um, thanks?" Molly took them.

"Wear them, they'll keep you safe." May insisted.

Molly eyed the small pins, each one an odd hue of unfinished grey metal. She slid them into place around her hair ribbon.

"And this is for you." May held out her other hand to Talie. "It's a knucklepick, useful enough to get through locks with simple enchantments and wards."

Talie hesitated until May frowned and pushed her hand out further. A dull grey ring sat on her palm, the metal underside thick and the top part curved into a sharp point like a bird's beak.

"Thanks," she muttered.

"You're welcome. Hopefully you won't need to use them, but in the depths of the citadel they might come in handy."

"Let's get this first test done first," Demi suggested.

Molly shouldered a large rucksack over one shoulder and Talie took a second one. Wriggling it onto her back, she stood with her arm flush against Molly's as Milo held his hands out.

"Good luck," Demi said. "Remember, don't move an inch. Just call for Milo and wait."

Talie took Milo's hand with as minimal touch as possible and moments later her view of the tent wavered, obscured by wisps of swirling purple-grey. The haziness solidified almost instantly into a gloomy tunnel with barely any light, an ominous, stale stillness waiting in both directions.

"This is the labyrinth entrance," she murmured.

Milo nodded. "A short way into the middle path from the doors, yes. I'm going to skip out, then you call for me to make sure I can hear you. Then I'll be back to get you."

"That's it?" Molly asked. "Are there any fairies still

here? Or could you get us to the library?"

"No, and don't even think about moving. I'll be right back whether you call or not."

He disappeared and Talie glanced around. Several of the doors that had recently housed tortured fairies were now open.

"I don't see why we can't at least take advantage of the opportunity," Molly grumbled.

Talie sighed. "Because if we do, they'll never let us come back again. Are you calling for him or am I?"

"Together, to be safe."

Talie nodded. "Fine."

"Milo?" they chorused together.

He reappeared and held out both hands.

"Good, I can hear you both."

Talie took his hand, unable to hide the fond smirk lifting her lips as Molly muttered something irritable under her breath before taking his other one.

The royal tent came into view and Talie let Milo's hand drop. She waited until he'd turned away to wipe her hand on her trousers though.

"Now we map the core," Demi said, her tone heavy with weariness. "We need to bear in mind that there might be guards down there still, and we can't risk any rescue missions until we know more. If there is a dangerous entity down there, then we can use that as our justification for amendments to the covenant."

"That sounds long." Molly frowned.

"It's all I've got."

"What about the Fae needing homes?"

Demi sighed. "I've got people compiling a list of opportunities, and taking names of anyone who might be interested and their skills and trades, so we may yet be able to place some. As for the others, we can only ask them to hold on and hope the goodwill the nobles are currently feeding them with holds. Now, I need to think. Everyone out."

Talie tailed Molly out of the tent, but she had nowhere to be other than Molly's side. When Molly halted outside, she did too.

"We should be finding the core and Celeste," Molly muttered.

"What can we do if we do find her though? We need strength, and for that we need knowledge."

"We can't leave her to her own devices for long though. What if she hurts more people?"

Talie hesitated. "What if we go in to fight and she hurts them to punish us instead? That's how we ended up here after all."

Molly folded her arms across her chest, looking adorable in her puffy pale pink snow-coat and matching woollen hat. The tips of her golden hair were spilling out in tufts and Talie fought the instinct to smile.

"I know that. She used people to punish me before but we can't sit around doing nothing."

"What's your grand plan then, Princess? You usually have something mad thought up."

Demi's head popped out before Molly could answer.

"Molly, can we speak a bit?" she asked.

Molly nodded. She gave Talie a weary look and

disappeared back inside. Before Talie could set her sights on Molly's tent and the exhausting thought of finding Marthe to drum up some food, the sound of footsteps scuffed through the snow nearby.

"You shouldn't talk like that to the princess," a squeaky voice admonished.

Talie looked around. Then down. A small boy with pink cheeks and a ridiculously padded frock coat in peacock green with silver trim flowered up at her.

She frowned. "Like what?"

"She's not your equal. I'm not your equal either."

"Why not?"

He stamped his foot and she strangled the urge to laugh.

"She's a princess and I am a lord."

"Lord of what?"

"I am Lord William of the outer reaches of the Fauna Court. I have a title. What do you have?"

Talie thought for a moment. This was no doubt the same William that Sammy had warned her about. Somehow, she didn't see him being a major threat for Molly's heart, but against her better judgement she flicked her sleeve back to bare her wrist.

"I have daggers."

The little lord's eyes expanded instantly.

"Wow. Can I have one?"

"No."

"Why not?"

"Because… Because they're not toys and you're a child."

"I have bigger ones at home, but I'm not allowed to play

with them either," he admitted. "I do when nobody's looking. All they want me to do is study boring old maps, but I'm going to be a warrior when I'm older."

"I thought you were going to be a lord," she muttered.

She scanned the queen's tent for some sign of Molly emerging, but still nothing.

"I can be a lord and a warrior," he insisted. "And I'm going to marry the princess and be a king."

"Really not how it works."

Besides, Molly's mine.

"It will be when I'm in charge. You can be my bodyguard I suppose," he announced.

"Er... I'm spoken for, but thanks."

"You can't refuse!" He clenched his piddly fists. "I'm going to be king one day. My father says stranger things have happened, then everyone will need to pay attention to me!"

Talie had no idea what delusions his parents might be whispering in his ear at bedtime, but she'd had enough of him either way.

"If you say so. I'll take my leave, your lordship."

She dodged around someone passing by and slipped into the crowd, only feeling slightly guilty for leaving him behind. An idea was forming, and for that she needed Milo to agree to it before they put it to the queen.

It'll get me plus points with Molly either way. She grinned. *That's what matters.*

CHAPTER NINETEEN

MOLLY

"We'll be really careful," Molly promised.

She watched Demi pacing up and down the tent, but they had no other option and they all knew it.

"Where exactly are these maps?" Demi asked. "Give it to me in metres."

Molly glanced at Talie. This was her idea, and she was the one who knew where the specific maps were, although Milo's head shot up as though he was dying to answer the question.

"I don't know about metres, but it's about a thirty second walk across the main entrance hall," Talie said. "Down the stairs on the left side, through the long corridor with the scroll things, and then the citadel ones are in a chest at the end."

Demi stopped mid-pace and gave her a knowing look.

"You know a lot about hidden parts of the library?"

Talie shrugged. "I know a lot about a few things."

Molly bit her lips together to hide a smile as Demi rolled her eyes and resumed pacing.

"Straight in, grab the stuff, straight out."

"Said the-" Kainen fell silent as Demi shot him a warning look.

"Actually, don't grab the stuff," she amended. "Don't take anything out that isn't ours."

"Does that include people?" Talie muttered.

"At the moment, yes, unless they actively ask to come with you. No impromptu rescue trips either. If they ask, we can go back in for them."

"What if people are injured?" Molly asked.

Demi grimaced. "Even then. Make a list if need be of those who need extracting and we'll deal with it separately."

"Can we take aid in at least?"

"I…" Demi hesitated, then glanced at Kainen. "I can't be seen to interfere."

Kainen stood with a wicked grin. "Nobody would expect you to, your magnanimous holiness. I have a few safety measures to give the girls before they leave."

Molly eyed him, not sure what more he could give them after her sunshine and Talie's rain gift. Demi gave him a stern look then threw her hands up and strode to her desk.

"Fine. Report back the moment you're done."

Kainen herded them out of the tent and stopped in front of a couple of women Molly didn't recognise, both carrying hefty sacks over both shoulders.

"Demi can't be seen to interfere," he explained. "That doesn't mean us courts can't disobey her. The citadel nobles might not be able to go up to help, and I'm sure several wouldn't bother, but take these in."

"Supplies?" Talie asked doubtfully.

He nodded. "Self-sustaining food pouches we've been developing with the Flora Court. We don't get as much light in the Illusion Court as most of it is underground and in the mountains, so we've seen the odd short supply issue to know how important it is to grow your own food."

Molly fought the urge to question him about the specifics and took two of the sacks, one over each shoulder as Milo hurried toward them.

"Demi approved this?" he asked archly.

Kainen smiled. "Demi may or may not have insisted that she can't interfere, and may or may not have forgotten to say that I can't interfere either."

"I see." Milo hesitated. "We don't have time to ask. Are you both okay with arms?"

Molly nodded and shuffled so Milo could hold her forearm, and Talie grudgingly did the same on his other side.

"Be good, and if you can't be good, think 'what would Kainen do'," Kainen suggested.

"Do not do that," Milo grumbled under his breath.

The purple-grey swirl of the nether wafted around Molly's face and she held her breath as the shadowy calm and scent of paper and dust built itself around them.

"How do you know exactly where to go?" Talie asked quietly.

Milo folded his arms and stepped back from them.

"It would take far too long to explain. Go get what you need, dump the sacks as close to the entrance as you can without being seen, then we're out of here."

Talie frowned and walked away from the library entrance hall along the narrow corridor that ran between two stacking units full of circular scroll tubes. The scent of aged paper was almost enough to make Molly homesick, but it was the subtle rustle and rumble of voices drifting in from the entrance hall that worried her.

"I'll just leave these here."

She dropped her sacks beside Milo and hurried after Talie. At the far end of the corridor, Talie stood to one side and toed a dusty wooden chest with her boot.

"This one. If we're not taking them out with us, we'll need to be quick in reading and copying them."

Molly nodded. "Got it. Maybe you go and drop the sacks off and I'll have a look through?"

"Do you even know what you're looking for?"

"You said the citadel is in the shape of that symbol you had, right?"

"Have a habit of remembering things about me, Princess?"

"Only the stuff that matters, Sunshine. Go on, then we can take poor Milo home."

Both of them glanced back at Milo, stiff-shouldered and almost vibrating with anxiety, his head twisting back and forth between them and the other end of the corridor that lead to the entrance hall and the subtle hum of voices.

Talie trudged off with her sacks and Molly eased the lid of the chest open. She covered her nose and mouth against the cloud of dust that puffed up and blinked at the collection of aged papers inside, some scrolled and tied with string, others folded into neat quarters.

Wonder if Celeste ever bothered to check in here, or more likely had others do it for her.

She unfolded several of the smaller maps, but guessed it would be one of the larger scrolls she would need. Footsteps tapped behind her and Milo crouched down at her side.

"Talie is keeping watch," he said. "I know how to handle antique documents, give those here."

Molly eased to her feet as he knelt in front of the chest and started to unroll the first scroll.

"Most are marked in the outward corner when rolled," he explained. "It lets you know which one is which, except we can't get to the inventory."

"Where is it?"

"At the front desk. I can't bear the thought of what folk might have done to it."

Burned it for fuel by now probably. She didn't dare say it out loud.

"I'll get it, hang on."

"Molly!" He hissed after her as she turned and set off down the corridor. "No!"

She couldn't remember if he knew about her stealth gift, but she slipped into it easily enough. Talie lifted a suspicious head and sniffed as she swept past but didn't say a word, so Molly hurried on toward the entrance hall.

The sheer chaos that hit her the moment she stepped into the wide open space was palpable. People sat in huddled groups around collections of blankets, and the sheer wave of icy air that hit almost made Molly stumble back.

Celeste's turned off the heat power to the library, she must have.

Someone definitely had, and a few food pouches were going to mean nothing if they didn't get a whole cartload of blankets in as well immediately. A few people nearby were shuddering and she swallowed down a rising wave of bitter fury that threatened to set her sunshine gift free at the sight of so many pale and sad faces.

She set off toward the reception desk, mindful to keep her footsteps silent, and eased around the chair. The inventory was a huge leatherbound folio, and she had the distinct feeling she could probably take a hammer to it without causing a single dent in the cover.

Her stealth gift absorbed her clothes into the zone of its power, but she wasn't sure if she'd get away with taking a hefty book. With painstaking slowness, she eased the book toward her chest and managed to inch it underneath her sweatshirt.

With both arms clenched protectively around it, she crept back toward the corridor. She expected someone to notice her, or shout about a mysterious floating book, but nobody even lifted their head as she passed.

Milo gave her a despairing look as she let her stealth gift slide away and slipped back into the corridor to give him the inventory. He snatched it and ran a loving hand over the cover with a sigh.

"Needless to say we won't tell Demi about this unless she specifically asks," he warned.

Molly nodded. "Okay."

"How long will it take you to find what we need?" Talie

asked as they marched back toward the chest.

Milo frowned. "I can't say exactly. This is a very specific process, honed over several-"

"Yeah, but how long?"

"Give me five minutes," he muttered.

Talie folded her arms and faced Molly next.

"Don't do that again."

Molly frowned. "Do what?"

"Sneak off like that. You just vanished."

"Aww, worried about me?"

"Well, yeah."

She hesitated, her mind shooting backwards to the entrance hall.

"It's hideous out there. They've cut all heating and everyone's in huddles shivering. The food will go down well but if it's in pouches it'll take time to grow, and they need blankets."

Talie took her hand and knitted their fingers together as Milo made a soft huff of triumph, but the bold move surprised her as much as it comforted her.

"They're doing a bit better than any fairies further down though," she said.

Molly sighed. "What do we do? What can we do? We can't leave any of them, not like this."

As Milo pulled out an orb and started scanning it over the mess of scrolls unfurled around him, Talie tugged Molly by the hand until they stood a short distance away.

"We should go down to the cells," she whispered. "Just to see what the situation is. Then we can take a full report back."

"He'd never agree to it."

She's going to tell me to use my compulsion gift. Molly tensed as the thought flickered into her head.

Talie shrugged. "We ask, or you could also pull rank."

Somehow, the princess suggestion was marginally less horrific than the compulsion one, and Molly rolled her eyes.

"We should really make sure the maps are correct before we use them," she suggested. "Milo? What if those maps are out of date? We should skip down to… ascertain the legitimacy of the data."

Talie snuffled over a laugh, but Milo's head tipped to the side as he started to fix the mess in front of him.

"There's merit in that, but Demi won't like it."

"It'll be two seconds," Talie added. "Skip down to where we rescued the fairies, look left and right, then skip back to the camp. Take us in a tiny bit further than we know, to be safe."

Milo said nothing as he collected the scrolls and maps back together and placed them neatly into the chest. He stood and Molly readied herself to beg, until he held out both hands.

"No more than two seconds, and you don't let go of my hands. Got it?"

Molly nodded and nudged Talie when she hesitated. They took a hand each and Molly's insides flared with worry as the nether wrapped around them.

Grey stone walls fell into place around them set with dark iron doors at regular intervals. Some of the doors were open but the air was full of pained and mournful sounds.

"There's still fairies down here," Talie muttered.

Milo nodded. "And we don't do anything without Demi's say so."

His hand tightened around Molly's and given Talie's wince, he'd done the same to her. He led them along the corridor lined with cells and Molly didn't dare look too closely at the face-height hatches lined with bars. The sounds were awful enough on their own to endure.

"Hey!"

A deep shout echoed behind them and they twisted as an awkward gaggle of arms and limbs. Molly gasped as Talie wrenched her hand free of Milo's and darted in front as a guard ran toward them. Molly drew a protection warding around them, a mere quiver of energy as it hit the absolute wall of Milo's and more guards appeared, some manhandling barely conscious people between them.

More fairies. Molly shuddered even as her anger spiked.

Milo reached out to grab Talie but she dodged him, her stance ready to fight as the guards hit the edge of his warding.

"You can't fight all of them," Milo snapped.

Talie scoffed. "I can try. If we take even one fairy back it's one less they've got."

Molly eyed the nearest guard as he reached for a long strip of metal, the kind of iron that pierced wardings, given the smug look on his face.

Panic flared and she forced herself to Talie's side with her gift winding over her lips.

"Where's Celeste?" she demanded.

The guard grimaced. "Rumour has it she goes deeper in past the cells a lot."

He gasped, the sound almost comical as he realised what she'd just compelled out of him. He took a wary step back, and she channelled her inner Kainen with a wicked smile.

"Where's Marcus?"

"He's managing most things, but everyone is saying he's annoyed that Celeste is too busy digging deeper to find the core of pow-"

He squeaked over the last word as the woman beside him let go of the fairy she was holding and slapped a hand over his mouth. Molly saw the opportunity as the fairy swayed toward them, his eyes glazed over and his clothing all but ruined. He smelled awful as she dodged to catch him, but Talie anchored her arms tight around them both and Milo's hand clamped over her shoulder as the nether curled around them.

The queen's tent appeared and Molly checked Talie was there with them before bristling with irritation.

"What the-"

Demi stalked toward them and the temperature in the tent, normally cosy, dipped into frozen territory as her eyes flashed icy.

"It was an... okay, it wasn't an accident, but I kind of acted without thinking," Molly mumbled.

She let the fairy man go as Talie stepped away too, but he wasn't able to support his weight.

"Orbs, get him into this chair." Demi hauled one over toward them. "I can't believe this! Is he from the library?

Did he ask to come with you?"

"No, but clearly he'd want to be here instead of there given the state of him," she tried.

Demi folded her arms and stalked back to her desk.

"Milo, get a healer. If he's up to answering, and I can get him to say he wants to be here, then we're safe from the covenant."

Molly bit her tongue on the retort brewing, because accusing the queen of Faerie of only caring about covenants would probably not go down well, no matter how liberal she was.

"I take it given the state of you both, all flushed, the library wasn't as calm as we hoped?"

Talie glanced at Molly with a 'your arena' look. Molly rolled her eyes back.

"We wanted to make sure the maps we found were at least initially accurate," she explained.

"So, you left the library."

"Kind of, yeah. Only for a second, but then we got jumped by some guards. I compelled one of them to tell us that Celeste is going further in to find the well of power as well."

Demi groaned and the fairy echoed the sound with more torment than Molly could ever imagine possessing. She shuddered, and even Demi stilled.

"I would have done the same," Demi admitted grudgingly. "I'll find a way around it, but please don't make a habit of it. The reason we abide by the laws is so that we can keep everyone safe, otherwise we're no better than them."

She lifted her head as Milo hurried in with someone who instantly dropped to her knees in front of the fairy.

"Orbs, this is savage. What's been done to him?"

"Faerie only knows," Demi muttered. "Can you take care of him? If you can get an agreement that he's happy to be in our care as well, that'd be a big help."

The woman nodded as two more came in with a stretcher.

"No worries, we'll see to him. Do I have permission to take him back to Arcanium?"

Demi nodded. "Might as well, whatever you need to do. If I'm understanding it right, he probably belongs in one of our realms anyway, so if you can get a location out of him you can even return him home, but under extreme care, okay? We don't know what they did to him."

The woman nodded, a grim understanding passing across her face. The moment the healers and the fairy were out of the tent, Demi braced her hands against the desk and folded over it.

"I'll hang her on her orbing obsession with power," she muttered. "We know they're testing for gift extraction, but kidnapping people and using them like cattle is beyond vile."

Molly took a tiny step back as Demi slammed her hands on the desk and a squall of icy wind fluttered through the tent. It dissipated as quickly as it arrived, but in that moment she knew whatever power she might have gained as a princess, she wouldn't ever be able to rival the queen.

That's what Celeste wants. She wants to be unrivalled, unbeatable.

"What is that?" Demi asked, her tone lethally quiet.

Molly looked around in alarm. Then down.

"I had to!" Milo wailed, a suspiciously familiar library book clutched to his chest. "It's the inventory for the entire library."

He didn't seem to be as awed by Demi's temper, but it had faded already and she groaned with both hands slapped over her face.

"Orbs, Milo, this is ridiculous. You can't steal books!"

"Exactly, this is what I've been trying to tell you. Books and knowledge should be freely availab-"

"*So* not what I meant. I'll deal with you later. Did you at least get what you needed in terms of maps and things?"

He nodded. "I got orb scans of the maps, yes. I'll need to transfer them but they should be accurate enough."

"We need to send more stuff in as well," Molly insisted. "She's cut power to the library, or heat at least. It'll take a while for those food pouches to grow as well so they need instant food and blankets and bedding."

"I can't. I want to more than anything but my hands are tied. If there- what do you mean *more* stuff?"

Oops.

Molly hesitated but Talie stepped past Milo to stand beside her.

"We took some food pouches in." Talie shrugged. "It's still not enough."

Demi sighed. "These would be the food pouches the Illusion Court have been working on? And I'm guessing Reyan wasn't the one to give them to you?"

"No, but it's not enough, and I'd do it again."

"The less I know the better," Demi said. "At this rate, I'm probably best off pretending you two don't exist, and what you do with his lordship has to be beneath my notice with all the other stuff I've got piling up. Be queen, they said. It'll be fun, they said."

It was as much of a green light to misbehave as Demi could give them, and Molly smiled with relief.

I can take loads of stuff out from that wardrobe Marthe keeps filling. She can give me blankets and probably food, and if I need to trade for them I will.

She flinched as Demi appeared in front of her, blue eyes tinged with frost and seriousness.

"Take tonight to rest. If you're going into the citadel then go tomorrow morning. Do what you have to do, but don't do anything rash or dangerous, I mean it."

Molly nodded and hurried out of the tent. She needed to find and organise as many supplies as possible, then she just had to bribe Kainen to bribe Milo to take them in for her.

CHAPTER TWENTY

TALIE

The hint of morning blended swathes of dusky peach over the inky blue horizon, the snowy forest spread out all around like a sea of glittering white gems. Talie watched her breath plume in short puffs as the peach turned to a blaze of gold, lighting up the five dark towers of the citadel. Molly stood in front of her, a soft glow haloing her body as she watched the sun rise.

"You crept out," Talie muttered.

Molly shrugged without turning around, her gaze fixed on the horizon as Talie stood beside her.

"It's so... vast, and this is only one realm of countless others."

Talie shrugged. "I imagine the necessities and niceties are the same whatever realm you're in. Here."

She held out the hot pastry wrapped in napkins, rubbing her fingers as Molly took it.

"Come on, it's beautiful," Molly cajoled. "The fresh air."

"Cold."

"The snow."

"A pain to walk in." Talie tried to hide her smile.

"The sunrise."

"Pretty, if you like that sort of thing."

Molly nodded. "I do."

"Then yeah, I guess it is beautiful. So beautiful it hurts. Eat while the food is still hot."

Molly bit into the pastry and her eyes widened.

"This is almost like Merry's," she mumbled.

Talie ducked her head as relief warmed her insides. She'd been up long before the sun trying to get it right, so much so the head cook almost insisted Marthe have her thrown out of the kitchen tent.

"That's something then. Took me ages. Come on, Princess, let's get warm before Marthe has my head for letting you be out here too long."

"You made this?"

She nodded. "It's nothing."

"You have to show me how though." Molly inhaled the crumbs and looked longingly at the empty napkins. "I want to be able to make them myself. Merry never shared the secret."

"And neither will I."

"Mean!"

Talie grinned. "Sensible. That way I know you'll always come back when you want feeding."

Molly rolled her eyes and started back toward the camp. Talie trudged along beside her in silence. She didn't want to ruin Molly's mood by mentioning what they would likely have to face later, but there was no avoiding it.

The citadel was in ruins, Celeste was burrowing deeper toward the well of power, and Molly still hadn't explained what she hoped to gain by going further into the labyrinth under the tower's core.

I'm not buying the whole 'we need to map it out' excuse. She's going after Celeste, and I'm not letting her get hurt doing it.

Even though it was still early enough for most of the camp to be in silent stillness, the queen's tent flap lifted and she emerged blinking sleep from her eyes.

"This is a fact-finding mission only, got it?" Demi insisted.

Molly nodded. "The core is huge, so chances we'll run into people the further in we go are slim. We've got Milo's maps, and Milo to fetch us once we're done. We'll have far too much to carry thanks to Marthe as well."

As if summoned, Milo hurried over to them with his sweatshirt on backwards and two large rucksacks hanging from each arm.

"I'll be on alert for whenever you call," he said. "Don't leave it too long or we'll start to worry."

"We won't. We have the orbs as well just in case."

"Orbs likely won't get past the stone, but it'll give you the information you need. I've put everything on there I can think of. Ready?"

Talie shouldered one rucksack then took the other as well. She ignored Molly's protest as Kainen ambled through the snow toward them in a t-shirt. He held out his hand to Talie with a well-worn black leather jacket hanging from it.

"Take this," he offered. "Your coat's worn through."

Talie stared at it for a moment. "I'm fine, but thanks."

"Isn't that your lucky coat?" Demi asked.

He nodded. "Figured a bit of luck can't hurt. I've got several others."

Talie bit her lip. She guessed he didn't mean anything by it, but it was still weird.

Then again, Molly's got the kind of coat that could be buried under mounds of snow and still warm. Mine might as well not be there.

She slid off her coat and took Kainen's instead.

"Just to borrow, don't worry," she muttered.

Demi gave him a wary, sideways look, as though she wasn't quite sure what he was up to. Talie wasn't sure either but at least the coat was warm and smelled like grapes and woodsmoke.

She held her arm out to Milo.

"Good luck," Demi said. "Remember, no heroics. No challenging anyone and check in regularly. Come back as soon as you need to rest, and no using your gifts unless you absolutely have to."

Talie didn't bother to nod as Milo grasped her wrist on one side and Molly's on the other. Talie took a deep breath and shook the lingering haziness from her mind. She needed to be sharp and ready for whatever mad plan Molly had come up with.

The gloomy stone tunnels of the Menagerie labyrinth came into view, each cell door shut. Talie listened but couldn't hear any signs of pain or life behind them like there had been on her last proper visit.

"Remember, keep it short," Milo insisted.

Molly nodded. "We will."

"Keep notes as well, any deviations from the maps. Stick together no matter what so I can get you both out. Make sure-"

"We'll be fine," she said, her tone soft and soothing. "The deeper we go, the less chance there is of seeing anyone anyway, so we'd better get on with it."

Milo pulled a doubtful face and vanished. Seconds later, Molly sagged with a sigh.

"Right, let's get started. Which tunnel should we take first?"

Talie shrugged. "Start with the left, I guess."

Molly set off and Talie kept right beside her, close enough that their elbows brushed as their footsteps tapped quietly on the stone floor. Molly pulled out a shining blue orb swirled with gold and swiped her finger over the surface until the hazy grey orb-cast of the core's floor plan hovered in front of them.

"I can carry my own bag," she muttered.

Talie bit back a smile. "You focus on the spying, Princess."

"What's your job then?"

Talie shrugged. "Everything else."

Molly rolled her eyes and focused on the map bobbing in front of them as they turned a corner and hit a fork.

"Ah, this one's not blocked off on the map." She frowned as she muttered to the orb to update the image's notes. "That would have taken us around an outer loop according to this."

Talie glanced around at the endless halls of bare rock. They'd left the cells behind already and the air was chilly with an oppressive stillness. Her rain gift woke to the cloying dryness and tiny beads of perspiration dotted her skin. She tensed as Molly glanced her way with a frown.

"Are you sure you don't want me to take my bag?" Molly insisted. "You look a bit flushed."

Her insides twisted with shame and she clung to the straps of each bag in each hand with a huff.

"No. The rain is acting up, that's all. Don't ask again."

"Fine."

Talie sighed as Molly stalked off before she could dredge up an immediate apology.

Great start.

She hurried forward to catch up as Molly turned down the right-hand hall, no more than a dim tunnel lit by lamps behind small metal cages. As she turned, the bags swung her momentum off balance. Her arm slid across a jagged edge of the wall and she seethed at the burn as it scraped a deep cut to her skin.

Molly whirled around and Talie got dazzled by a momentary carousel of light as the map passed right over her face.

"Here, let me look," Molly said.

Talie closed her eyes and forced down the instinctive urge to snap like a wounded animal.

"It's fine."

Molly sighed. "I don't think we've been given anything for healing either."

"Do not even think about calling Mi- him." Talie

opened her eyes immediately. "It's fine."

Molly gave her an exasperated look and started rummaging through the bags while muttering under her breath. Talie stood obediently as she got shoved around with the bags and her irritation faded instantly. She'd had cuts and scrapes and even a couple of breaks far worse before, but Molly was fussing like it was the injury of the age.

Like she cares.

The water warmed as it beaded over her skin and soaked the cut, but it was a cosy sort of heat.

Molly came back to face her empty-handed, then untied one of the ribbons around her wrist. Talie's heart picked up and her gut went into a delighted freefall when she recognised them.

"I got you those." The words were out before she could stop them.

Molly frowned. "You did? I figured Sammy got them and put your name to them. We were barely grunting at each other at that point."

She wrapped the green hair ribbon around Talie's arm until the cut was fully bound. Talie didn't have the heart to tell her it'd be soggy in no time given the way her gift was behaving.

"No, they were from me. Poor trade for a dagger, but still."

Molly smiled and the tunnel looked a bit brighter for it.

"Yuletide gifts aren't about trades, they're about being thoughtful. The dagger was easy for me but good for you. Hair ribbons are infinitely useful for me."

"If you say so. I'll wash this one and give it back."

She readjusted the bags and gave Molly a warning look when she lifted a hand to take one.

"Stubborn." Molly sighed, but it was a wicked smile she turned to walk down the tunnel with. "Besides, I hear it's the fashion to wear your girl's hair ribbon."

Talie stared after her.

Molly hadn't made any mention of the moments they'd shared before, or the bed-sharing either. The closest they'd come to declaring anything was Talie kicking Sammy out of a seat, but the blunt admission sent tingled of excitement all the way to her toes.

Only when she realised Molly was almost getting out of reach did she speed up to keep pace.

"Hurry up, Sunshine," Molly called over her shoulder.

Talie grinned. "I'm not sunshine. You are, remember? I'm the rain."

She drew alongside, unable to take Molly's hand because of the bags she was now absolutely regretting having anything to do with.

Molly glanced back with a soft smile.

"You're still sunshine to me."

Talie grimaced as her gift latched onto her emotions and gleefully evaporated from her skin into the air above them, but Molly laughed softly as the water dropped again moments later in tiny sprinkles. Talie had no skill with sucking the water back in, but she tried imagining it collecting over her skin again and absorbing.

Molly lifted her face to it and a soft glow of light pulsed over her outstretched palm. Moments passed as sunshine and rain danced together, until the faintest hints of a rainbow arced between them.

Molly smiled in awe but Talie couldn't take her eyes off Molly's face or the reverential magic in her eyes, so tranquil blue in the soft light that the muted hints of green were visible.

When Molly looked up and caught her staring, Talie dropped her gaze down a few inches, then back up, mesmerised. Molly inched closer. Talie tilted her head.

A loud crash echoed down further down the tunnel.

The rainbow faded and Molly's glow with it.

"Orbs, that scared the life out of me." Talie swore under her breath. "Take your bag and hold my hand. We can't risk getting separated."

Molly regained control of her shock quickly enough to give her a withering look.

"Oh *now* I'm allowed to manage my own bag," she muttered.

"So not the time, Princess. That noise was right down the hall."

Molly took the bag and slung it over her shoulder, but Talie didn't move an inch until Molly's fingers were threaded with her own.

"Sorry, it's a bit clammy," she mumbled.

Molly shrugged. "Barely notice if you don't keep going on about it. I have my stealth gift so I could go and see what's down there."

"No separating."

"Argh, fine, but if there's Fae down there they'll be able to see you."

When Talie drew the sword Taz had given her in answer, Molly disappeared. Talie had seen her do that before but it still unnerved her, especially when she was now holding an invisible hand as they crept side by side to the curve of the tunnel ahead.

"If the hall is still lit, it means it's being used," Molly murmured. "It's not standard Faelight either. The hue is much darker and it's flickering so that means it's actual fire, probably pre-dating what we're used to."

Talie wanted to ask how exactly Molly knew and noticed so much about the clues others would find irrelevant, but they reached the end and peered around the corner before she could.

What she saw beyond the glow of firelight flickering high and low ahead, swept any hope of words away.

CHAPTER TWENTY ONE

MOLLY

Molly clenched her free fist around the strap of her bag and tightened her other hand around Talie's fingers.

The tunnel opened out beyond the corner into a wide cavern. It had similar stone pillars around the edges to the Menagerie's main hall, but there weren't any fancy furnishings and no windows of colourful glass. The main space of the cavern was littered with wooden tables, each with a lethal array of tools on stools nearby. Further on, a few circular baths held some kind of bubbling pale goop, and several fires had been set in makeshift pits ringed with stones.

Fae moved around the space with purposeful strides, some carrying vials and trays, others holding books or sheaves of loose paper.

Molly gazed past them in horror to the figures shackled on the tables, all in varying states of pain that would frighten even her nightmares.

"This is depraved," Talie whispered.

Molly sensed the subtle step back Talie took. She

loosened her grip on Talie's fingers and took a breath.

As she hauled her hand free, ready to run further into the room, Talie's arm anchored around her waist.

"Oh no you don't."

Molly squeaked as Talie almost lifted her off her feet and dragged her back into the tunnel.

"We can't do nothing!" she hissed.

Talie couldn't see her but she clung on tight, which put their faces almost side by side.

"We're not going to do nothing, but we are going to be smart about it."

A pained groan echoed through the air. Molly froze, then winced as the groan turned into a jagged scream.

"We can't leave them," she insisted.

Talie grimaced and looked back to the source of the noise.

"You can't get them out, not without Milo, and he can't interfere on the queen's behalf. There are too many to save in one go and more artificers and guards than we can possibly take on."

"Then what?" Molly asked, frustration jittering in her veins.

She caught the rueful look in Talie's eyes moments before she realised what was about to happen.

"Don't-"

"Milo," Talie called out quietly.

"I can't believe you just did that!"

"I'm not risking your life for whatever unplanned mania you're considering," Talie muttered.

"What about that?" Molly swiped a hand toward the

pained echoes.

Talie frowned and Molly realised she was still invisible, but it gave her an edge so she stayed in stealth mode. She also didn't mention anything about Talie's arm still anchored around her waist, or the cool fingers now wrapped tight around her own.

"Are you saying my life is worth more than theirs?" she asked.

"No." That surprised her into stillness. "But we can't rescue them without help."

Molly glanced around. "Yeah, about that..."

"Milo?" Talie risked saying it a bit louder.

Moments passed and Molly's heart sank.

"No Milo," she said.

Talie grimaced. "Typical."

"Maybe he's busy."

Talie scoffed. "I can't imagine what would be more important than picking up the crown princess of Faerie."

"Orbs don't call me that! It's clear he's not coming."

"Or can't, which means we need to find another way through this place until we can either hide out or find the exit, or Milo reappears."

Molly let her stealth gift fade to avoid draining her energy. Marthe had packed plenty of snacks but they'd need to be careful until they had a better plan, or until Milo came back for them.

"We'll take a walk back to where we came in," Talie insisted. "See if he can hear us. Check for suitable dead ends we can use as a base while we walk."

Molly sighed and held the orb up, swiping across the

map that projected in front of them. It wasn't as easy one-handed, but she didn't make any attempt to remove her hand from Talie's firm grip.

"The way we came in will be full of guards," she countered. "Look, turn left up ahead, then take a right and there should be a small dead-end we can stop in."

Talie nodded. "Lead the way. Milo?"

They hesitated, but after a few moments and still no sign of him, Molly led them along the tunnel and to the left. As soon as they reached the dead-end, nothing more than a short slip of tunnel unfinished, Molly dropped Talie's hand and palmed hers together to hold the orb and the image steady.

"There might be a way out, there to the left of the tunnels. I imagine they'd need an emergency exit in case anything went wrong, and it looks like it comes out on the guild levels."

"Unless that's how the guild members are getting in," Talie suggested. "Risky if it is."

"Or it could be a way out, and from there we can try calling Milo again."

She didn't voice the other thought rumbling around in her head. Talie seemed to be taking the whole 'protect the royal' thing seriously, and she likely wouldn't agree to any kind of plan that involved mass danger and setting free the fairies first.

Either that, or we'll need a diversion of some kind and a way to sneak them through the Menagerie itself.

The window that led out onto the levels near Marcus's office that she'd used countless times would likely be unwarded to let the assassins and spies slip in and out as before. If she could somehow get the fairies up there and out into the citadel, she could beg Phoenix to shelter them.

Celeste wanted me. If I have to be the diversion, so be it.

Thoughts of Ru filled her head and she shook them away as her gut plummeted.

"Hey." Talie's voice turned soft. "We'll figure this out, okay?"

Molly nodded. "We will. Are we checking out this guild level tunnel then?"

"I guess we've got no other option, but the first sign of trouble you slip into stealth and get yourself somewhere safe and hidden, got it?"

"Yes, Sunshine," she sighed. "Whatever you say."

Talie rolled her eyes. "Somehow I don't think you mean that. Need me to take your bag again?"

Molly pulled a face and set off back the way they came.

"There should be a gap or a turning or something up ahead," she announced. "It's not marked as an opening but there's a jagged line. If not, this tunnel takes us further inward."

She glanced ahead and slowed to a halt.

"Ah."

The tunnel ahead was in darkness, the firelit lanterns on the walls not going any further. Molly lifted her hand and let the warmth of her sunshine gift flow over her fingers.

"Not going to last us long, Princess," Talie said. "We can't have you tiring out too fast, and you've already used your stealth gift."

Molly shrugged. "The gap is almost in front of us. It won't take long."

She set off again with Talie right beside her. Every few steps, Talie muttered Milo's name, but he was either out of reach or unable to get back in to them.

"There." Talie pointed. "Is this the cavernous dark hole you were hoping for?"

"I think so."

They stood side by side and stared at the roughly knocked through archway that led into complete darkness.

"I'll go through first," Talie decided.

"Why do you get to go first?"

"To make sure it's safe, and that we can both fit. It might be a dead end, or a bottomless pit. Or a tight squeeze."

Molly sniffed indignantly. "You do dip a lot more than I do."

She reached out a hand and tapped the bone at the base of Talie's neck, amused when Talie closed her eyes momentarily instead of tearing the offending finger clean off.

"Well, I don't need extra mass to be strong," she muttered.

Molly glanced down. "Are you saying extra mass is a weakness?"

"Absolutely not."

"Well, I may curvier than you but I can still climb better."

Talie's gaze seemed to linger a fraction too long before she shrugged.

"You can climb better because you practiced far longer, like I've practised sparring much more than you."

"And that automatically makes you stronger?"

"Well obviously. You want to fight me, Princess? Test it out?"

"No need, Sunshine." Molly had to laugh. "I won't lower myself to proving you wrong."

Talie snorted and reached out a hand. Molly didn't say a word as Talie's fingers closed around hers, but she squeezed softly and pointed to the ominous crevice.

"We go in together," she insisted. "But sure, you can take the first step through."

CHAPTER TWENTY TWO

TALIE

Talie stalked after Molly through the endless darkness with a tiny smirk on her face. She kept close behind, so close she was almost tapping Molly's heels with her toes, because without the soft glow from Molly's outstretched hand she'd be lost in the dark tunnel completely.

She thinks she's so sneaky. As if she's not already looking for a way to get the fairies out.

"What's the plan then?" She had to ask. "After we find out where this tunnel goes I mean?"

Molly shrugged and Talie waited for the inevitable word tangling that would come next.

"Investigate all the options. See what the safest route out is."

Talie caught the hint of effort in Molly's tone and frowned.

"What's the map say? Is it much further?"

Molly stopped and held up the orb, the faint image shadowy against the glow of her gift.

"If this is to scale, then we might have a bit of a walk

yet. We're sloping down, which is expected, but the curves and turns are taking us almost in looping curves somehow."

Talie didn't need to see the map to be able to imagine the labyrinthine paths through the tower's core.

"No knowing what's on the other side," she said, careful to keep her tone casual. "We should take a break now and have a snack."

Molly hesitated, then nodded. "There's another off-shoot tunnel up ahead by the look of it."

Talie followed her to the short stretch of bare rock that served as little more than a passing place. The moment they stopped, she swung her bag off her back and reached inside. She set out a blanket with enough room for them to sit side by side, then pulled out a couple of sturdy paper bags.

"Cold, but they'll do," she announced.

Molly eased herself down to sit against the wall with a groan and reached out to take the cold meat pocket.

"You think I'd get sick of these, but I never do."

Talie smiled. "You're a fan of habits and routine."

"Am not."

"You are. You love nothing more than working in the workshop all day, you eat the same food over and over, your clothing is all very similar, and I bet you have no problem watching the same reruns on the orb channels."

She said it teasingly, but even in the dim light of Molly's gift, which flickered and faded momentarily, she could make out the hurt on Molly's face.

"I want to see other realms. And anyway, so what if I

know what I like? What's wrong with that?"

Molly fixed her gaze on her hands as she methodically started wrapping the half-eaten food back in its paper. Talie's insides twisted at the sadness on Molly's face and she leaned forward.

"Nothing, I didn't mean anything by it. I mean, it's true though."

Molly nodded. "I guess so. Maybe I'm just predictable, although nobody knew I was in the Menagerie for over a year, and that's..."

She trailed off as her frown deepened. Talie bit her lip.

The one time I actually need Sammy to be an absolute pest and she's not here.

"Well, I knew," she reminded her. "I caught you falling, then sneaking around on the beams."

"So I'm cruddy at that as well as predictable, great."

"That's not how I-"

"Forget it. I can't spy, I'm not interesting and the only thing I have going for me is a psychotic mother and some royal blood."

Talie stared in horror as the words spilled from Molly's lips, but it was the almost wooden expression that didn't fit with the bite in her voice, as if she was more than used to the ideas rolling out of her mouth.

That's really what she thinks?

Fae couldn't lie.

Talie grabbed strands of her hair in a panic and started weaving a neat line.

"That's not true," she tried. "You're strong, and brave, and too kind for your own good sometimes, but it's honourable."

"You think I'm some naive idiot who thinks more of herself than she is, running into problems like getting kidnapped by Ru because I wasn't smart enough with my own safety, or being seen by you instead of being stealthy enough to go unseen, or-"

Talie lifted a hand and pressed her fingertips gently to Molly's lips. Anything to stop the waves of venom pouring out. She had no idea where it was coming from, but until Milo returned Molly only had her to lean on and she was screwing it all up.

"Stop. I don't think any of that. Do you do rash things? Yes, but it's from a good place. We wouldn't have the information about the whole gift extraction thing if it weren't for you."

"Celeste wouldn't have it either if it weren't for me."

Talie shrugged. "She'd have found another way. We wouldn't have known about this well of power from chasing guilds all over the place either if you hadn't suggested it."

"It was only one guild, hardly all over."

Talie smiled and risked moving her hand to smooth straggles of hair behind Molly's ear.

"And if it weren't for you, I'd probably still be there swinging from that hatch. Or worse."

She sagged back against the wall and tugged at another clump of her own hair to plait it.

"I wouldn't have left you."

"I know, and you're not going to leave these fairies either, I'm not dim. We'll find a way, but no heroics. No sacrifices. Okay?"

Molly nodded. "Okay."

It wasn't a promise, and Talie knew Molly wouldn't hold to it if she had a chance to do the "right thing", but at least she had calmed down.

"Is that really how you see yourself?" she asked quietly.

"Not often. It's more, how other people see me. Ru... he used to point all those things out, like me not thinking things through before acting or being able to take care of myself."

Talie hid her clenched fist under her knee.

"I think you can take care of yourself well enough," she said. "If he didn't believe that, then he didn't deserve you, friend or otherwise."

"He thought he was protecting me."

"He talked down to you and bossed you about. He sided with your mother enough to kidnap you. He kissed you pretending to be me-"

"How do you know that?"

Talie winced. *Me and my stupid big mouth.*

"It was talked about among the nobles. I was there as Lia, and I overheard."

"I remember." Molly sighed.

"Anyway, he kissed you under false pretences and when you were vulnerable. Orb-muncher behaviour at its worst. You need to stop thinking everyone thinks of you like that, because the right people won't."

"Don't you? Think of yourself like that I mean?"

Talie hesitated. "I do my best not to think, Princess. Not about myself. Nothing good can come of it and I have

Sammy to look after still. And you, so finish your food and we can get moving again."

It was bittersweet relief as Molly unwrapped the half a meat pocket with a sulky huff.

"I can look after myself," she muttered grouchily.

"Of course you can." Talie started a third braid in her hair as Molly ate. "But no harm in letting people who care about you share the load."

Molly's grin was beautiful in its sudden wickedness.

"You care about me?"

"Not what I said."

"Kind of."

"Not really. Come on."

She stood and grabbed the blanket before Molly had fully vacated it, unsure how a girl could have her so instantly flustered. She didn't say a word as she packed the blanket and Molly re-centred the map on the orb, and they set off down the tunnel in silence.

"Talie?"

She could hear the amusement in Molly's mockingly sweet tone, and the tunnel ahead was lit that little bit brighter.

"Yeah?"

"I'm not really saying that I care about you too."

Talie groaned to hide her grin.

"Faerie give me strength."

Molly didn't answer but her head shot up. An echo of footsteps came from behind them and Talie glanced over her shoulder.

"There's another gap up ahead," Molly hissed.

"Quick!"

She grabbed Talie's hand and Talie barely managed to cast a warding before Molly's dropped over them. They surged forward side by side, sacrificing some speed to avoid the slap of their shoes on the hard ground. The orb-cast of the map bounced in front of them but Talie couldn't see it clearly enough, let alone figure out which one of the darker lines of path they were meant to be on.

"STOP!"

"Crud," Molly muttered. "We won't be able to outrun them and the map won't keep still."

Talie slowed to a halt and turned back as Molly closed the map and shoved the orb in her pocket.

"We fighting?" Talie asked.

Molly grimaced. "If they're not warded, I'll compel them to leave. If they are…"

She left it unspoken but Talie took a step forward all the same. Molly might have compulsion and her sunshine gift but she was no great fighter in combat, no matter how much she grumbled otherwise.

Talie made sure Molly was a step behind her and kept her hand ready on Kingkiller as two guards in the standard boots uniform of dark colours and hefty boots stopped at the edge of their warding. The man towered over all of them with a fierce glower on his broad face, but the woman gave the warding a gentle tap and a dismissive smirk.

"What are you two doing all the way down here then?" she asked. "Too young to be in training, aren't you?"

"You don't know who we are?" Talie scoffed.

She would keep Molly's identity secret, but if they

could brazen it out without a fight it would save energy. Her Fae connection was awake and already raging, but she ignored the ill-timed trickles of water beading on her palms and up over her wrists.

The woman frowned. "Should we? Either way, you shouldn't be this far down. Come along. The mistress can decide what to do with you."

"Who is your mistress?" Molly asked.

"You don't know? Are you fairies or Fae?"

It wasn't an answer, and Talie took that to mean they had wardings up.

Fighting it is.

"We're not going anywhere with you," she said. "Leave us be and go on your way, or you'll be sorry."

The guards exchanged a bewildered look, then both burst into laughter. The man lifted a hand and flicked it in their direction, and Talie braced as a swirl of energy hit the front of their warding. The moment it dissipated, Molly folded her arms and cocked her hip to one side.

"What's that supposed to do? We're clearly all warded so this is just a waste of time all-round. We've been given a task to do by the highest authority, and we're doing it one way or another."

Talie kept her gaze welded to the enemy, even as a strain of pride calmed the damp climbing up her arms.

I need to be careful she doesn't try word-tangling on me, she's scarily good at it.

Again the guards looked to each other.

"When you say the highest authority..." The man trailed off.

Molly nodded. "The highest there is. The fact you don't know who I am either means you definitely can't be in Celeste's inner circle, or Marcus's. We can do this the hard way if you like, but I'd prefer to get on with it. She gets tetchy when things aren't done quickly."

Smooth and tricksy without a single lie. Talie clung to her hand and focused on calming her water gift back into her hands the way Molly had told her to. If she did have to fight, she'd need to at least hang onto the sword.

"We've no guarantee," the woman muttered. "I say we take them in."

"And we say we're not going anywhere," Talie snapped.

She drew Kingkiller and held it aloft. The tip of it seemed to sing as it came to the edge of their warding, and she felt the subtle puncture in their energy as it poked right through.

The woman laughed, but the sound was pinched and uneasy.

"You're barely what, fifteen? You think you can best grown Fae in combat? I've trained for years. Put the sword down and stop being silly. If you're truly on task for Celeste then we'll take the consequences of slowing you down, but we can't let you go without a guarantee."

"The Menagerie doors are guarded and the wards are near impenetrable," Molly countered. "Beyond that, there are guards at the entrance to the labyrinth and no doubt roaming throughout. If we weren't meant to be here, wouldn't we have been found by now?"

The woman cocked her head. "Maybe. And maybe

we're the first to find you. I don't want to fight kids, but I will if I have to."

Talie rolled her shoulders and let the rucksack drop to the ground. She kicked it a safe distance away against the wall, grunting under the weight of it, and faced the woman again with Kingkiller ready.

"I haven't had a spar in weeks. Do your worst."

If she could distract the woman enough to get her warding down, Molly could swoop in with compulsion.

"Stay behind me," she muttered out of the corner of her mouth.

Molly snorted. "Don't be dim. I can fight."

"I say this lovingly, Prin- I say this with all the care in Faerie, but no, you can't."

"I can!"

She dropped her bag and faced the man, but he seemed more than content to lounge back as the wardings of both sides met. Talie feinted forward and the woman arced back with a startled look on her face.

"What… how did you do that?" She took another step back. "Orbs, that sword is *metirin* iron! Look, it's been tipped. Where did you get that?"

Talie had no idea what *metirin* iron was, but there were all sorts of mentions of special irons in the library, and in the stories she'd read. She shrugged.

"Someone lent it to me. Why?"

She lunged the sword forward again and both the man and the woman stumbled sideways.

"We've still got gifts," the man said. "Screw the wardings."

Talie frowned and glanced at Molly, who looked as confused as she was, then at the sword.

Is it some kind of magic warding-destroying sword?

Perhaps that's why Taz had given it to her, to cut down the protection of their enemies so Molly could compel.

"What do you mean?" Molly demanded.

"I mean screw the wardings, we don't need them." The man grimaced. "And that one has compulsion, I can taste it."

Molly grinned. "I've got another gift too, but I'll spare you that. For now. What's Celeste doing down here?"

The man opened his mouth to answer and the woman did too, but the woman covered her mouth to muffle the words and slapped a hand over his also. Before Molly could ask again, the woman barrelled forward and slammed herself against the warding. The force of it sent them both stumbling back, and Kingkiller gouged a tear in their warding large enough for the woman to reach through and grab Talie's arm.

Molly launched forward but Talie swung her free arm out and slammed it over Molly's chest to force her back.

"Keep yourself warded," she snarled.

Molly tried to follow, but Talie tore herself out from the joint protection and shunted her shoulder into the woman's chest next, sending her reeling. With Kingkiller aloft as protection, she ducked and punched and kicked. Her elbow caught the man in the cheek and he hit the tunnel wall with a sickening crack.

She couldn't risk a second to check if he was getting up again but had to trust Molly would watch her back. The woman ducked and weaved as quick as she did, but for all her practiced grace, Talie was panicked and furious and not willing to hold any savagery back.

She gave the woman's shoulder a swift jab and lifted her other hand to the back of the woman's head, ready with the hilt of the sword to slam her from both sides.

The woman tumbled to the ground with a hand to her head and didn't get up again.

"Is she…" Molly trailed off.

Talie peered over her, then flicked a glance in the man's direction. He was still groaning but with no sign of him getting up again either.

"Unconscious. What do you want to do with them?"

Molly blinked. "What do you mean, 'do' with them? What can we do?"

"Compel them to walk away and not mention you were here? That's your arena."

The man groaned something and Molly rolled her eyes, the pink high in her cheeks suggesting she was fast moving from panic to planning.

"I don't know if compulsions work when people are unconscious."

Talie frowned, then the idea hit her. She dredged some water onto her palm, fighting to keep it from leaping all over the place. The mere concentration it took exhausted her more than fighting ten guards, but she splashed it onto the woman's face.

The woman's eyes opened and Talie levelled the tip of Kingkiller to her throat.

"You won't mention anything about us, or seeing us, or

anything that's happened here in this tunnel, not unless we're in mortal danger and someone needs to come in and find us," Molly compelled. "Tell me you agree to this."

The woman nodded but Talie pressed Kingkiller that little inch closer.

"Words."

"I agree to it," she spat.

The man's sluggish head lolled as much as it nodded.

"I agree to it," he mumbled.

"Good." Talie sheathed the sword and wiped her soaked hands over Kainen's jacket. "Off we go then. Might want to take a quick rest first. Sorry about the heads."

She shouldered her rucksack and winced as a sharp pain tore between her shoulder blades. The woman had gotten some savage blows in of her own, but Talie hadn't noticed under the adrenalin.

"You okay?" Molly asked.

Talie nodded. "Yeah, I'm fine. Let's go."

Molly's brow lifted doubtfully but Talie didn't wait around to hear it. As they fell into step with each other and continued on down the tunnel, Talie focused on keeping each step painfully measured. It would make sense to stop and rest but she wanted to get Molly as far away from the guards as possible.

We didn't even ask what they were doing this far down, or if there are likely to be others.

It didn't matter because she would fight all of them to the death if she had to, but given the throbbing ache in her back, she'd rather not have to risk it.

"Oh orbs, come here."

Molly's low muttering drew her attention. She twisted around to check they weren't being followed, but Molly dodged in front of her.

"What is it?" she asked through gritted teeth.

When Molly didn't answer, Talie lifted her head and pain sliced down her neck to her shoulder. Molly lifted a hand wreathed in gentle, pulsating light and Talie held still as the glow passed her face until warmth settled on neck beneath the collar of Kainen's jacket.

The heat eased some of the ache in her neck, but she couldn't ask Molly to shove her hand down a bit further, so she stood soaking in the contact instead.

Her eyelids fluttered closed, and if she hadn't been relying solely on her hearing she might have missed the rhythmic thud of boots echoing in the direction they'd just come from.

Molly hadn't noticed the sound, too busy focusing on the warmth glowing from her fingertips, but Talie stared along the tunnel as a figure came into view. Her insides chilled and Molly's heat spiked in reply, but Molly had her back to the man now blocking the tunnel. His broad shoulders were levelled and his dark hair seemed to shimmer pale momentarily, but his face was a picture of cruel amusement.

Marcus, head of the Menagerie, looked directly into her eyes and smiled wider. He definitely wasn't someone they wanted to deal with, but before Talie could get Molly's attention, Marcus dashed a hand through the air and stepped back.

A loud rumble shook the tunnel around them, violent

enough to send crumbles of rock dashing down. They tumbled into the tunnel and obscured Marcus from view, blocking the path back completely.

Talie winced as Molly hauled her into a small cut in the side wall. She clung to Molly's arms and manoeuvred them so that she had her back to the tunnel and Molly was protected. Bits of rock shaken loose thudded against her back and shoulders, but she gritted her teeth and held firm against the onslaught until the shaking settled.

"Are you hurt?" Molly asked.

Talie flinched as the warm hands that had been cradling her neck moved to her cheeks.

"I think I'm okay."

"Amazing, those weren't tiny pebbles. Are you sure? I did my best to cover your head."

Talie blinked and reached up to grab Molly by the wrists. The glow of Molly's gift still illuminated the tiny gap between them, but Talie hissed in dismay at the dark lines on Molly's skin.

"You're all cut up."

Molly shrugged. "Better my hands than your head. Come on, we need to grab the bags and move."

Talie didn't dare drop her hold on Molly's arms as they shuffled back to the tunnel. She glanced over her shoulder and gulped down a squeak of pain, but Molly was already grabbing both bags with a grimace.

"No way out," she said. "That's cruddy luck."

Talie shook her head gently. "Not luck. That Marcus was there, waved his hand about and it started crumbling."

Molly stared at the rock now covering the way they'd

come from, then shook her head.

"Not exactly a surprise. He isn't dim enough to trust Celeste fully, even if he pretends otherwise." She lifted the orb and swiped back to the map. "We go on then."

Talie sighed. "Not got much choice now, have we?"

CHAPTER TWENTY THREE

MOLLY

The tunnels twisted and turned endlessly, and Molly worried the orb would either give out its connection or eventually run out of map. They stopped to rest regularly, but even the odd stint of sleep they took in turns didn't ease the ache behind her eyes.

She lifted her head as they reached a wider length of tunnel. It opened out large enough to become a cavern, the low roof giving way to one a vast height higher. A subtle echo of whispering filled the air and the scent of something unpleasantly living wrapped around her.

Talie lifted the lantern she was carrying so that the light illuminated higher and Molly flinched.

"Orbs, no," she muttered.

The shadows of several winged creatures hung from the roof, and more were pressed into furrows and dips in the rocky walls.

"They're bats," Talie said. "Not birds."

"Still beasts that can dive at your head and probably scratch your eyes out. Maybe there's another way."

"Is that what the map says, there's more than one way out?"

Molly hesitated. She hadn't admitted that she was searching for a way further in yet, because finding Celeste and ending the madness had to be her first priority.

I shouldn't have dragged her into it, but she wouldn't have let me go or let me leave her behind.

She murmured a non-committal noise and fiddled with the orb to swing the map image back and forth in front of them.

"Show me."

Molly froze. Too tired to work out a suitable excuse or word-tangle the question aside, she looked Talie's way. Talie lifted her eyebrows to reinstate the question, but her lips were pressed thin and Molly's heart sank.

She knows.

"I... there are many routes through the labyrinth," she tried.

Talie snorted. "Which says absolutely nothing at all. We're going after Celeste, aren't we."

That time it wasn't a question, and Molly bit her lip as she nodded.

"Or we would be," she said. "We'll need to find another route though."

She shuddered as she risked another wary glance upward to find a few pairs of eyes now glowing white in the lantern light.

"Is there another route then?" Talie asked.

"You're not going to blame me?"

Talie sighed. "No, I figured out you'd probably do

something like this. You're too noble for your own good. Is this way a dead-end then?"

Still amazed Talie was taking the whole thing suspiciously well, Molly lifted a hand and angled her finger upward.

"We can't risk going underneath them."

Talie tilted her head back. "If we walk quickly and quietly, they probably won't even notice. I'm guessing they're probably Shrieker bats so they won't bother if we don't make too much noise."

"Library?"

Talie nodded. "Of course."

She lifted the lantern again to highlight the path ahead and show the entrance to another tunnel in the opposite wall. Molly eyed several dark patches that loomed on either side, gaping holes in the floor that probably led to more nested bats.

"Is there another path?" Talie prompted.

Molly scanned the map one more time, but it didn't look like it. The focus of the map was a large circle swirling inward on itself at the centre, and she guessed this was the well of power everyone was after. If not, it was as good a place as any to hunt around.

Common sense was long gone and the idea of trying to sneak through the Menagerie with it. She wouldn't be able to free the fairies on her own, not enough to get them all safely out of the Menagerie, let alone out of the citadel somehow. Without Milo, they couldn't do much of anything except venture inward.

End Celeste and all of this ends with her.

She had no hope that Marcus and Phoenix would play nice afterwards, or that either of them would guarantee her freedom to leave the citadel again, but she had to hope Milo would find a way back in somehow.

"There's no other route, not that wouldn't take us back around on ourselves for ages," she admitted. "But... I can't."

She flinched as Talie's hand brushed hers and snared tight.

"Do you trust me?" she asked.

Molly stared into the amused hazel eyes ringed with amber that were shadowed and smoky in the lantern light.

"Yes, but-"

Talie smiled. "Maybe I should blindfold you."

Molly heard the echo of old memories. "You'd have to keep steering me."

"Or I could let you bump into things."

"I'm loud when I bump into things."

She forgot about the bats and Celeste and the entire wretched labyrinth around them as Talie's face came mesmerizingly close to hers.

"Maybe I should cover your mouth as well then." Her voice turned husky. "Want to kiss a commoner, Princess?"

Molly nodded. Bolder than she could ever remember being in the light of a cold day, when Talie hesitated, Molly covered the tiny gap between them and pressed her lips to Talie's.

A hand landed on her hip to pull her closer, and she had the maddening realisation that it was technically her first proper kiss.

Then there were no thoughts at all, only the warmth in her bones and the sensation of Talie's embrace matching hers, and the subtle scent of earth after rain in the air.

She tensed as Talie broke away, but Talie only uttered an inaudible grumble and pressed closer for more. Molly smiled into the kiss, too weary to feel anything other than comfort but revelling in it all the same. When Talie lifted her head, Molly almost complained.

"I meant it about the blindfolding," Talie said. "If the bats bother you, you can close your eyes and I'll lead you across."

Ah yeah, the bats and the potentially life-threatening endless hole we're stuck wandering around in.

She bit her lip, her cheeks still hot.

"There are massive pits in the ground, it's not safe. What if they're hiding super-bats or something?"

Talie shrugged. "Never heard of a super-bat before. Come on. We can get into the next tunnel and have something to eat."

Molly took one last look around, then dimmed the image of the map on the orb and held out her hand. The moment Talie had a secure grip on it, she took a deep breath and closed her eyes.

"Just walk normally. Nothing to worry about, and if I need to steer or stop us, I will."

Molly clenched her free hand into a fist around the orb and took the first few steps. Her mind whirled with wild visions of the bats waking and a sweat broke over her skin, her sunshine gift grumbling awake in reply.

"Okay, maybe turn the glow off," Talie muttered.

Molly grimaced. "I'm trying. It's reacting to the fear."

"Okay the snake is out," Talie muttered.

"Excuse me?!"

"The snake, the big snake with fangs is… shadowing us."

Molly risked cracking one eyelid open and her jaw dropped. Her sunshine illuminated the path ahead of them but a circle of shadow contained it, the edges flickering reminiscent of scales that pulsated like a snake slithering in a coil.

"Thank you, Betty."

As she opened both eyes, she made the mistake of looking up. Hundreds of glassy grey eyes blinked and winked down at them from above and the fear slammed back into her chest.

Talie squeezed her hand. "There's nothing wrong. I've got you. Close your eyes again."

She had no idea how Talie could sound so sure, or so soothing at the same time, but it wasn't working. She closed her eyes again as the scent of freshness after rainfall filled the air and Talie's palm grew soggy.

"Look."

Molly shook her head, her eyes welded shut as she continued shuffling forwards.

"Okay, just squint forward a tiny bit."

"I can't."

"You'll miss it otherwise."

Molly risked cracking the tiniest hint of a gap between her eyelids and saw a hint of colour.

"We're making rainbows," she whispered.

"Yeah, and we're halfway across now, safe as anything."

Molly followed Talie guiding her sideways around one of the holes. Through the arcing rainbows around them, she saw glinting eyes in the wall they were heading towards and couldn't decide if she should close her eyes again or make the most of the beautiful swathes of colour that swirled and danced with them.

"Orbs there's one right by the tunnel," she hissed.

Talie marched faster. "If it causes trouble, I'll deal with it."

"You can't hurt it."

"Seriously?!"

Molly closed her eyes tight with a soft wail. "Well, we're in their home. Just because I can't stand them doesn't mean they deserve to be hurt for existing."

"Friend to all aren't you, Princess. Fine, I won't hurt it. Defence only if necessary. We're not quite there yet. Got your eyes closed?"

"Yeah."

"Okay. Want me to tell you when we're going past it?"

"I don't know. Maybe. But then it's probably best-"

"Okay, we're through."

Molly stumbled to a halt and her eyes snapped open. She twisted around to see the mouth of the tunnel a short distance behind and no sign of bats around them. No sign of Betty either, but Kainen had warned her that might happen.

"Phew." She sagged against the wall. "Thank you."

Talie shrugged. "It only stared at us. They won't harm

you if you don't bother them. Think of them like Aurora."

Molly sighed. She missed Aurora already, and Sammy and the camp. She missed her workshop too, and the familiar citadel lanes she'd grown up in.

Talie swung her bag off her back and rummaged inside but Molly stayed with hers on her back.

What happens when this is all over? Do I go back home to the workshop? Will I be expected to be a princess now? Can I somehow choose a bit of both?

Talie glanced up at her with a frown.

"You took last watch. We eat, then you get some sleep. Can you work out how far wherever we're headed is?"

Molly pressed her back against the wall, her bag providing a suitable cushion in between. She let her head drop back as well with a sigh and pushed the orb into her pocket.

"It's a rough estimate but I'd say maybe a day? The orb is keeping time but I'm not sure how accurate that would be, or even how the orb waves are still working."

"Orbs are made to feed off the power of Faerie and the nether, so they'll work anywhere. That's why it takes so much effort for the citadel to block communications going in and out. If production and programming was left unchecked, orbs would be dangerous things in the wrong hands."

Molly managed a small smile. "Library?"

"Yep. Here." Talie handed her a messily made pretend meat-pocket. "Eat then sleep. Just promise me, if we find her or this power well, we talk it through first. I'm not going to stop you doing what you need to but we do it safely, got it?"

Molly nodded and smiled to herself as she ate. She couldn't have asked for anyone better to be stuck in an enemy lair with. The moment she finished her food, Talie pointed to the ground.

"Sleep while you can. I'll take the next once we're a bit further in."

Molly slid to sit on the ground with her bag rucked up behind her like a pillow. She wouldn't lie down, but a quick rest would probably be wise.

"You're bossy, Sunshine, you know that?" she grumbled.

Talie nodded. "I care. Now sleep, Princess."

Molly closed her eyes and focused on untensing her muscles bit by bit. She would need strength and everything else to face Celeste, and she still had to figure out a way to get to her without Talie being in the firing line. Talie would whisper Milo's name every now and then when she thought Molly wasn't paying attention, and the moment he arrived Talie would probably body-slam her to the ground to get her back to the camp.

When we do find the well of power, how do we even deal with it? What if Celeste is all powerful?

She frowned as a soft voice danced into the hazy half-dream state her mind was in, like the echo of a deeper, more primal consciousness she couldn't quite remember having.

What if the power could be harnessed? Used for good things? To build and prosper.

The dream swayed and she grasped for her fading sense

of self, flailing bodiless through the dark.

We can't take risks with power. Celeste is proof of that. It's dangerous.

She tried to wake herself, something she'd been able to do before, but the dream clung on.

What if power only needs goodness to wield it?

CHAPTER TWENTY FOUR

TALIE

Talie watched Molly sleep, uneasy about the occasional twitch and the constant frown on her face. She'd seen Molly asleep before and often she had the faintest glow of sunshine that slipped free over her skin, or her face was at least relaxed. She wondered if Molly was having bad dreams, but she didn't want to admit that she'd been having strange and wild ideas that didn't feel like her own for hours on and off, an unfamiliar tangle of thoughts in her mind like a tiny pebble in her shoe.

No sense worrying her. She has Celeste to deal with yet.

"Milo," she whispered, just in case.

She'd given up hope of him hearing her, but she'd try it all the same. Molly would be furious if he turned up and they ended up back at camp, but if the chance to keep her safe came, Talie was taking it.

Molly flinched violently and her face contorted. Her head slid sideways from its perch against her bag and Talie crouched beside her.

"Molly, wake up."

Molly muttered something inaudible and Talie took her chilly hand. No hint of the sunny warmth lingered in her skin.

"MOLLY."

Molly's eyes snapped open and she gasped a ragged breath. Talie shifted so she wasn't blocking the light from the lantern and Molly could see her clearly.

"Bad dream?"

Molly nodded. "Weird one. Doesn't matter. Your turn."

Talie sank onto the ground beside her, mimicking the position with her bag as a cushion behind her shoulders. Hers was lumpier than Molly's with less of the soft blankets and clothing changes Marthe had packed, but she didn't mention it.

Not ready to close her eyes until she knew Molly's mood had settled, she grabbed a chunk of hair and started weaving the dark strands around her fingers.

"Do you want to talk about the dream?" she asked.

"No, I can barely even remember it now, but the feelings linger sometimes."

Talie nodded. "I know. You hungry?"

"Not really. I can wait." She nodded to Talie's fingers weaving fast through her hair. "You do that so quickly."

"It's a silly game I started as a kid, braiding wishes into my hair. It was just some old superstition I read about in the library. Then I had to learn to do Sammy's hair so I ended up fiddling with mine as well. It calms me sometimes."

"I wouldn't have thought you got nerves often."

Talie smiled. "I'm still Fae, Princess. As breakable as

any other."

"Be careful then."

"Once this is over I'm planning on never leaving the citadel ever again. Perhaps never even leaving the room. Sammy might drive me mad though."

Molly laughed softly. "Maybe consider leaving your room occasionally then. Once this is done, the citadel should be freed. It could even open to other realms and trades. Think of all the amazing things that could be achieved with that."

Talie ignored the sudden stab of anxiety clawing its way through her chest. She'd not given herself time to consider that Molly might not want to come back to the citadel now that she'd had a taste of freedom, but she chose her next words carefully.

"Sure, but more importantly as soon as we get this done we can go home. Sammy will be safe and you can go back to your workshop, and everything will be fairer, as it should be."

Molly sighed. "Have you never wanted to see what's outside the citadel?"

Talie thought about the maps she'd snuck into the citadel library to pour over so many times, parts of mad plans to get Sammy out somewhere safe, where she could have a future. She hadn't thought of the wider realms of Faerie as anything other than a necessity before, but now the idea of it frightened her. In the citadel she had Sammy and the gym, Phoenix and her routine. It wasn't much but it was all she knew.

Better to fix and build than risk stepping outside into

something that might not be any better at all.

"The citadel is home, or it will be once it's safe again." She shrugged. "No doubt you'll dip in and out to see your fancy friends."

"I guess so. Not going to happen either way if we don't get through this though, so get your sleep while you can."

Talie smiled. "And you call me bossy."

She closed her eyes and settled her head back against the wall. Sleep wasn't anywhere near but she had to rest to be able to protect Molly properly. Celeste was no doubt already drawing from the well of power, or heavily influenced by it at least, but Talie had plans of her own to keep Molly safe.

Safe so she'll skip away the moment she can. She frowned. *She always said she wanted to see more of Faerie, but if she gets the chance to do it safely through the courts then she'll soon realise that there's no better place than home.*

She fidgeted against the ache in her back from so much walking and the fighting before. The urge to open her eyes and check Molly was still beside her swelled, but her body wouldn't cooperate.

You could give her what she wants. The thoughts that didn't feel like her own bubbled forward. *Why deny the power when it could change the fortunes of so many?*

She jolted as something landed on her arm.

"Did you hear that?"

Molly's voice roused her and she snapped her eyes open. Molly dropped the tight grip on her arm and scrambled to her feet.

"Hear what?" Talie asked warily.

She stood up with a groan, not able to hear anything.

She's destined for great things, the insidious voice whispered. *Why not take the power needed to stand beside her and do great things too?*

Molly glanced up and down the tunnel, then pointed ahead.

"We need to go that way, now."

Talie frowned. "Wait, what did you hear?"

"We're close." Molly dodged around her and set off. "We can end this and stop all the fairy testing, the inequality of the nobles against the higher levels, all of it. It'll all end when she does."

Talie stared in horror as Molly strode off, then realised she should be running after her.

"We said we'd talk about this," she insisted.

"I know but we have to stop her. My compulsion won't work on her, but my sunshine gift will."

"What are you planning to do with it though, roast her alive?!"

A shadow of doubt flickered across Molly's face but she didn't slow down.

"Hopefully it won't come to that." She stopped dead and Talie crashed into the back of her. "You should go for help. Here, take the orb and use it to get yourself to the Menagerie. Glamour to get out and see if you can call Milo from there, or the library. If not, go to the workshop and see if Kainen's checking there instead. Let them know-"

The words babbled out until her voice broke and Talie's heart twisted tight, even as anger rose white hot and burning. Her rain gift leapt to her skin and hot water beads appeared but she didn't bother to swipe them away.

"I'm not leaving you. Sammy's safe, Kainen promised he'd look after her, and I'm not going to let you go in there and face this alone."

Molly hesitated, her gaze twitching around. Talie saved her the trouble of arguing by gripping her hand tight and dragging them nose to nose.

"I'm. Not. Leaving. You."

"You should," Molly said, her tone riddled with doubt. "I can go in with stealth before she even sees me. I can call her out and use my charm to get her to come back to the citadel. Then we can find a way to call Milo and he can get all three of us."

Talie sighed. "It won't work, but either way we're doing this together or not at all."

"I can't let you."

"You can't stop me. Going to burn me unconscious, Princess? If not, then let's go."

Molly huffed loudly and started walking again.

"Stubborn arse."

Talie nodded. "Right back at you. Is that light ahead or is the lantern skewing?"

"Turn it off and we'll use sunshine for now. We need both hands free."

Talie extinguished the lantern and stowed it in her bag, but the light glowing ahead wasn't anything to do with Molly's gift either. It was bright white and pulsating, like some kind of lure to draw people in.

"Lead on then," she muttered.

Despite the mention of keeping their hands free, she didn't say a word as Molly's shaking fingers slipped through hers and their joint protection warding domed tight around them.

CHAPTER TWENTY FIVE

MOLLY

They crept toward the light at the end of the tunnel and the exit it seemed to be coming from. Molly slowed as they reached the end where the tunnel opened out into another cavern, but this one wasn't full of bats. Worse, it was thrumming with the skin-tingling tinge of power that set her hairs on end, the pulsating light leaping up from a deep chasm in the ground to plume through the air as raging white smoke.

At the edge of the chasm with the power rolling over her body, Celeste stood with her arms lifted at her sides and her head tipped back as if in prayer.

Molly slipped into stealth on instinct, but she couldn't do anything about Talie fully visible beside her.

"Maybe if you glamour into Marcus we can brazen this out," she whispered.

Talie rolled her eyes. "Not unless you're planning to push her in while I distract her. What is your plan?"

"It's rude to whisper in company, girls."

Molly flinched as Celeste's voice boomed around the cavern, magnified with sizzling strength.

"She can hear through our warding," she muttered.

Talie nodded. "Looks like it. You don't have a plan, do you?"

Celeste turned to face them before Molly could answer. Aside from the stiffness in her limbs, still held out to her sides, Celeste's eyes were pure white and crackling with raw energy. Talie tugged on Molly's hand as she took a step back.

"Orbs, that's not good," Talie said. "I read something once about channelling pure power and the eyes going white. We can't do this."

Celeste's laughter wrapped around them like a suffocating blanket, and Molly clung to her warding with all her might as the realisation that she was foolish for even considering it thundered through her head.

Power, the strange voice she'd been dreaming of whispered. *Accept it. Own it. Let it fill you and you can best her.*

Molly shook her head as Talie drew Taz's sword and held it in front of them. Their warding twanged as the metal got closer to the boundary, but Molly was too busy fighting off the seductive thought of borrowing just a little power to get Celeste to back down.

You wouldn't have to keep it. Just siphon enough, then let it flow back out.

"Don't listen to it," Talie muttered through gritted teeth. "The voice, it's not going to lead us anywhere safe."

Celeste laughed as she advanced, but whether she was

aware of their warding or simply toying with them, Molly couldn't risk finding out.

"There is nothing to fear from power," Celeste said. "Those born to harness it have nothing to worry about. Wielding it is as easy as breathing for those whose bloodlines have honed their skill and power over the ages. Bloodlines like ours."

Molly pushed through the unending anger rising up and focused on Talie instead. If she was going to get her out safely and back to Sammy, she had to think fast.

"So, this is the fabled well of power then?" she asked.

Celeste nodded and spared a quick glance over her shoulder.

"The edge of it, yes. Nobody knows how far down it goes but I will find out someday."

"When you drain it dry?" Talie scoffed.

Celeste smiled. "I doubt even I would be powerful enough to manage that. It feels almost limitless, but never say never. Several of the books on the citadel's history mentioned it being built on a nether well, but not many know that it was made specifically to be a prison for some ancient powers."

Molly winced, asking the question even though she already knew the answer.

"And you've freed them?"

"Not quite. The Omens have specific conditions, much like gift extraction does. That's working remarkably well by the way, thanks to your eventual input."

Molly didn't even bother to fight the flare of heat as sunlight burst over her skin, but she focused on keeping the burn of it free of Talie, who had to let go of her hand to shield her eyes.

Keep her talking. Burn just enough to make her unconscious.

It was all she had and she went for it.

"Our morals definitely don't align on that, but I won't blame myself for being manipulated and coerced. Was this always the plan then? You and the Oak Queen plotting to get to this well of power?"

She inched sideways away from Talie, determined to split their joint warding so she could distract Celeste's mind elsewhere.

"Ah, yes." Celeste sighed. "I'm still used to thinking of her as mother, but I suppose for conversation's sake we can call her your grandmother."

"Oak Queen's more than fine actually."

"As you wish. She knew Elvira was aiming for the Apocalyptians long ago, so she sent me to take over the citadel. It took a few years for me to ingratiate myself into the Menagerie, but they were little more than thieves and petty bureaucrats then."

Molly wanted to ask more personal questions but held her tongue.

"I took a short break to find a suitable noble with a satisfactory enough bloodline and have you of course, although he's dead now. I couldn't risk him asking questions or expecting favours further down the line. But the Menagerie was finally taking shape and I managed to get access to the core."

Celeste turned away to face the enormous pit and Molly

moved away from Talie in one swift leap that severed their warding. Talie reached for her but she firmed it around herself.

"Go back," she mouthed. *"Get help."*

Talie stood with the sword in hand and shook her head. As Molly shuffled forward, Talie followed as close as their protections would allow her to get.

"From there it was easy enough to track the labyrinth," Celeste continued. "Now the nether is demanding the power back, such is the ebb and flow of it, and I've been holding it off until the artificers found the way to extract gifts. I can feed the nether and myself from them, and also duplicate them to ensure we always have enough. With a library of gifts at my disposal, nobody will be able to stop me."

"You're mad if you think people will stand for that," Talie spat.

Celeste faced them again with a wide smile.

"You're naïve if you think anyone can stop me."

Her arms lifted and the white smoke billowed toward her. Molly darted sideways to shove Talie back into the tunnel, not sure if it was more dangerous to concentrate Celeste's attacks in a small space or a better chance for them to run.

The smoke spasmed toward them as Molly threw herself in front of Talie, who had made herself wilfully immovable behind her warding. Celeste whipped a hand up at the last minute, but Molly winced as the slightest hint of the raw energy scraped the edge of her protection.

"You think a few minor gifts and a sword is going to

protect her from me?" Celeste laughed. "Dearest, I can have several more suitable girls brought in from any noble family you choose. She doesn't even have a known family."

Molly sucked in a breath full of rage and pushed it down. Right down, until she was able to blow out a gust of lethal calm. She dropped her head to one side and let every essence of Fae wickedness she possessed enter the game.

"Why'd you pick her then?" she demanded. "Why gift her to take my memories and keep an eye on me?"

Celeste shrugged. "I needed someone untraceable. There are others, although I've lost track of most now. Marcus has the relevant files somewhere."

Careless. Molly managed not to clench her fists. *She's arrogant on power.*

"Okay, well I'm good either way. If you stop threatening her, I might be more likely to consider leniency."

Pretty words that meant nothing at all, because her leniency or lack of it wasn't something she was worried about gambling with. She might be more lenient with her opinion, but only by the tiniest hint in an ocean of hatred, so tiny it would barely signify either way.

"Oh, child. I don't need your leniency. It would be tiresome to wait for another daughter to grow though, and I don't much fancy bothering with sons. Your grandmother is delighted with you already and it'd be a shame to disappoint her."

"And I already know the Holly Queen well." Molly put a hint of petulance in her tone. "And I'm favoured by one of the courts as well."

Celeste's expression soured. "The Holly Queen will be dealt with. She is not a good influence for you. I can only assume you're talking about Kainen Hemlock's court and, while he has his uses by many accounts, I wouldn't spend much time with him either."

"Nobody's asking you to, thankfully. Don't want you making me look bad to people that actually matter."

She took strength from Talie's hysterical snort of laughter behind her, and how close behind her it sounded. Talie was planning to be with her to the end, and it would be the end because neither of them were equipped with endless power.

You could be. Take it for yourself. Beat her.

She shook the persistent voice away, but it gave her an idea.

"Is that how you hear it?" she asked. "The well? Is it a voice in your head telling you to take advantage of it?"

Celeste smiled. "Ah, yes. It came to me in dreams. Those are the Omens, and they want us to help them be free."

"Yeah, not happening. They were probably imprisoned for a good reason."

"By Fae less adept at controlling them maybe. There are three, and what would you know, there are three of us here."

"I don't like the sound of that," Talie muttered.

Molly didn't either, but short of running she couldn't think of a single thing to do other than keep Celeste talking.

"Let me guess," she said. "The Omens will need to take

possession of our bodies, like the Apocalyptians tried to do in the War of Queens?”

Celeste frowned. “I’ve heard scant tales of that. What do you mean, take possession?”

Molly’s heart beat faster, a glowing sliver of opportunity opening in front of her. She leapt for it.

“You mean you don’t know? Your mother didn’t share that with you? To think the Holly Queen is sharing more with me than the Oak Queen is telling you. Fancy that. The Apocalyptians were essences of vices and virtues, and they used her as a host body. That’s how they got rid of Elvida.”

“Elvira,” Celeste snapped. “She… well, even so, that’s immaterial.”

“Very not immaterial if the Omens are planning to escape the same way. Haven’t you even done any research yet? Were you literally going to skip into the well and let them run riot with your body? Weird.”

She put every essence of irritating attitude into her voice, channelling her inner Sammy as best she could. Celeste’s eyes shuttered momentarily, and she shook before storming toward them.

“Enough. I’m powerful enough to manage any entity now. I’ve been clever enough to imbue myself with power. You think a tinpot sword and some sunshine can stop me?”

Molly glanced at said sword as realisation slammed through her.

She doesn’t know what Kingkiller is made of. She’s been holed up here with only rumour and tall tales from nobles and the Oak Queen. Maybe she doesn’t even know what metirin iron is, or what it can do.

She hadn't mentioned Talie's mind-wipe gift either. Molly saw the plan unfold like a giant orb-cast and she whipped around to face Talie with her back to Celeste.

"Sword, warding, mind-wipe," she mouthed.

Talie frowned for several seconds before she made the connection and nodded. Molly stepped toward her and almost breathed a sigh of relief when their wardings merged together again.

Talie took her hand and held on tight as Celeste stalked closer. Molly shuffled a few steps back to draw her to the tunnel.

"What do you think you can do?" Celeste demanded. "None of your fancy friends are here for you now, are they?"

Molly shrugged. "They're friends, not resources. If they were able to get in here then they'd be here to help. Them at least I can rely on."

She called her sunshine gift forward, mindful to keep it away from the hand Talie was holding. Drops of moisture beaded over the inside of their warding and Talie grimaced with concentration as it started to rain. The warding began to glow, colours forming a kaleidoscope of prisms that danced around them.

Talie lunged forward. The sword sliced a hole in their warding and punctured a hole in Celeste's too. Even as the surprise registered on Celeste's face, the rain faded.

How do we get her to talk?

Molly hadn't considered it as Celeste darted backwards and Talie ran after her. Molly kept pace with them, but she was concentrating on keeping herself free as Celeste fought back with her hands and erratic stabs of white smoke.

Take the power, the Omens echoed. *Just a little bit, enough to strengthen your gifts.*

Molly bit her lip. Kainen had once told her compulsions had to be exact, but considering Celeste was immune, she might benefit from trying the opposite approach.

"Why are you doing this?" she screamed as loud as she could. "The power won't be helping you in the long run."

Celeste grimaced as Talie dodged and ducked every attack sent her way, stabbing and hacking and whirling with lethal grace as she attacked back.

"Harnessing this power is vital!" Celeste shouted.

"Why?"

Celeste stumbled and took a second to right herself as Talie attacked again. Molly had to hope Talie knew to be wiping whatever Celeste said, to confuse her and cause so much mental chaos that she offered enough for them to take her need for power away.

As Talie and Celeste fought on the edge of the well, she had to hope it would work.

CHAPTER TWENTY SIX

TALIE

Talie let all her rage flow down her arms and into the sword as she sliced at Celeste's warding. Not even so much for herself, but for all the torment Molly had suffered at the hands of the awful woman in front of her.

She could barely hear the incessant echo of the voices from the well through her fury, but she knew they would leap on a chance to snare her the moment the fight was done. She had to be strong, had to get Celeste down whatever way she could then grab Molly and drag her out of the labyrinth completely.

Wielding her mind-wipe gift was easier than the fighting, and she let that flow too as Molly shouted questions. The subtle tug of Celeste's answers unspooling from her memory wrapped around her, but she couldn't let herself feel guilty about it. That could come later.

"Why even try coming down here in the first place?" Molly demanded.

Talie didn't dare look away from Celeste for a second, and her rain gift soaked over her skin at the pure effort she was expending, but she kept going.

"Because I needed…" Celeste faltered. "Because, I came to the citadel. I built the Menagerie. I... there was a child."

Talie flinched back. *I can't take the memory of Molly from her completely, can I?*

Celeste stumbled and rubbed a hand at her head as she looked around at the cavern, and at the roiling smoke.

"We're supposed to go down," she muttered. "We're supposed to take the power."

She wouldn't remember why, Talie had seen to that, but the memory of Molly as a baby would still be in there.

"No, we need to leave," Talie insisted.

She turned to face Molly, to nod that it had been done. They could even try getting Celeste out with them if they absolutely had to, and off to Taz and the rest of their family.

"NO!" Molly shouted.

Talie twisted in time to see the top of Celeste's messy blonde head in front of her, and to feel the unflinching weight of arms anchoring around her waist. She tilted her weight back away from the well but Celeste had already yanked against her. They flailed forward together, Celeste's grip never faltering. Talie dropped the sword and reached her hands out as they tumbled down and the edge of the well shot past. Through the growing haze of white smoke she lunged for the lip of rock and dug her hands over it.

Molly's frantic face appeared above her, but Talie winced as Celeste started kicking her legs to haul them further down. Talie clung on, her gaze fixed on Molly's face.

One last look.

"Let me go," she insisted. "I'll take her with me and the consequences. Get out with stealth, get to Phoenix and keep calling for Milo."

She clung on, wanting one last look, but Molly shot out a hand and clamped it around her wrist.

"Don't you dare," Molly seethed as tears rolled down her cheeks. "You said you wouldn't leave me, remember?"

Talie managed a pained smile. "Luck's run out, Princess."

Molly grabbed both her arms to pull at the same time Celeste gave one almighty kick against the edge of the well. A sickening crack suggested she might have even broken a knee or an ankle to do it, but the momentum hauled Talie downward and her hands slithered away from the edge.

She twisted her hands to free Molly's grip on her wrists, but as she tumbled into the well, Molly clung on.

Stupid, irritating idiot!

She couldn't get her mouth open to shout as the white smoke engulfed them and air rushed against her face, but she twisted again so she could grab Molly's arms and work her way along them to get her closer. She couldn't see a thing with her sight obscured by the endless brightness either, but the sensation of Celeste anchored around her waist disappeared.

Relief swirled moments before she felt the crushing weightlessness of Molly gone too.

A sharp thud vibrated through her bones, the absence of Molly a chill creeping over her like a shroud.

Talie fought the darkness folding in around her but it dragged her ever further down, until the last thought in her head was of Molly and rainbows.

CHAPTER TWENTY SEVEN

MOLLY

Molly flailed through the brightness, her eyes scrunched as she searched for Talie. The sensation of tumbling jolted and she winced as she hit something solid chest first. Scrambling to get her hands and knees steady underneath her, she lifted her head.

The fierceness of the smoke had dimmed to a curling haze that glimmered gently and illuminated another vast cavern. Imposing black stones towered over her, five of them all lined with veins of dark purple rock.

She couldn't see any sign of Talie or Celeste, but as the smoke curled tighter and solidified into the vague shape of a Fae, she pulled a shaky protection warding around her and faced it.

"Welcome, little princess."

The voice echoed around the cavern, a whisper like the rushing of the wind through the lanes of the citadel. It was the same one that had called inside her mind in the tunnels above.

She shook her head and pulled her Fae connection

closer around her.

"I might not be able to fight you, but I'm not going to succumb either," she announced.

The spectral smoke figure roiled taller and the vision of a perfectly aligned face formed to match her own. Only one, whereas the Omens suggested there were more, and she had to hope that Talie and Celeste were okay facing theirs.

"Power is nothing more than energy," the voice insisted. "For good and ill. It feeds those strong enough to wield it and breaks those too weak to control themselves."

Molly remembered what Milo had said, something about the Omens swelling against the constraints of Faerie, harnessed ancients needing to grow and using Fae to do it.

"You're not just power though, are you?" she countered. "There's intent there. You're ancient but you have your own will and your own desires."

She glanced around at the cavern, but she couldn't see any sign of stairs or even rough enough dips for hand-holds in the sheet-like rock.

The whispering echo of laughter scraped off the cavern walls.

"We have been known by many names. The Omens is perhaps the latest, but we are the manifestations of the nether's limitless energy. We feed Fae gifts and give power to balance Faerie's order."

Fae couldn't lie but she had no guarantee that these ancient entities couldn't either. She backed up as the figure stalked after her.

"Where are the others that fell with me?" she asked.

There wasn't a single length of rock she could use to climb up, even if she did manage to somehow contain the Omen she faced.

"They are facing their own fate. Accept the power we offer, use it, and you may yet be able to save them."

Thoughts of Talie flew through her head. She couldn't be sure whether Talie would succumb or not, but Celeste most definitely would, and easily.

"Take the power," the Omen urged. "With freedom comes chaos, with eternity comes stagnation, and power brings entitlement. You can be the balance that is needed. Uncage the prison this structure has become, for all of us."

Molly bit her lip. "The citadel wouldn't be a prison if it was fairer, and Celeste has been the problem with that. Keep her here with you and let me go."

It was a pointless angle to take, because of course the Omens wanted their freedom to wreck chaos across the entire expanse of Faerie, but she needed to keep them cajoling her while she found something that might get her out.

"Take what we offer and your citadel can be rebuilt with fairness and equality for all Fae. You could be the firstborn of a firstborn to be crowned a queen of all things."

Molly grimaced. "I don't want to be queen of all things, or of anything."

The figure swelled and she clenched her eyes shut as it suffocated around her warding. She fought the sudden breathlessness it forced against her until it ebbed away again. With a pained grunt, she opened her eyes.

Does it look ever so slightly hazier?

She focused on putting all her strength into her warding as Milo's words filled her head, that ancient entities like the Omens fed off belief as much as the nether. They were conduits that desired to grow strong.

The more I resist, the weaker it gets.

With memories of Talie calling her stubborn anchored in her mind, she squared her shoulders and lifted herself as tall as her aching limbs would allow.

"No thanks. Power's overrated. You picked the wrong girl, so if you just tell me how I get out of here."

She braced all her will behind her warding as the figure shattered and the smoke rolled bright and angry. It plumed around the circle of stones with the echo of a roar thundering through it, and Molly winced as it shattered her warding to pieces.

The breathlessness tore at her chest as the smoke enveloped her in dizzying light, and the smash of her knees and hands against the ground was lost in the chaos.

Submit. The voice demanded inside her mind.

"No."

She slumped onto her side and clutched at her head, trying desperately to cover her mouth and nose with her hands to conserve what little air she might have left. The brightness burned against her eyelids.

SUBMIT.

She shook her head as panic tore through her and her sunshine gift flared. She could feel it burning pointlessly against the smoke, but it gave her strength.

I'll never take power I haven't earned.

The roar intensified and she moved one of her hands

from her face to her ear, pushing the other hard against the ground to ward off the sound. Her consciousness danced on the edge of oblivion, but the Omens needed three to free them according to what Celeste had said, and she wouldn't give them the satisfaction of using her.

Do your worst. My answer is no.

CHAPTER TWENTY EIGHT

TALIE

Talie's consciousness surfaced and she lifted her head with jumbled thoughts and a jarring, jagged pain slicing across her back. Rolling onto her side, she stared at the towering circle of enormous black stones around her, five of them.

More Fae circles.

She eased to her feet, her vision swaying until she caught sight of a body lying still nearby. A gasp hitched in her throat as she stumbled across the rocky ground.

Molly's face was far too pale.

Talie barely even winced as she dropped to her knees beside her. She grabbed Molly's wrist, but the skin had a blueish tinge and she couldn't feel a single thud of life.

"No, no no no," she muttered.

She swiped her hands over Molly's face until Molly's head lolled to one side. A subtle kernel of heat pulsed between her eyebrows and Talie stroked it with a forefinger. She had no healing abilities, no skill with anything other than fighting, but she clung to Molly all the same.

Her tears rolled down her cheeks and just as quickly evaporated along with the moisture leaking from her skin, a soft rain falling down over them. She sheltered Molly's body with her own, unable to turn off her gift as the agony clawed at her chest until it choked her.

"Take the power we offer, and you can bring her back."

The voice that had taunted inside her head on their journey through the labyrinth echoed out through the stone circle like the rushing of water over rocks. She turned her head and sucked in a pained breath as she stared at the wavering white smoke behind her. It had taken on a crude imitation of her, but if it weren't for the stupid smoke bewitching Celeste, Molly would never have even needed to come find it.

She refused to answer and focused on Molly instead.

"Please wake up," she begged. "Please."

"Take the power, and you can both have an eternity to live the lives that Fae have denied you," the voice urged.

"Please Molly, *please*. If you're in there still, give me a sign. Anything."

She sensed the smoke at her back but ignored it.

"She never had a chance to choose," the voice taunted. "and you have lived a life thinking the next day might be your last, going short so others wouldn't. What harm is a little power to rebalance the unfairness?"

It made sense. Talie glanced around the cavern beyond the stone circle, but even she with no climbing experience could tell there was no way out by hand.

"Take the power. Harness it. You could get her out safe and alive and vibrant."

Talie hesitated. Molly looked peaceful, the small dip between her eyebrows that was often there non-existent. Talie hadn't seen her like that often.

Would it be a cruelty or a kindness to take the tiniest bit of power, and the downfall that inevitably comes with it, to save her?

Molly had a royal family out there waiting to give her every safety and luxury, and Talie knew Molly would happily absorb Sammy into that.

It's barely even a sacrifice, as long as I don't go back up with them.

"How would it work?" she asked. "What do I do and what power will you give me to save her with?"

The smoke surrounded them, glimmering and bright. Talie thought she saw flashes of images inside it, barely there, but she returned her focus to Molly.

"Ask and it shall be yours. What gifts would you ask of the nether, of the ancients who would wield them alongside you?"

Warning bells pealed in her head.

Molly would tell me not to. Talie smoothed her fingertips over that warm spot on Molly's forehead again. *She'd say it's all tricks to get us to free them.*

But Celeste had harnessed the power before, enough to build the entire Menagerie for herself. Talie had no idea what she should even ask for. The Omens had offered gifts, but she couldn't think of a gift that would somehow wake Molly back up and get her out of the pit, let alone back into the citadel or out to the royals.

"What happens after? I ask you for gifts, and you give

them. What then? What do you take in return?"

The smoke billowed thick with distorted faces in the mass as it circled them. A truth within the trickery, she realised.

"We rise with you. As you grow strong with power, we grow with you."

"And a little bit would never be enough." She scoffed sadly and lowered her head to kiss Molly's forehead. "Goodbye, Princess."

She dredged all her effort into a warding around them and stood.

"Thanks, but no thanks. I'll take my chances."

The smoke spasmed angrily, fighting to form itself into a Fae shape again, but through its fitful movement she could see someone else facing the smoke from the other side, like a garish orb-vision being played out.

"Take the power," the voice urged.

Celeste edged closer. "How do I take the power? What will it give me?"

"Take what we offer. For those strong enough to harness it, there will be untapped power. You could hold dominion over all, a queen with the only crown and power to level the entire land of Faerie. Rebuild it as you choose."

Celeste's eyes lit up and she raised a hand to smooth it through the smoke. She didn't seem to see Talie or Molly on the other side.

"That would be a blessing," she said. "No half-breed brothers to take my claim or mothers to keep me humbled."

"You cannot be this dim!" Talie shouted.

The smoke whirled thicker between them and became

solid wall when she tried to slam her hands through it, wild thoughts of choking Celeste unconscious for her stupidity and arrogance filling her head. The smoke shivered around her forefinger as the knucklepick scored a tiny hole in the mass of it, but it wasn't enough to carve through.

"You could stop her," the voice insisted. "You could claim the power for yourself, have her subdued and the other awakened. It can all be yours, if you're strong enough to take it."

Talie eyed Molly as panic pounded in her ears. The temptation roared loudly and she hovered on the edge of desperation as Celeste raised both hands aloft with a greedy smile.

"I accept your power, all of it."

CHAPTER TWENTY NINE

MOLLY

Molly rubbed a hand over her forehead to ease some of the tingling as it quickly became a stabbing headache. The faint echo of a voice filled her ears and she opened her eyes to a carousel of glimmering white and solid darkness.

Memories slammed back in and she rolled onto her front, her hands sliding and her muscles straining as she fought to get to her feet.

Talie stood with her hands outstretched, her warding somehow holding against the onslaught of thickening white smoke that battered against it. Molly took a ragged breath and found her connection, weak but still there inside her. She focused on protection and lending hers to Talie's as she inched forward with her head still pounding.

Talie flinched when Molly reached her side, her eyes wide.

"Keep going," Molly said, then coughed loudly. "I didn't give in. I didn't accept anything from them."

Talie's cheeks beaded with tears and Molly lifted a shaking hand to wipe them away.

"Are you real?" Talie asked.

Molly nodded. "Hurts enough to be real. There's no way out but we'll face this together, okay?"

She reached up and grabbed Talie's hand, their wardings knitting seamlessly together.

"Don't let go," Talie insisted.

"Never."

They faced the smoke, thin enough for them to see it channelling toward Celeste, who stood with her hands outstretched and a look of determined euphoria on her face.

"I will wield this power to bring about change, and fortune," Celeste called out. "I shall offer you those girls over there as a sacrifice to the nether."

The white smoke billowed around her face and her eyes turned white, until the smoke dissipated into her body with a final, satisfied puff.

Celeste faced them in the centre of the stones and Molly fought the urge to back away. Where her hair had been dishevelled, Celeste's honey-blonde waves were immediately silken once more, her posture regal, but her eyes were still pure white.

"How useful you both were," she crowed. "I knew you'd both have soft enough hearts to refuse the power the Omens offered, and now I can siphon it all for myself."

Molly winced. She hadn't considered that, but beside her Talie bristled.

"I removed your memories of all of it, so how can you know that?" she demanded.

"I do not need memories, foolish girl. There are some gaps but the Omens are whispering everything I need of their wisdom. You tried to trick me into sharing power."

"No we didn't!" Molly shouted.

Celeste advanced, the pulsating waves of power clouding around her like an aura.

"Lies. I will not be lenient."

"How can we lie?" Talie scoffed. "We're Fae. The Omens aren't though. They can lie at will and you're drinking it up like a good little puppet."

Talie ducked as a whip of fire lashed toward them and Molly almost didn't duck in time at all.

"She means it," she muttered.

Talie nodded. "What can we do?"

"What have we got?"

The bags were far above and beyond reach, and Molly knew she had nothing useful in her pockets. Talie held up her hand, the knucklepick deceptively dull-looking between her other rings of black and silver.

"Short of this or you throwing your hairpins, we're screwed, Princess," Talie muttered. "The pick must be special iron like the sword because the smoke was cut by it briefly, but I doubt it's enough to save us."

Molly lifted a hand to her hair and tugged the pins free. As she glanced around at the stones, Milo's words echoed back to her like a blessing.

"Circles of three contain all that be, with Fae iron from point to point."

Talie frowned. "Nice, but can you maybe think of something helpful?"

"I am. I don't know if this will work, or be strong enough, but it's all I've got. Keep the pick on but point it down so the iron is on the outside, okay?"

Talie nodded slowly as Molly dropped one of the pins in front of them and angled one behind.

"And that does what?" Talie asked.

"I'm really hoping it's like a special warding, but we'll see."

She faced Celeste. "What's the plan then? Weren't you going to sacrifice us or something?"

Celeste laughed and sent a wave of smoke from the palm of her hand rushing toward them. Molly tensed as the smoke domed around their warding, but instead of suffocating it and beating against them, it raged against something unseen.

"How…" Talie grimaced. "Never mind how. This buys us a bit of time but unless we can find a way out, we're at a stalemate."

A loud screech tore the air before Molly could admit she hadn't thought any further than the iron warding. She lifted her head upward in time to see something hurtling down, and launched sideways to shove Talie out of the way as Kingkiller clattered to the ground at their feet. The smoke raged on around their protected bubble, but Molly recognised the second screech that echoed quieter with growing distance.

"Aurora," Talie guessed. "She's here, which means the others might be too."

Molly nodded. "We can only hope. Taz mentioned something about the hilt, didn't he?"

Talie ducked to pick Kingkiller up, sparing a wary look for the iron pins that rattled angrily as she moved with the pick on her finger.

"The iron won't hold forever." She ran her fingers over the hilt of the sword with a frown, then handed it to Molly. "You're good with crafty stuff. Figure out of there are hinges or something."

There weren't any hinges, but Molly lost a few seconds to the innate need to marvel at the flawless craft on the hilt, including the strangely curved metal guard. Unlike the grip and the pommel, the guard was the same dark iron as the blade, with a hair-thin line either side.

"Um, Molly…"

"Just a second." She followed the line and pushed against one side of the guard, gasping in amazement when one side of it popped out, leaving half the guard remaining on their side of the blade. "It's like a boomerang, look!"

She lifted her head as one of the hairpins ricocheted under the pressure with a loud pop and flew out of the circle. Molly panicked and shoved the blade of Kingkiller in its place, swiping at the smoke trying to fire in with the boomerang.

"Okay, now what?" Talie asked, even as she inched the edge of the circle with her to Molly's side.

Molly bit her lip. She had an idea, a mad one, but it was all they had. She ignored Talie's shiver as she leaned close to whisper.

"I'll distract her. Use the boomerang to cut her wards and the smoke, then your gift to take everything you need to take."

Talie gripped her hand tight and squeezed.

"Okay, Princess. If we don't make it out of this alive,

it's been an honour and an absolute pain in the behind."

Molly couldn't help the smile that flickered across her face.

"You too, Sunshine. Pick your moment carefully."

She shook Talie's hand free and walked as close to the edge of the circle as she dared. Celeste's possessed face was twisted in a sneer, but Molly recognised the vein of anger than ran beneath the mask.

"See, that's the problem with Fae like you," she began. "You're so arrogant that you've forgotten the old ways, and the tricks that effort teaches you. You're lazy with borrowed power and nothing else."

"And what do you know, child? A simple iron warding won't hold out the power for long, and then you're nothing more than fodder for it to feed on. At least I've honed my strength to wield it."

"Maybe, but for how long?" Molly paced a few steps sideways, emboldened when Celeste turned to keep her in sight. "You're the puppet of ancient entities until they find a better conduit, and they're only ancient conduits for the nether itself. What are you even planning to do with it anyway? A bigger office?"

Celeste laughed, the sound rolling across the cavern with chilling clarity.

"I will overthrow both queens. I might have lost some memory of recent years, but I have been planning this most of my life. Why do you think I went to all the trouble to induce labour and ensure you were born on midsummer?"

"What does that achieve?" Molly asked.

She held her breath as Talie threw the boomerang right

through their iron warding. It sliced through the smoke which parted and swarmed angrily on the fringes of the path it took, but Celeste didn't seem to notice it whirl dangerously close to the top of her head.

Is Talie trying to kill her?!

She hadn't told her not to and thoughts of Ru filled her head at the worst possible time.

Celeste sighed. "You will become the Oak Queen. I already plan to birth another child to become the Holly Queen, and then I shall rule over both of you. It will be a new style of family tradition, or rather an ancient one long since forgotten."

Molly fought the wave of acid rising up her throat.

"You're not…"

Celeste smiled. "It took some convincing, and there is a risk the child will be more powerful for being conceived while I was channelling the Omens, but you shouldn't worry about being upstaged, dearest. We will be a family."

"You remember who I am?" Molly asked.

"I don't have to. You look like mother, and Mayflower a little too. You look like our family, and the Omens recognise you as my daughter. When the time comes, we will rule the whole of Faerie together as it always should have been. Mother grew weak from the moment Oakthorn was born. I should have strangled him in his cradle like the others suggested."

Molly shuddered as Talie gave her a weary grimace and a nod that she was ready. She took a deep breath and focused beyond the pain of unfortunate bloodlines to the gritty truth of what had to be done.

"So tell me how it happened then?"

She put all of her charm and compulsion behind the demand, even though Celeste was immune to the compulsion, she had to hope the charm would be enough.

"It took a lot of trickery," Celeste said, her tone turning purposefully pensive. "When Oakthorn was born, mother named him the crown prince. She had some deal with Faerie and there he was. I hated him. Well, not him specifically, but what he represented. I started a few rumours about the citadel, and soon enough mother sent me here to keep track of the place."

Molly saw the boomerang swing overhead again but focused on holding Celeste's gaze.

"The rest is tiresome," Celeste said. "A multitude of deals that I'd rather not dwell on with Fae I'm glad are now dead for the price of it. They saw me as expendable and I made myself invaluable from it."

"Then you what, had me, built the Menagerie and found this well of power to tap from?"

Celeste hesitated. "You know, it's all rather a blur. I can feel the power though. It slides through my veins. I always heard rumours about the citadel and its power, and now here… we are here."

She frowned and glanced around at the cavern, then at Molly and the smoke.

"What about me?" Molly asked. "You know who I am?"

Celeste nodded, her expression clearing as she smiled wide.

"Yes, of course. You're the sacrifice, for the… for…

Stop going on at me, I'm doing it!"

She snapped the last words at her shoulder, and Molly guessed the Omens were still whispering in her mind. The smoke flared angrily over and over but it was getting thinner beyond the iron warding.

She doesn't remember me. Talie's taken all memory of her from me.

She took a deep breath. "So, you don't have any children?"

"Children? Orbs no, why would I want children? Nasty things, always crying, like Oakthorn wailing in his crib."

Molly nodded at Talie. "Enough."

Talie sagged and tucked the boomerang under her arm so she could wipe her face with her free hand. Her other arm was vibrating wildly as the pick held its part of the warding, but with the smoke still simmering, they couldn't risk letting it go.

"What do we do?" Talie asked. "Feed her to the well?"

"Of course not. She's… there's a…." She doubled over as the realisation swarmed in. "Oh orbs, she's pregnant."

I'll have a half brother or sister, with no clue who our fathers are. Our mother is mad, more so now Talie's messed with her mind.

"Okay, no feeding her to the well. So what next?"

Molly wiped both hands over her face and glanced at Celeste, then at the pillars around them. The Omens were contained in their prison or they would have broken free by now. The smoke still roiled in Celeste's eyes but there was no telling whether it would follow her out or be ripped from her body by whatever great protection kept them in.

"We need to find a way out first," Molly murmured.

"There's no way out though, unless there's some magic way of translocating?"

Molly shook her head. She just needed time to think but her mind wouldn't stop sputtering and spinning, and the iron warding around them was rattling more violently with each moment that passed.

"Translocation?" Celeste piped up. "I am *excellent* at translocation. We have a mad aunt who gave it to all of us. Insisted on it."

Molly lifted her thudding head. "Could you translocate us out of here?"

"Molly…" Talie shook her head in warning.

Celeste nodded. "Oh, most definitely. There's an art to it, you see. You need to be able to know where you're translocating to of course, but she liked me the best, so she gave me the ability to take others with me."

Molly bit her lip. They would need to time it so carefully. She still had to face the risk that the Omens might be torn upward with them, or Celeste might be ripped to shreds as part of them, but she had no other choice. Thoughts of the baby simmering inside Celeste's belly thundered through her mind but she only had the one option.

Talie had scratches all over her skin and her eyes were lidded and hazy. She didn't look like she'd survive another fight either.

"Okay." She faced Celeste. "Can you remember the Menagerie entrance hall?"

Celeste smiled, a frightening stretch of her lips beneath

the swirling white eyes.

"The one I had built with the stained glass windows? Oh, I do remember that, yes. Would you like me to show you?"

Molly nodded. "We really would. We'll hold your hand on each side."

"Are you sure?" Talie asked.

Molly inched alongside her and leaned close as the smoke raged even harder, as though it knew exactly what they were planning.

"We need to time this," Molly said. "I'll grab Kingkiller and on the count of three we grab a hand each."

"What if it's a trap, or she takes us somewhere completely random?"

"With her memories gone, it'd probably be the queen's court, and we're safer there than here at least."

Talie nodded. "If you say so. On three or after three?"

"Always on three."

Molly grabbed Kingkiller and hissed at the sheer effort it took to lift with the warding vibrating through it. The white smoke surged toward the gap beneath it.

"One, two, three!"

She darted forward on unsteady legs toward Celeste with Talie beside her, both of them struggling against the pull of the warding trying to keep itself secure. Talie twisted into a spin to sever the connection and Molly stumbled sideways at the sudden impact of it releasing.

She grabbed Celeste's right hand as Talie grabbed the left one.

"Go!" she shouted. "To the entrance hall!"

Celeste huffed. "Yes, alright, alright, don't rush me. Who are you anyway?"

Molly's panicked growl of frustration got lost in a sudden swathe of grey and purple that dulled the brightness raging toward them. She reached out on instinct, searching across the space in front of Celeste for Talie's hand. Her fingers snared over Talie's wrist and slithered away as the swirl of nether dissipated and left them staring at absolute chaos.

Molly choked over a sob as several people in the Menagerie entrance hall stared at them in horror, but it was the ear-shattering yell that tipped her over the edge as Taz stormed toward them.

"WHERE THE BLOODY HELL HAVE YOU BEEN?!"

CHAPTER THIRTY

TALIE

Talie had no idea what a hell was or why it was bloody, but guessed it was some kind of curse used outside the citadel. It was enough to make Molly cry though, and she shoved Celeste back so she could wrap her arms around Molly's shaking shoulders. One glance at Celeste's eyes, hazy from lack of memory but turquoise instead of pure white, and Talie let the breath tumble out of her mouth in one swift huff.

"Is she okay?" Taz demanded.

Talie frowned. "Which one?"

"Molly obviously."

Physically and mentally yes." Talie shrugged. "Emotionally, probably not."

"I'm fine," Molly sobbed.

"We need to get you back to camp immediately, Demi's furious." Taz wiped a hand over his face with a groan. "Milo came back and then couldn't get in to you, Reyan went in to find you and couldn't get through the shadows."

Talie nodded and let her hand rest on Molly's head as

she caught Taz's gaze and looked pointedly at Celeste.

"We've lost some memories," she explained. "We found what we needed, but there's a lot still needs sorting."

Taz frowned. "How long until the memories come back?"

"They won't. They're not her memories anymore. To her, none of it ever happened. Whether the mentality is part of her, as in would she do the same a second time, nobody knows."

He nodded and pulled a reluctant face before a Fae-like smile flickered over his face and he laid a firm hand on Celeste's shoulder.

"Oakthorn, I take it?" Celeste sniffed. "You've grown. I don't think I've seen you since you were a squalling child. You look like mother."

Taz pulled a face. "Ouch. Come with me, Celestial. You're going to have tea with Belladonna. You always liked Belladonna."

"Did I? I thought she hated me."

"Er... yeah, close enough. MILO."

Milo appeared, his eyes wide and ringed with shadows.

"Take Celestial to Demi first, straight to the tent. Make sure she has others with her, then come back for us."

Milo nodded and reached out a tentative hand to replace Taz's on Celeste's shoulder.

They vanished and Talie let her shoulders sag under Molly's weight as Taz inched closer.

"Anything broken?" he asked.

Molly lifted her tear-streaked face. "No, but she's pregnant."

"Who is?"

"Celeste."

He blinked. "As in…"

"As in with a baby," Talie offered drily. "No clue who the father is, we didn't get that far, but the danger is still down there."

She flinched as the Menagerie doors banged open and Phoenix strode in with his silver hair flapping loose about his shoulders.

"I've been hearing rumblings," he announced.

Talie nodded. "Enemy number one has been downed, or passed off, or whatever. There's still the other one floating about though."

She thought back to Marcus appearing in that tunnel, and the smirk as he crashed the exit to smithereens behind them.

And the subtle flicker of silver hair in the firelight.

Talie held Molly closer as Taz turned to face Phoenix with them behind him. His flaming wings flared ever so slightly open, but Phoenix was wearing his 'friend to all' smile that meant he was definitely up to something.

"The girls are coming back with me," Taz announced, his tone possessive with warning.

Phoenix nodded. "I'm sure that's their choice. What happened?"

"Celeste has been causing trouble. She won't be doing that anymore."

"She's still alive?"

Taz nodded. "It's a family matter now, but she's no longer in the citadel and she won't be coming back."

Phoenix wiped a hand over his forehead to sweep back his hair.

"I see."

"You'll need to discuss any citadel matters with whoever succeeds her. I believe Marcus is the name we've been hearing, but not sure who that is."

Phoenix chuckled and Talie's skin beaded with sweat as he swept his pale hair back over his shoulder. It was only a suspicion but she couldn't shake it, which meant so many tangled truths that she couldn't even begin to work out which one to tug at first.

I'll have to take Molly back and make sure she's okay. Sammy's going to be impossible for days.

"You leave Marcus to me," Phoenix insisted.

Milo appeared before Taz could answer and Talie tensed as Phoenix looked her way.

"If Celeste is no longer causing trouble then it'll be safe for you to come home," he said.

Talie hesitated. *Is it? Am I being over-cautious?*

She couldn't say a word, couldn't decide, until Molly's arms tightened ever so slightly around her waist. It was only a moment, then Molly let go and stepped away, but it was enough.

"I'll think about it. I need to go back to get Sammy if nothing else."

Milo took Molly's arm gently and held out a hand for Talie's. As she obliged, she caught Phoenix's unrelenting gaze once more. Then the nether swallowed them up and dumped them in the middle of the royal tent. There was no sign of Celeste, but the queen was perched on her desk alone and looked in no mood for dramatics.

"I'm one step away from sedating your sister," she announced, her tone utterly weary. "Tell your side quickly for now."

Talie detailed the basics when Molly didn't speak straight away, only pausing when Kainen and Taz came in until Demi nodded at her to continue.

"We thought you might have to fight with iron," Kainen said. "It seems to be the failsafe option of Faerie, but considering we're lucky to have the amount we do, we need to start being more careful what wars we fall into."

Demi snorted. "That almost sounded wise, be careful."

"That wounds me, your majesty."

"Wouldn't be the first time." She stuck her tongue out at him. "Celeste is in containment so we can consider her crossed off the list as an immediate threat. You should both go and get some rest for now."

"If Marthe gives you anything pink to drink, it's a sedative, fair warning," Taz added.

Talie definitely wouldn't be drinking anything pink, although the thought of slipping Sammy a little sip until she was in a better mood to tell the tale entered her head. She grabbed Molly's hand and led her out of the tent.

"I wonder how many days we've lost," Molly mumbled.

Talie frowned at the faraway weakness in her voice. It was probably the shock of everything but it worried her more than Molly shouting or crying. She didn't know how to deal with frailty.

"Orbs, get inside both of you!"

For once, Talie couldn't contain her relief at the sight of Marthe hurrying toward them. She swept them through the snow into Molly's tent, and Talie didn't argue as she was rushed through a change of clothing and a forced face-wash. She wasn't exactly hungry but she knew she should be, so she ate while Marthe made Molly wash and change too.

Molly shook her head when Marthe insisted she eat, and she refused the bright pink drink Marthe summoned in a tiny glass with a click of her fingers. It didn't look like a lot would be needed and Talie kept the one Marthe gave her in her hand.

"You want me to make you a meat pocket?" Talie asked.

Molly hesitated, and that was all the prompting Marthe needed.

"Meat pocket, of course. Leave that to me. It took a fair bit of trading with the kitchen tent for them to tell me what the secret was, but luckily for me I have deep pockets."

She left the tent and Talie picked up the cup full of pink liquid while pointing to the bed.

"She'll be back soon. If you need space, pretend to be asleep."

"She won't fall for it," Molly said, even as she clambered beneath the covers. "I don't… We were in the darkness for days, and…"

Talie sighed as she crawled onto the bed and settled herself next to Molly.

"I have to face Sammy yet, so I could do with pretending to be asleep as well."

"What about the rest of the citadel, Phoenix and Marcus, and the Omens are still down there-"

Talie laid a gentle fingertip over Molly's lips, hoping with everything she had Molly didn't notice the slick of pink on her skin.

"We figure all that out tomorrow after rest and food. Sleep, Princess. I'll watch over you until then."

As Molly's eyelids fluttered shut, Talie settled against the pillows with a sigh.

Rest and food, and Sammy. Then I need to figure out what to do next.

CHAPTER THIRTY ONE

MOLLY

Molly sat in bed with Talie passed out beside her. Early morning light filtered in through the fluttering entry flap of the tent, but she didn't want to risk going outside yet and getting snared by anyone else.

Marthe would no doubt be bustling in soon anyway and her stomach growled in anticipation. She glanced at the table but there was no sign of fresh food prepared, so she stayed in the comfort of the covers.

Celeste was only my mother by blood. She's still alive and no doubt the queens will decide what to do with the baby. Neither will risk any harm to them either.

The question she couldn't quite face circled around and around. The citadel wouldn't be safe, not now Phoenix and Marcus knew about the well, and she had to guess Marcus knew about it. She couldn't risk leaving the fairies to their fate either because she didn't trust either man to be benevolent enough where potential power was concerned.

Talie snuffled in her sleep and Molly sighed softly.

She had no guarantee that Talie would see the benefit

of staying outside the citadel, not even for Sammy's future, but she couldn't imagine holing herself up inside it again either. She still had her debt to the Menagerie to consider but if she gave up the workshop, that might make Marcus let her go.

He won't let me go. Phoenix might not be allowed to control me now, but Marcus will try it.

She wrapped her arms tighter around her legs and pulled her knees to her chest.

Marcus, who'd had a soft spot for Ru, was still her 'employer'.

A soft rustle outside the tent caught her ears and she sat up as Marthe bustled in.

"Oh, you're awake." Marthe eyed Talie in the same bed with a thinning of her lips. "There's been a summons from the citadel and the queen has asked for you. Wash and dress, then I'll bring breakfast."

She disappeared and Molly shook Talie's arm. Talie shot upright, her gaze wild for several seconds until she saw Molly and recognised where they were.

"Everything okay?" she asked.

Molly shrugged. "There's been a summons from the citadel. We're to get dressed and go with them."

"Phoenix?"

"Or Marcus." Molly groaned out of bed. "They probably want promises the royals won't interfere."

Talie opened her mouth but another voice echoed out before she could speak.

"You've kept me away more than long enough!"

Sammy charged into the tent and looked them both

over. A flicker of a smirk crossed her face as she saw them both in the same bed, then she kicked off her boots and took a flying leap onto the end of it with them.

"You've been summoned," she announced.

"So we've heard." Talie rolled her eyes as Sammy hugged her, but Molly smiled to see it.

First step, dress and eat. Perhaps I can get them to promise to free the fairies at this summons.

She dressed while Talie gave Sammy a light version of what happened and shuddered as the memories see-sawed back and forth. By the time Marthe reappeared with breakfast, Talie had changed too and Sammy had moved onto a rant about some young noble who was causing trouble around the camp.

Molly grabbed a pastry in one hand and an oia berry ring in the other, ready to go. As Talie scoffed down two pastries, Sammy settled down at the table at a much more leisurely pace.

"You two go do whatever it is you do," she said. "I'm fine here."

Molly ate her pastry as she crunched through the snow toward the queen's tent with Talie beside her. She wondered if she should check they were both on the same page, or at least reading the same book, but Talie didn't seem inclined to say anything either, her gaze stuck on the snow in front of her feet.

"There you are, good." Demi beckoned them in. "Milo's going to take you two in, and hang around in case you need him. Let Taz do the talking."

Kainen grinned. "Is that wise?"

He ducked the sandwich that flew at his head a second later.

Molly held out her arm for Milo to take and a moment later the nether whisked around them and dissipated to reveal the gym. She smiled to see it, a momentary gap in all the worry, and a quick glance at Talie showed her shoulders lowering with relief.

This is her home. Molly bit her lip. *What if she doesn't want to leave and I don't know if I can stay?*

"Thank you for coming." Phoenix strode toward them, all easy smiles. "You'll have to excuse the state of it, but we've been using this as a hub of sorts."

He held out a hand to a table and chairs near one of the training rings and led them across to it.

Molly took a seat beside Taz and watched with faint amusement as Talie and Milo had a brief silent squabble over who sat beside her. Talie won.

"There is a lot to discuss," Taz began.

Phoenix nodded. "There is. Thank you for coming. This is going to take some explaining, but I ask that you indulge me."

Taz stiffened and Molly felt the subtle increase in heat as his wings opened slightly. Her sunshine gift woke in answer but she calmed it before it glowed over her skin.

Seeing he had their attention, Phoenix leaned back in his chair. For a moment, nothing. Then his hair shortened and darkened, his angular face becoming broader as his eyes turned blue.

Molly stared Phoenix, except it wasn't Phoenix staring back at them.

It was Marcus.

Her jaw dropped but she couldn't see any sign of surprise on Talie's face, only grim acknowledgement.

How long has she known?

Foreboding stole through her mind and her chest clenched tight.

"Explain," Taz demanded.

Molly didn't need to look to sense the sheer defensive wall of a warding he'd cast around them.

Phoenix nodded. "Of course. When I was young, my father gave me the gift of truth. It wasn't always kind, but when Celeste arrived and started championing her own endeavours, I knew who she was. The citadel wasn't flourishing as fast as we needed and Fae were starving, so I integrated myself into her social circle, then her inner one. It wasn't difficult to play to her vanity either."

Molly's mind whirled and the headache from the previous day threatened to stage a comeback. She rubbed her hand over her forehead but other than Talie's subtle twitch of a glance in her direction, nobody spoke as Phoenix continued.

"So, on we went for years. The Menagerie grew off the back of Celeste's collaborations with the guilds and nobles. I have no shame in admitting she knew far more about manipulating supplies and support out of people than I did at the time. I also knew she had a child somewhere, but not who it was. I kept watch on several of the Menagerie's interests, and at first I thought it was Ru. She seemed extremely fond of him, sending him on missions, recommending him to me."

Molly tensed as he glanced her way with a frown.

"She must have taken particular precautions to shield you, even from me. When I met you, I thought it was your proximity to him that had my gift alert. I suppose I expected someone more hardened, more like her, which was my mistake. You need to understand that I will do anything to keep the citadel and those within it safe. The citadel must function in order to keep its place among the other towers, and there are more than covenants keeping everyone in line."

Phoenix shook his head and released the Marcus glamour with it.

Unless the Phoenix persona is the glamour and Marcus is who he really is. Either way they're the same person.

Taz hadn't moved a muscle beyond the odd flicker of the fire on his wings, but he tilted his head to the side.

"It's easy to word-tangle and even easier to hide truths. Are you the one dealing with the other towers, or did Celeste handle that?"

Phoenix sighed. "Celeste left that to me in the latter years. This tower was her test subject with the guild."

Molly almost opened her mouth but Taz beat her to it.

"Test subject for what exactly?"

"That's citadel business, I'd gather."

"Not when there are fairies still stuck in the confines of it that were stolen from other realms of Faerie. That makes it the queen's business, which makes it mine."

The air crackled with unspent energy and Phoenix eyed Taz for a long, silent moment.

"The fairies will be freed, you may have my word on

that."

"When?"

Phoenix glanced over his shoulder as Nia came through from the back rooms. She apologised softly but paused long enough to give Molly and Talie a relieved smile before retreating again.

"That's essentially what I've asked you here to discuss. All displaced citadel Fae can come back immediately. We need all the help we can get to rebuild."

"And any that don't want to return?" Taz asked.

Phoenix hesitated. "That's their choice I suppose, but this is their home."

His gaze swept over them, and Molly averted hers to the table instead.

I can't choose, not straight away.

"The citadel Fae will return as soon as you can send them, starting today ideally, and we will be releasing the fairies in the Menagerie's keeping-"

"In the citadel's keeping, you mean," Taz interrupted.

"Yes, we have no intention of keeping any back. Gift extraction was Celeste's project and not one I plan on continuing. The cost of finding coalbane alone is extortionate."

"Not to mention illegal," Milo muttered.

"I've had guards go down into Celeste's lair." Phoenix ignored him. "They're bringing the fairies to the Menagerie's entrance hall where you can collect them and see them safely home."

"How many?" Molly asked.

Phoenix smiled. "After several were mysteriously

removed from the cells last time, there are about twenty or so left. Celeste never had a chance to arrange another import."

Import, 'removed'. Molly did her best to hide a shudder. *Like they're not people at all.*

"What about what lies further beneath the citadel?" Talie asked.

Phoenix frowned. "I've ventured down a short way, but past Celeste's lair I have no idea exactly what lies down there."

Not exactly, but I bet he knows more than enough, even if Celeste never told him about it.

"Your family used to rule the citadel, didn't it?" Taz asked, his tone suddenly conversational. "I'm going to guess that's all you have in mind going forward."

"Yes, the citadel and no more. If those outside it leave us be, all will be well. Once we've registered all the returnees and finished with those on the various levels, we'll be able to tell if there are any spies. Celeste allowed far too many slip-ups on all sides."

It was an obvious warning, but Molly clenched her hands under the table at the mention of registration.

"When you say registered…"

Phoenix shrugged. "A necessary formality and nothing more. Once we re-raise the wards, it won't matter so much for most, as only the nobles go in and out anyway, and we may find a way to manage that better too."

"So, the wards were your idea all along," she clarified.

"They are. Wards are tricky things and there are sacrifices of a sort." He caught her expression and smiled.

"No sacrificing people, don't worry."

"Did you at least try to sneak any of them out? The fairies?"

She shifted as Taz laid a soft hand on her wrist, to silence her probably, but she stared Phoenix out to wordlessly demand an answer.

"I don't expect you to understand, Molly. From what Celeste told me, and from what I've seen, a heart as soft as yours won't see the delicate balancing act that's sometimes needed for governing."

"People need to stop saying that!"

Taz squeezed her wrist briefly then leaned forward to brace his arms on the table.

"You're planning to restore the previous allowances for nobles then?"

Phoenix nodded. "For now. They won't be getting a free ride anymore, but we do provide some wares on the higher levels that they make good use of."

Molly thought back to the disastrous dinner she'd had with some of the nobles while in Celeste's keeping, and she couldn't help wondering if Fae were being traded in other ways besides for testing on.

"The nobles tend to handle many trades," Taz said. "It's a tradition that we've never bothered to unravel, but as we don't have any direct royal trades with any of the citadel towers, perhaps there's time to change that."

Phoenix caught the surprise on his face well and masked it with a cheerful smile.

"We can definitely have the discussion. There will be minimal communication channels for the foreseeable future like we've had previously for our protection, but if you want to name a noble of yours to trade on your behalf, we can add them to the list."

Molly glanced around as panic rose in her gut. She would be asked to choose sooner rather than later, to either wall herself back up in the citadel with Phoenix finding ways to draw her into his machinations, or outside with the entire realm of Faerie at her feet. The queens would no doubt see her as a potential ally no matter where she ended up, or in the Oak Queen's case probably a shiny new toy to replace the previous model.

"You need to give everyone a chance to decide for themselves," she said.

Phoenix frowned. "I am. They don't have to return if they don't want to, but I imagine most will."

"No, all of them. Even the ones inside the citadel who never left. To not even give them the choice to leave or secure other options before you raise the wards again is cruel."

"I get what you're saying, Molly, but we can't afford to lose anyone with the citadel in such a state, and people are already scared for the future. Keeping everyone in safely until things settle is a sacrifice we have to make, and people don't miss what they've never known."

She stood, irritation flaring deeply enough to bring her sunshine gift to the surface.

"I did. I can't be the only one looking out and wanting freedom enough to choose for myself."

Phoenix only shook his head sadly at her and turned his attention back to Taz.

I could compel him to change his mind.

Temptation itched at her to do it, to make him listen as Taz stood and Milo hurried to wait between her and Talie.

Talie, who was still in her seat.

"We'll send word when the fairies are ready to be collected," Phoenix promised. "And in the meantime, if you could see the citadel Fae back to the base levels where we can welcome them back, that will be our agreement."

Taz nodded. "Any who want to return will be returned safely. I'll expect word on the fairies in the next day."

When he held his hand out to her, Molly took it without argument. She looked to Talie who sat staring rigidly at the table.

"Our deal about Molly still stands," Taz added. "If she chooses to return to the citadel, she's absolutely off-limits."

He's thinking Kainen can get to me through the shadows, or maybe Milo can get in via the nobles and his realm-skipping abilities.

It wasn't the comforting thought she expected it to be, because Phoenix had already made her decision for her.

"That promise still stands whatever she chooses, but the citadel has been her home all her life," Phoenix said.

"I am here you know," Molly muttered. "But being walled in here without any way out isn't giving me a choice."

"Think about it though. The wards won't go up until all the returning Fae have been accounted for and processed, so that gives you a few days to decide if you want to come home."

"What would we be coming back to?" Talie asked quietly. "We've earned our place in the citadel now ten times over, and I want more for Sammy than that one room."

Molly sucked in a breath as the realisation dug sharply in.

Phoenix nodded. "Of course. As Phoenix I have certain limitations, but as Marcus, I can ensure you're all taken care of."

Until we cause problems. She couldn't see him as Phoenix anymore even though he'd taken that persona back visually. *He's still the Marcus that orders assassins about. He's the reason Ru died a killer.*

"The resistance do need their chance to govern for what they fought for," Talie said. "It's what we've been wanting, right?"

Molly couldn't bear to look at her, the jagged edge digging ever deeper as the unfortunate truth separated them.

She can't bear to leave, and I can't bear to stay.

"Come back to the camp and decide," Taz suggested. "You need to pick up Sammy if nothing else, and if you decide to come back then you can help the others returning."

Phoenix nodded. "That's a great idea. You've beyond proven yourself, Talie, and you're going to be instrumental in building the citadel back to how it should be."

"Because of my gift?"

"You're strong and have a good heart, but more importantly a sensible head. You both have, and the citadel needs all the good minds it can get. I might have to ask you to renounce your heritage openly, Molly, if you do choose to come home. Then again it could come in handy for getting the nobles with deep pockets back to get things jump-started."

Surprised Taz wasn't saying a word, Molly realised he was still holding her hand firmly.

He's letting me decide, which is all I've been asking everyone for.

"Can I have a word, Talie?" Phoenix asked.

Talie hesitated, but when nobody said a word she got up and followed him across the hall.

Molly squinted to try and read their lips but couldn't make anything out. Phoenix looked serious, but Talie had her arms folded and was muttering. When they returned to the table a few minutes later, Talie held out an arm to Milo without a word.

"I need to see what Sammy wants to do first," she announced.

Phoenix smiled. "Of course. Take some time, talk it over. I'll send word tomorrow morning with an update about the fairies."

Molly fought the urge to tear down and go pulling them out one by one. With Milo, she might even be able to manage it, but Taz had a firm grip on her and realm-skipped them away before the thought was fully lodged.

They appeared in the queen's tent a moment later and Demi lifted her head expectantly. Taz pulled a weary face, but the moment he let go of Molly's hand, she stormed out of the tent and ploughed through the snow.

She didn't have to look behind her to know Talie would be following, but she could already feel the choke forming in her throat that meant tears and a wobbly voice wouldn't be far behind. She turned to face Talie the moment they were safely out of earshot of others, right beside the water's edge where Talie had revealed herself and she'd pushed her in.

"Are you going to give her the choice?" she demanded.

Talie frowned. "I will, but the citadel is safe now so there's no need for her to leave, or you either. We just need to humour Phoenix until things settle and he'll start to relax the precautions. The nobles go in and out anyway, and he as good as said you could play go-between to keep them sweet."

Molly's chest crunched tight. "Yeah, he's planning my future already without even consulting me, how generous. Fine to shush me like a kid at the big meeting but now he wants to use me as his poster girl?"

"He thinks he's doing what's best for us, all of us. There'll be some adjustments of course, things to cope with for a while, but it's supposed to be for the best in the end."

"Funny, that's exactly what Ru said about Celeste."

Talie's jaw dropped. "That's not the same."

"It really is." Molly folded her arms over her chest. "There's a whole world of Faerie out there yet you want to wall yourself and Sammy into more of the same, I don't get it."

She turned back to face the camp, determined not to let Talie see her until she could regain control of her temper.

"Ah. Too good for us already then," Talie muttered. "Makes sense. I guess I always knew deep down."

"Knew what?"

"You and me, it was never going to work, Princess."

A cold chill stole over Molly's shoulders, trickling down into her chest, over her arms. She didn't dare turn around. Couldn't.

"The citadel is all I've ever known," Talie added. "It's home to me, and Sammy, and she'll want to go back. Phoenix is offering us more now as well."

"It's not right. The wards should stay down. Closing the citadel off will just create the same problem under a different banner. Why can't you see that?"

"It'll be different this time-"

"No." Molly clenched her fist in her pocket. "It's never different. People always repeat the same cycles. I should have never forgotten that. My mistake."

"What are you-"

"Go. I hope for your sake, and Sammy's, it's the fur-lined cage you're expecting and not a doomed one."

She held herself still, unable to turn and let Talie see the tears coursing down her face. She stared instead at Kainen a short distance away, and followed the track of his gaze which told her Talie had walked off the other way.

One foot in front of the other.

She took unsteady steps toward him and focused on fixing her expression, a mask of bland nothingness to hide the agony tearing at her insides.

For once, Kainen didn't say a word.

Not a single smart quip or awkward reassurance, even

though he kept a pace behind her all the way back to her tent, where she wasn't entirely surprised to find people waiting for her. She didn't argue as Marthe fussed around her, but she drew the line at having her hair brushed and tugged the comb free before Marthe could attack her with it.

"I've announced the return to the citadel to the people," Demi said.

Molly nodded. "They should get to go home if they want to. Do they know they'll be stuck inside again?"

"I did tell them that, but I think they prefer that to imposing on people they don't know from other realms."

Is that what I'd be doing if I don't go back too?

She caught the lightning quick eye roll Kainen sent Demi's way.

"Not that I'm saying that's what you're doing," Demi added hastily. "We're definitely happy to have you in our court."

"Or ours," Kainen offered. "Much cooler and far less crazy."

"Watch it," Taz grumbled without any real heart behind it.

"You're still a princess, Molly," Demi added gently. "We need to ensure you're safe wherever you choose."

"Unless I choose to go back to the citadel. Nobody but Phoenix can interfere there apparently."

Molly took the drink Marthe pressed on her, noting that even Taz got his after she did.

"Oh hush," Marthe huffed. "You're a princess wherever you go, even there."

Molly took a swig of *offke* and let the familiarity of it swill over her.

"I should be championing your return to the Oak Queen's court," Marthe added. "But perhaps going with your uncle to Arcanium would be better for you."

Molly choked over her drink at the same time Taz did, except she managed a discreet cough whereas he dribbled half of his over his chin.

"We are not referring to me as an uncle," he insisted. "It makes me sound ancient."

Marthe rolled her eyes. "Nonsense. Your great aunt Euphebia May Belle is younger than you, and her sister is twice her age beyond that."

"Fae royalty is weird," Molly mumbled. "Look, I might be blood, but I don't want to be a princess and get stuck at a royal court. I definitely doesn't want to be under the Oak Queen's thumb either."

Demi nodded. "I figured as much. There's always a place for you at Arcanium and yes, Kainen, I know you're offering the Illusion Court as well. I think the whole of Faerie knows by now."

"I don't have any intention of being one of your EDPs or whatever though," Molly insisted.

"FDPs, and we wouldn't expect you to be. We could get you working with Milo in the library, or wherever you feel most comfortable."

"I don't want to trade on my heritage for favours either. If I wouldn't get the job just being anyone, then I don't deserve it now."

"I respect that." Demi sighed. "But like it or not, you're

family so we'd prefer to send you to a court for your safety."

Molly wrapped her arms around her middle. She couldn't bear the thought of going back to the citadel, not now she knew there was a whole land of Faerie out there and actual family who wanted to get to know her.

Maybe May can teach me how to send Aurora with a letter. She can get herself in and find Talie. I can explain why I had to do this. Maybe she can even send a letter back.

She had no idea if Talie would even bother. Wild thoughts of Talie using her to get rid of Celeste at Phoenix's command filled her head, but it hurt too much to dwell on so she shoved it aside.

I'll let it lie for a day or two, then write a letter once I'm less worked up about it.

She flinched as the shadows twisted in the corner of the tent, but the roiling movement was dark, not bright white. Kainen strode toward them and a bodiless hand dropped something into his outstretched palm before retreating again.

"Ah," Kainen said, dramatically with a big pause. "I've been waiting for this."

When nobody answered, Molly took pity on him.

"What is it?" she asked.

He held up an orb and swiped the surface until a monochrome vision of a room loomed between them. Molly squinted and leaned closer.

"Is that…"

"A workbench, yes. We've been doing a collaboration with the Flora Court, or Reyan has. They're using extra space at our court so we've had a workshop put in recently. Now they're finished with the project or whatever it is, and the room's been abandoned. I'm going to have to find something to do with it." Another dramatic sigh, then, "maybe I should knock it down."

It was beyond obvious, and she had no idea if he'd somehow had a workshop built to entice her to their court for devious reasons yet unknown, or there really was a conveniently abandoned workshop, but it was almost enough to sway her as the shadows curled together once more.

"We also needs someone to help with Kainen's ridiculous pile of paperwork," Reyan's bodiless voice added irritably. "He keeps ignoring it, so it wouldn't be charity or anything. It'd also be a good way to learn more about how Faerie works in case you ever do decide to go back to the citadel."

It was basically a kindness, but Molly knew she wouldn't get as helpful a compromise as that again.

"Okay, Illusion Court it is," she announced, then flinched as Kainen let out a deafening noise.

"HA!" He pulled a triumphant face in Taz's direction. "I win!"

CHAPTER THIRTY TWO

TALIE

The Menagerie entrance hall was loud and full of activity. Talie stood by the base of the stairs with the sensation of being swamped and overwhelmed prickling at her skin. She'd never understood the whole 'deep breaths' thing, but it turned out that was the only thing that seemed to work at keeping the rain gift at bay.

She hadn't waited around after Molly stormed off. The first waves of citadel Fae were already packing up when she joined them, so she and Sammy followed them back to the citadel.

Sammy, to her credit, only asked once about Molly, and hadn't mentioned it since after Talie sadly shook her head.

Now a day had passed and the fairies were all clustered in the entrance hall to be collected. There were seventeen in total, and several were so cowed and shaken that they didn't seem to even recognise where they were.

Talie had insisted on sending Sammy upstairs to rest with Nia to keep her company, because Phoenix had commandeered the Menagerie and let his Marcus persona conveniently slide aside. All the citadel would know was that Celeste was the enemy that had been bested, and Marcus would no doubt be forgotten in time.

He was the hero of the hour, their leader by birthright, and Talie couldn't find it in her to be anything other than sickened by how easily he smiled and played into the part.

Molly's safe outside with her family. Sammy's safe inside with me. She wiped a hand over her face. *And I will find out what Phoenix is really planning one way or another.*

His request to talk to her the day before had given her an unfortunate temptation she couldn't say no to. She guessed he was using it to his full advantage rather than out of any actual desire to do a nice thing, but she couldn't risk letting the opportunity pass.

If Phoenix had ways to find out who Sammy's family were, Sammy deserved that much.

If Phoenix was really the one who brought that tunnel down on us to trap us in there, I'm going to find out why.

She hadn't dared let herself dwell on that thought too much since arriving back at the citadel or when they were collected in one of the carts to go back up the levels. Phoenix's gift was divining truths and she had no idea how deep that ran, whether it was through spoken word or simply knowing, but she wasn't going to let him get away with whatever he was planning.

Talie bit her lip and glanced around the entrance hall again. She didn't need to be hanging around and Phoenix had actually told her to take a day off, but she had nothing to do with a day off. She would eventually have to venture to old haunts, but seeing any of the ones she'd shared with Molly would only make her more miserable.

Phoenix had also hurried off early that morning to speak to representatives from the other four towers, and Talie wondered what the power dynamic there was. If Phoenix was in control of all, as he obviously wanted to be, then she had to tread even more carefully.

The air shivered near the doors leading out to the lane and Talie's heart lifted traitorously as Milo appeared.

Then it sank like a stone.

She'd secretly hoped all night that Molly would be with whoever came for the fairies, but Milo was alone. He said something quiet to Phoenix, then in a whirl of disappearances he whisked the fairies away two at a time until there were none left.

Phoenix lifted his head and found her hovering.

"Wanted to see the job done?" he asked.

She gulped down the uneasiness and nodded.

Keep it boring. Don't show any emotion that he can feed off or use.

"Thought Molly might be with them, but oh well."

He sighed. "It is a shame she couldn't see sense but we can press on without her. As it is, I want to give you something to thank you for your loyalty."

"Like what?"

Her insides squelched as he beckoned for her to follow him. Not a word was spoken as they climbed the stairs, each step a reminder that she was almost as trapped there as Molly had been with Celeste. The opulence of the place passed her by, and in time she'd be able to rationalise

Phoenix's role as Marcus and find out what he was really planning for the citadel, but then he led down a corridor she recognised.

She guessed which door he was going to open before he opened it, but he stood aside to wave her into Molly's old bedroom. She didn't dare say a word as her gut twisted and water beaded on her palms.

"Sammy's got a room down the hall, so you'll be close to each other," he said. "I've asked Nia to keep an eye on her and make sure she gets some training too. I thought this room would be ideal for you."

Talie turned around and stared at the familiar walls, and at the bed Molly had slept in. There would be clothes in the walk-in wardrobe that Molly had worn, or at least had a quick look at before wrinkling her nose at the opulence of them.

He knows. She resisted facing him for a few more moments, needing to compose herself first. *This is all a test to see how I'll react, and where my weaknesses and loyalties really are.*

Fury flared but she breathed in deep and locked the glimmering thought of Molly and all the hope she represented deep in her mind.

When she turned to face Phoenix, she had herself in full control.

"Well, this is better than I've had before, so thanks I guess."

Phoenix chuckled. "That's not all. You've more than earned your place in our inner circle, so I've come up with something to mark the occasion."

He lifted the sleeve of his shirt to reveal the resistance symbol, a circle with looping lines inside that mimicked the shape of the labyrinth beneath them.

Her pulse began to thud. "A tattoo? You're going to brand people?"

Inner circle, isn't that the same thing Celeste called it? And the Menagerie branded their people, like the silver cage Molly has on her wrist.

Because of course, Phoenix was aware of all of it as Marcus, possibly even behind it.

"It's a badge of honour, Talie," he said. "You don't need to have it if you don't want it, I won't force you. I'd have thought you wanted to claim your place though. Like you said, you've more than earned it."

And if I refuse he'll wonder why.

"Can I pick the design, or does it have to be that one?" she asked.

He smiled. "You can pick any design you like of course. I'm not a monster. Let me know what you decide and I can ink it on."

"Don't need time, I know what I want." She pulled up her sleeve and held her arm out. "I'm no artist to design it though."

"No problem, I'll fetch Nia. She's creative with these things. She and Sammy both seem to be artsy in that way."

Talie's skin chilled as he strode out of the room. She had no idea how he knew Sammy was creative, and she certainly wouldn't have ever mentioned that to him herself.

More potential dangers.

All she wanted to do was collapse on the bed to cry but

with the door still open she didn't dare. That could come later while everyone was asleep.

Nia came in a minute later with Phoenix, who shut the door behind them. Talie eyed the pad Nia was holding and the bag slung over Phoenix's shoulder. She'd secretly admired Molly's tattoo a few times, even despite what it represented. Now she would make one of her own.

"What am I drawing then?" Nia asked.

Talie sank onto the edge of the bed. "*Akiai* plant growing in moorgrass with the sun shining over them."

She hoped with everything she had that Phoenix wouldn't make the connection. He wasn't stupid, so he'd know she was still upset over Molly not coming back, but if she played it carefully in time she could get his mind off Molly and onto trusting her with whatever long-term plan he was following.

The room was silent except for the rapid scratch of Nia's pencil on paper, and Talie walked to the window.

"Are Celeste's wards still up?" she asked.

"No, shouldn't be. You can leave if you want to go to the gym or to get your things, but the tattoo may make you feel a bit dizzy afterwards as the ink takes root."

Talie shrugged. She would go and get her and Sammy's things eventually, but if she remembered right there were some of Molly's old clothes hidden away from when Celeste forced her into dresses.

She stared through the window to the citadel glass beyond. It would take time for them to replace the glass, but she guessed Phoenix would have the wards in place all the same. She wanted to ask about the Fae still filtering in from outside but she couldn't find the energy to say it.

One day, I'll see her again. Once I know what he's playing at, I'll find a way to get a message out to her, but I can't risk him letting those Omens out or worse, and the royals aren't allowed to interfere.

"How's this?" Nia asked.

Talie eyed the single red *Akiai* flower, the many vibrant petals tinged with pink edges on its darker red stem, and the stalks of green moor grass bent at strategic angles so that they looked like they were swaying in a soft breeze. Haloing the *Akiai* flower was a golden sun the exact shade that Molly's skin turned when her gift shone through.

Talie nodded. "It's perfect."

She tensed as Phoenix appeared beside her, but he didn't notice as he opened his bag and pulled out a long needle and a vial of murky dark liquid that shimmered different hues of purple, blue and green.

She took a deep breath and tapped the back of the wrist to show him where she wanted it. Nia gave her a sympathetic smile as she left the room, but Talie focused on the bite of the needle as Phoenix started stabbing the ink into her skin.

"Not too painful?" he asked.

"It's fine."

The sting gave her something to focus on even as queasiness churned up in her gut.

I'm doing this for her. She promised herself. *One day, we'll see each other again and there'll be no more Phoenix, no more Omens and I'll be able to walk away without any guilt holding me back.*

As Phoenix doubled over to focus on his work, Talie allowed one single tear to slip down her cheek before she forced it to evaporate into the air.

<u>CHAPTER THIRTY THREE</u>

<u>MOLLY</u>

Molly opened the door to the queen's quarters, her new home at the Illusion Court, and kicked something with her foot.

After a fractured night's sleep where she tossed and turned between waking worries and jumbled nightmares, she'd woken with no idea what time it was, because very few parts of the Illusion Court tended to have windows.

Now she was in the same clothes as the day before, and she'd opened her door only to go foot first into what looked like a huge pile of lavish gifts.

"What the…" She crouched down to grab the nearest tag. "Welcome to the Illusion Court, compliments of Lord-oh for orbs' sake!"

The door opposite hers opened and Reyan's sleepy face appeared. She eyed Molly, then the gifts, and grimaced.

"Morning. Yeah, that's a necessary evil of people knowing who you are, but news got around far quicker than we anticipated. This is them trying to bag your favour."

"Oh really. Well they can take their bags and their gifts and whatever else and shove it up their-"

"Why are we yelling?" Kainen appeared, his eyes barely even open. "No, more important, why are we yelling so early?"

"Control your courtiers," Molly snapped.

Kainen blinked, then noticed all the stuff.

"Wow. Okay, if you don't want it, I'll have it. Maybe not the fur shrug thing, and I'm guessing I wouldn't suit that puffy skirt thing in the corner. Ooh, oia berry puffs!"

Molly sidestepped the chaos as Kainen dove straight in. She couldn't tell if he was being mad to cheer her up or just being himself, but she suspected a bit of both. Either way, she didn't want gifts so he could help himself.

"Perhaps we should step into the office," Reyan suggested. "Just toe those into the room for now."

Kainen did as he was told, but he grabbed the oia berry puffs in their neat wicker basket and hugged it happily to his chest. Bemused, Molly let herself get sandwiched between him and Reyan as they swept her through their bedroom and toward a door at the back.

"It's easier this way," Reyan announced.

Molly barely even had time to see their room, the walls bare rock like much of the rest of the court, with fine dark green furnishings and a curtain similar to the one in her room that hid a balcony from view. The walls in her room were much lighter, and being the queen's quarters, the décor was festive red and green with strains of glimmering white like snow.

It had taken all her energy to insist that they didn't need

to build an aviary for Aurora, who had doggedly followed them to the court and taken residence on top of yet another mirror. It wasn't home and it didn't even feel all that comforting, but Molly had decided during the night that she would take over the workshop Kainen had all but promised her and build herself a little living space there.

I can style myself as the eccentric princess and they'll all forget I exist.

Reyan opened the door and ushered her into an office, insisting she take a seat while Kainen shut the door behind them.

"We're going to need to get you a companion for when you're not with us," Reyan announced. "I know you're not going to like it, but it's necessary and Demi's insisted on it. We tried to get you Ace but he's busy with something else apparently, so until we find you someone you'll have to put up with one of us instead."

Molly blinked. In all the mentions of her safety, she hadn't once considered they'd decide she needed minding.

Talie would have been ideal.

She winced. "I'm fine by myself."

"Of course you are, we're not doubting that, but it's not just for safety. They'll be able to keep the nobles away from you. I asked Demi about Beryl or maybe Hutch but they're busy too, so she's going to send some suggestions."

"What difference does it make? I'm just here to help with paperwork, right?"

Kainen sank onto the edge of the desk with a wicked grin.

"You really think Phoenix is all happy clappy shiny and

nothing is going on there?" he asked.

Molly frowned. "No, I reckon he's going to be a different kind of bad to Celeste, even if he's not going after the Omens, otherwise why would he want to seal the citadel off again? I don't trust him an inch."

"Good, because Demi doesn't either. She can't be seen to be meddling, but he worries her and she's an impeccable judge of character, mostly. Still not convinced about Taz." He ducked as Reyan threw a sock at his head with a roll of her eyes. "Don't make a mess, sweetheart. No, we'll be keeping an eye on the citadel through the shadows, and I figured you'd be the best person to tell us everything we need to know about it."

"You don't have to of course," Reyan added.

"No, you don't. No obligation if you don't feel comfortable. You're here to help us with the court and be safe from the chaos that is the Faerie nobility. Oh, your grandmother is also demanding you take tea with her, so we'll have to pencil that in by the way. But yeah, if you want in on the espionage then ours is the best court for that."

For the first time in what felt like ever, Molly's heart lifted. She'd thought over and over about what she might say in her letter to Talie when she finally got around to writing it, but every time she ended up with the damning realisation that it didn't change anything.

"I'm in," she said. "The people in the citadel deserve the choice to come and go as they please, and I'll never stop fighting for that."

"Good. Some of our nobles are already talking about

going back to be nosy. Worst case they'll decide to close up their holdings there and we can't stop them, but I reckon at least one will be amenable to staying."

"Because she's your number one fan lately," Reyan retorted.

"I simply gave her the chance to take the prime noble spot at court. It was either that or allow that other orb-muncher to make lewd comments about you and I wasn't having it. Besides, it suits our ends to have her in place."

"Who?" Molly asked.

"You'll meet her soon enough I'm sure, but she's currently top dog among the nobles here and determined to keep that hallowed title."

"I wouldn't like to go against her if I weren't lady of the court to be fair," Reyan said. "Glennoria Featherdown is scary when she wants something."

Molly gasped. "Lady Featherdown? I met her. She was… not kind exactly, but she could have been worse."

"That's perfect," Kainen snorted loudly. "She could have been worse sums her up exactly. Want to meet her again? I'm sure she'd be delighted to have first tea with the princess."

"She probably already expects it as a given," Reyan muttered.

Molly hesitated. Demi had told her before they left for court that Celeste was safely incarcerated and the baby would be taken care of, with Molly informed every step of the way if she chose to be. But any mention of the Oak Queen and her hand in the whole thing had been suspiciously absent.

"Not yet," she said. "We should do tea with the queen first."

Kainen groaned. "Really? She hates me."

"She hates me more, so don't even think about it," Reyan said. "Get Demi to go with you, and Taz. Rope May in too, and Marthe."

"No need." Molly stood and pulled out the orb Demi had given her. "I'll contact May and ask her to come get us. I need to ask her a few questions first. She can let Taz and Demi know we're all going to have a nice family reunion with a heavy side order of questions."

Reyan and Kainen exchanged a glance, then Reyan puffed out a weary breath.

"Yeah, I get what you mean now. She does that scrunchy face thing Taz does when he's planning something."

Molly ignored that, even though a wave of sadness washed through her at the thought of Talie saying something similar once before.

I'm doing this for her. If the citadel is open for all to come and go, it won't be such a hardship to see it as home again, for both of us.

May would be able to teach her how to get Aurora to take a letter to Talie, or at least she would have a bird able to do it if she asked. She would ask May that first, then she would go to the queen and demand answers, hopefully without getting pulverised in return.

"May Elverhill," she announced.

Moments later, the orb-cast of May's face loomed in front of them.

"First of all, I forgive you for choosing the Illusion Court of all places over coming to stay with me," May announced, then her face enlarged as she peered closer. "Oh, no offense you two."

Molly smiled as Kainen huffed loudly in mock offense. Talie might be stuck inside the citadel with Phoenix and whatever he was planning, but one day they would see each other again.

Even if I have to shake the citadel and the rot inside it right to the ground.

ACKNOWLEDGEMENTS

A huge thank you to every reader who has walked with me through Faerie and is still coming back for another visit! To those who've shared on social media, done ARC reads or just given me compliments about the book to keep me going, thank you!

To my family and also my writing family as always, your support means everything to me – Aerin Apeltun, Katina Wright, Estelle Tudor, Maria Oliver, Anna Britton, Sally Doherty, Marisa Noelle, Emma Finlayson-Palmer, writing Twitter, the amazing ARC readers (who have caught so many printing blips it's not even funny…), the wider writing community and everyone who joins #ukteenchat, WriteMentor, SCBWI, and especially libraries and schools who've taken a chance on the previous books, shops that are still stocking them and giving this indie author a chance to reach more readers *deep breath* and most importantly to the readers who will find these books in the future:

THANK YOU!

ABOUT THE AUTHOR

While always convinced that there has to be something out there beyond the everyday, Emma focuses on weaving magic realms with words (the real world can wait a while). The idea of other worlds fascinates her and she's determined to find her own entrance to an alternate realm one day.

Raised in London, she now lives on the UK south coast with her husband and a very lazy black Labrador who occasionally condescends to take her out for a walk.

Aside from creative writing studies, an addiction to cake and spending far too much time procrastinating on social media, Emma is still waiting for the arrival of her unicorn. Or a tank, she's not fussy.

For the latest news and updates, check the website or come say hi on social media:

www.emmaebradley.com
@EmmaEBradley

www.ingramcontent.com/pod-product-compliance
Lightning Source LLC
Chambersburg PA
CBHW030533190726
48283CB00006B/1893